The Secret Meaning
of Blossom

GW00467588

The Secret Meaning of Blossom

By T.M. Parris

A Clarke and Fairchild Thriller

The Clarke and Fairchild series of novels

is written in British English

This book is dedicated

to the real Takao

with apologies, and thanks.

Chapter 1

Funny, that, the woman showing up at his hotel room. But the oddest thing about it didn't occur to James until after she'd left.

When the knock came, James assumed it was Housekeeping and did a double-take when he saw her standing there. Yellow was the theme this time, from top to tail, as it were: strappy sandals with enormous heels, a short – very short – dress with a bit of frill about it, and some kind of band or other in her hair, with flowers. The whole effect was, he had to admit, rather pleasing.

"James-san! It's so good to see you!"

"Mirai! You too, of course! What a wonderful surprise."

She seemed to expect him to ask her in. So he did. She leaned in delicately to deliver two pecks on the cheek that James had to stoop to allow. He didn't realise kissing was the done thing in Japan, but he was generally the kind to go with the flow. He got a wave of some floral perfume. Purple petals came to mind. Irises, maybe, or violets.

By the window of his rather small room were two chairs either side of a tiny table. Mirai, glancing at the bed as she squeezed past, sat in one of them and crossed her legs, revealing, James couldn't help but notice, quite a lot.

"Would you like a drink?" he asked. "I could order some tea."

"Tea?" She giggled, covering her mouth with her hand as if he'd said something shocking. Her eyes, terribly wide, were fixed on his face as she laughed.

"Maybe not, then. Terrific view from here, isn't it?" He pointed out of the window. "Fabulous city, Tokyo. It all seems rather futuristic to me. It's the noises, I think. The cars slide along so smoothly, but everything else seems to talk to you out there, even the billboards and such like."

She was frowning at him now. She wasn't following, was she? He'd been struggling generally with getting himself across out here. Fiona normally did the talking when they went abroad, or indeed anywhere for that matter.

"So, you enjoy conference?" she asked.

Good! A change of subject. James shoe-horned himself into the other chair. "Yes, very much. I don't know how my paper went down. Never had a paper accepted at one of these things before. Well, truth be told, I've never tried before. It was Fiona's idea, actually. My wife. I think I mentioned her yesterday, didn't I?"

"Yes." Mirai's voice was flat.

"Yes, well anyway, I did ask for feedback, got lots of nodding heads from the organisers. I expect you're used to that."

A slightly baffled smile. Of course she was used to it, you fool.

"And you?" he asked. "I have to say I wouldn't expect someone like you – I mean, of course, I'm glad that IT security is a subject you're so engaged in."

She'd been a striking delegate the previous day, in an eye-catching red outfit then, sitting amongst the tired-looking audience of global IT professionals, largely middle-aged men like himself. She couldn't be more than twenty, twenty-one, though it was hard to tell really. He thought he remembered asking her that, towards the end of the evening, when it got to the stage where they were laughing at everything. He rather lost track of how much whisky he'd consumed before finally persuading her into a taxi and staggering down the road to the hotel. All part of the experience, he supposed.

Mirai suddenly looked glum. "You go home soon."

"Yes, soon!"

"That makes me sad."

"Oh, well, I'm sorry to hear that." He didn't know what else to say, so started gabbling again. "My flight's tomorrow. Couldn't get one today. All booked up. So I'm just getting on with a bit of work."

He nodded at his laptop. She gazed at the screen curiously. He reached out and closed it. "Nothing interesting, believe me."

Her eyes snapped back to him. "You want to do something more interesting?" Her lips opened into a smile, no hand over the mouth this time.

"Well! Yes, I suppose it is a bit of a waste sitting in this hotel room when there's a city to explore. How about a walk? Looks like a bracing winter's day out there." He could do with getting out of this cramped little room. "You mentioned a park last night, that you like to go to."

A moment of blankness, then her face brightened with delight. "Yoyogi Park! You remembered!"

"Yes, that's it." He couldn't help feeling flattered that this pretty little thing was so bothered by what he thought.

Then her face fell. "But that's for weekend. Sundays. Today, nothing."

"You mean the park is closed?"

She frowned. "Closed? Not closed."

"But we can't go to the park?"

"Eh – tooooo…" She gave a low humming sound as if contemplating how to phrase something extraordinarily delicate. "So, Yoyogi Park, Saturday, Sunday. For music, cool clothes."

"Oh, yes! I remember." Something about dressing up to go there. Why that meant you couldn't go there during the week was rather lost on him, but it didn't seem to be an option anyway.

Her eyes had moved to the bed. She shifted in her seat, leaning over so that her front was full on to him. "We stay here a while. Maybe relax?"

"Oh, well…" What to say? "You don't want to go for a walk? A bit tired, maybe?"

"Tired?" She gave a kind of pout, as though he'd said something ridiculous. It was pretty ridiculous, to be fair.

"Not tired then."

"No. But walking. These shoes, not so good."

She held up one leg, giving him, he couldn't help noticing, a clear view up her skirt, and pointed to the strappy sandals.

"Oh, yes. I see your point. Must be tricky. Don't know how you ladies manage in them."

"I take them off?" she asked brightly.

"Oh, sure! I guess it's the Japanese custom, though doesn't seem to apply in these big hotels. But why not, if you want?"

James was wearing a pair of those disposable white slip-ons over his thick brown socks. It did cross his mind how silly they looked, but your toes got so cold in these sparsely-heated rooms. He was glad of his cardigan as well. Mirai was undoing her sandals and slowly pulling them off. Her skin looked terribly smooth. She ran a hand up her shin, taking his eyes up to her thigh, and then somewhat inside her legs, rather.

"I take off something else?" She lowered her head and blinked at him.

"Oh!" Good Lord. His mouth was dry. "Well, not on my account. I mean, I certainly don't want, you know—"

"But *I* want."

She stood up and faced him, then looked over to the bed again. Now she seemed a bit uncertain. She hesitated, then turned back towards James and did that pouting thing again while trying to back towards the end of the bed. But the space didn't really allow for such a manoeuvre and she stumbled.

"Oops! Careful how you go." James didn't know whether to get up or not but decided it was safest to stay put.

Mirai recovered and perched on the bed. They looked at each other, a bit of an awkward moment. "So, I get undressed now." She slid her shoulder straps down and reached behind herself.

"I rather think – well, it would be best if you didn't, actually." Damn this country! He'd read somewhere it was rude to say the word no, which did make things difficult sometimes. "Mirai, this is all very flattering, believe me, but I really don't think it's a good idea."

She'd unzipped something and was persuading her bodice downwards, giving James a partial view of her bra, which was exactly the same colour as the rest of her outfit. How did women manage these things? Was the underwear sold as part of the whole get-up? Put that thought aside, James. Time to take action.

He stood. "No!" He put his hand out like a police officer stopping a line of traffic. It must have looked rather foolish. But Mirai, thankfully, stopped. She looked up at him with those wide eyes. "We really can't be having this, Mirai. You're a lovely girl, but it just won't do. Now, I'd be delighted to take you down to the bar for a cup of tea or whatever, or, as I said, perhaps for a walk, although as you mentioned earlier your footwear might not be ideal, but…"

His voice trailed away. Mirai's face had crumpled into a picture of shame. She seemed to shrink as she got onto her knees to reach for her shoes.

"Now, now – I don't want to upset you." But from her pink cheeks it was clear that he had. She struggled with the tiny buckles.

James floundered. "As I said, this is all very flattering, it's just, you know, with the wife and kids, it's not the kind of thing I go in for these days. Though whether there were any days when I did go in for it is another matter."

She was still wrestling with the darn shoes, not looking up at all. One of them was done up but the other wasn't playing ball. The seconds ticked by. Eventually she climbed to her feet anyway and made a beeline for the door.

"Do be careful there." Her foot was slipping around all over the place. Come on James, try and be a little gallant about this. He stepped over and opened the door for her.

She glanced up at him just for a swift moment, but enough for him to see that her eyes had filled up. "Sorry," she whispered, stepping out. She walked unsteadily away, having to limp somewhat with the floppy sandal. James briefly thought about going after her, but what would that achieve, really? He closed the door, having to admit to a feeling of relief. The room smelled of purple petals.

Funny old place, Japan. But here's what was really odd: how did she know where he was staying?

Chapter 2

Rose knew, looking at the young man's face, that she would be the first person he killed. Lying on her back in a wet Paris street, she saw the barrel of his gun glitter as it trembled in his hand. But that wasn't it. It was in his face that she saw what was coming, a realisation in his eyes, a horror then an acceptance, a hardening of the jaw, a re-setting of the chin. He was going to do it, for sure.

But it was no big deal, as she said to the counsellor back in London, and as she said now to her boss Walter, sitting in front of her in a gloomy bistro near the Gare du Nord, a lightly dressed slice of cucumber speared on his fork.

"I've had a gun pointed at me before. Why all the fuss? I mean, a counsellor evaluation? What for? I'm still here, aren't I?"

"I think that's rather the point," said Walter. "I've seen this with other officers, Rose. This is a life and death game sometimes. But not always. It's mainly about patience and persistence, finding agents, cultivating relationships. Every now and then push comes to shove and we're up against our adversaries face to face. But most of the time we're dancing round each other, skulking in their shadows, trying to outguess them."

The cucumber was consumed, followed by the last pieces of tomato and dill. Rose stirred a bowl of brown soup. The bistro was almost empty. How did these places make money? They were only here because Walter had just got off the Eurostar from London. Had a couple of errands to run in Paris, he said. He wasn't here just for her. Like everything Walter said, Rose only half-believed it.

"I've taken on these things because you've wanted me to, Walter."

"Oh yes, yes, I'm aware of that. But sometimes people who've had too much direct exposure, well, they can get a bit…"

"A bit what?"

"They think their luck is always going to hold, because it has done so far. But it's a percentage game, Rose. Just like at rolling dice, your luck will only last for a while."

"You think I'm getting careless? That's nonsense."

"They tell me you didn't have to go after the man. You could have waited."

"No, Walter. He was getting away. He suspected me as soon as I walked into the store. He made some excuse and hightailed it through the back."

"He was running down an alleyway that was covered at both ends. You could have held back. He had a gun."

"How was I to know that?"

"You should have considered the possibility. Dead bodies are no use to us, Rose. Yours or his."

The waiter approached with some lamb edifice for Walter and a long white fish for Rose, drooping over the side of the plate. When he'd gone, Walter started tackling the lamb.

"He's not dead," said Rose. "And neither am I, as you can see."

"But you could have been. We're all flesh and blood. This line of work is all about weighing up risks and seeing the bigger picture, but we need to stay human as well. MI6 is about human intelligence after all."

Rose's fish stared up at her, untouched. "You think I'm losing my humanity? Is that what the counsellor said?"

"Well, not exactly."

"So what did the counsellor say?"

8

"A lot of things, but what it boiled down to is that you're too caught up in the work."

"Caught up? Caught up how?"

"You're wound up too tight and it's affecting how you're dealing with situations."

"Situations? The guy was detained. He turned on his colleagues. He's now an informant. With the help of MI6 the French now have insight into a radical Islamist group recruiting young Muslims for terror operations across Europe."

"You almost shot him."

"I gained possession of his gun and was holding him until the backup arrived."

"They only just got there in time. They had to prise the gun out of your grip."

"Who said that? Nonsense."

Her mind went back to the alleyway again, the desperate kick with her foot that sent him staggering, her fist hitting flesh, his yelp of pain. Grabbing the gun and gripping the trigger, the running footsteps stopped her, the hand on her arm: *we'll take it from here.* She'd put her hands in her pockets to stop them trembling as she walked away, the man on his knees now, surrounded, hands on head. Had it ever been that close before?

"Well, I didn't just take anyone's word for it," said Walter. "I sent you for a counsellor evaluation. But they backed it up, I'm afraid. Said you were in denial about how traumatised you were by it."

"And you go along with that, do you? Walter, you know me. How many years have we worked together?"

Walter sighed. A pink piece of lamb wobbled on his fork. Was there more to this than he was letting on? Walter had been around for ever, knew too much to be let go, people said. His soft voice and fondness for a waistcoat and cravat gave him a fussy air which masked a wit of steel. He was a mover in the present as well as the past, but a furtive one. Despite their long history, her last operation in France had given Rose reason to wonder more and more about Walter. She didn't look at him in quite the same way these days.

"Where's this coming from?" she asked. "Is it about the painting?" During the most recent operation, an extremely valuable masterpiece had met a sticky end. To Rose, it was a pragmatic decision but Walter had been shocked, and he wasn't the only one.

"No, not that, my dear."

"Salisbury, then?" MI6 Chief Marcus Salisbury was a man Rose found very difficult. Walter seemed to have some unspecified influence there – another mystery.

"No, Rose. It's much more simple than that. This really is about you and your wellbeing and abilities. You seem so single-minded about the work. As if there were nothing else."

"What's wrong with being committed? Loads of people in the Service live for the job. It's demanding work and it's important."

"It's also important to keep a sense of perspective."

"I'm supposed to be married with kids, am I?"

"Well, hardly. I didn't do that myself, did I? It's not about your private life. It's about your work. You're very – what do people say? – *hardball*. The way you dealt with Fairchild in Monaco, for example. You were working well with him and could have done with his help at the end. And there were things you didn't share. What we do is a team effort, at the end of the day."

Fairchild, always Fairchild. Walter was obsessed with John Fairchild. That was what guilt did to you. "You put me in a situation where I had to work with him despite my reservations, or walk away entirely. Sure, at times it worked well but he kept things from me, too, Walter. Including the fact that he'd had contact with one of my informants who then got herself into a lot of trouble. We have different views about the man, but I think it's a bit unfair if you're using that to form some theory about my personality defects."

She stabbed the fish and cracked its spine. "The op was a success. Despite Fairchild's absence for part of it."

Walter looked philosophically at the tablecloth and returned to his lamb. A long silence followed. Rose dissected the fish, and Walter's comments. No point in saying what she really thought: you wouldn't be saying all that about a man. But it was true. Hardball males were gutsy. Hardball females were damaged. Walter was always trying to talk up John Fairchild, making up for supposedly letting him down in the past. The truth was, regardless of what happened in the man's childhood, Fairchild had grown up to be a cynical, untrusting, self-serving operator with no loyalty to anyone and a serious grudge against the British intelligence service. It also had to be said that his cynicism made him very useful to Rose. After the Monaco operation, she and Fairchild had a conversation that changed everything, and it was one that Walter was never going to know about.

"So what are you saying, Walter?" she asked. "What does this mean for me? Paris was only going to be temporary. What next?"

Walter laid down his cutlery. "You need a break from operations, Rose. I'm assigning you to an analysis team back in London."

"London? I don't want London. Give those posts to people who want to settle down and send their kids to nice schools. I want a posting. One that lasts more than a few months. That's what I'm good at, Walter. I got you Grom, didn't I? We went after his money and we found it."

"Yes, indeed, Rose. There's been no sign of the man since Monaco. Hopefully he's too advanced in years now to make another comeback." Grom was the gritty street name for former MI6 double agent Gregory Sutherland, a man with a history of grudges against his former employer which resulted in many lives lost, including, a long time ago, Fairchild's parents.

"Then let me do more of that. I'm good, Walter. There are plenty of other dangerous people out there."

"In time, of course. But for now, you're out of the field. Go home. Take a break."

"I don't need a break. I need to get back to what I'm good at. What's this really about?"

Walter blinked. He rarely showed any signs of impatience, but she was sailing close to the wind now. "I've told you what it's really about. London is the only offer for now. We have analyst vacancies and you can be useful there. It's not forever."

"How long is it for, then?"

"I can't say."

"So what do I need to do?"

He sighed again. "Think about what I've said. Think about what's important."

Rose gave him a blank stare. "That's it? Come on, Walter. There must be more. You want me to do some training? More counselling? Whatever. I'll do it."

She could hear herself now, over-eager like a new recruit. Truth was, she couldn't see anything beyond this job. It was her life. Walter confining her to an analyst's desk in London was a kind of slow strangulation.

"We'll catch up over there in a couple of weeks," he said. "I'm sure you'll like it more than you think."

"I'm sure I won't."

Walter ignored her petulance. "Oh, I almost forgot! The internal mail arrived as I was walking out of the door. Something for you. Via the Foreign Office."

He handed her a brown envelope. Like many others at MI6, Rose worked under diplomatic cover, so getting mail that route made sense. But snail mail of any kind was pretty unusual these days. She opened it. Inside was a postcard, sent from Japan several days ago. She recognised her brother's handwriting straight away.

Dear Rose. I am in Tokyo, enjoying a few extra days after attending a conference. As you can see, the cherry blossom is lovely at this time of year.

She flipped the card over. On the front was a picture of a temple, formal Japanese gardens and a few boughs laden with blossom. The message concluded: *I hope things are going well for you in the diplomatic arena. Thinking of you, James.*

Rose put the card down and stared at it.

"Something troubling?" asked Walter.

"It's a postcard from my brother. He's in Japan."

"Ah! That's nice. Not many people bother with postcards these days."

That was exactly what Rose was thinking.

"You've never mentioned your brother, to my recollection," said Walter.

"Why should I? Lives in Surrey. Works in IT. Married. Kids. What's there to say?" Rose stared at the postcard.

Strange. Very strange.

Chapter 3

John Fairchild climbed from the old town square up streets so steep the pavements were steps. Mountains rose up, the dramatic backdrop to Riva del Garda, a town slotted into the narrow top end of Italy's Lake Garda, itself a water-filled gash amongst the vast peaks.

The house wasn't easy to find. Not obvious. That was probably deliberate. Old spies fell into habits they'd never break, always watching, always looking over their shoulder. By counting he knew he had the right door, but it had no number, name or bell. By the side of the row of narrow cottages lay yet more steps, rising up and round at the back. Fairchild took these and found himself on a level with roof terraces lined with geraniums. A woman with white hair was working with a trowel and some window boxes, absorbed. It wasn't her face that was familiar; it was something about her movements, the way she held herself. There were times when he thought he'd never find the woman. And now he had, just when he needed this the most.

"Penny?" He spoke softly. They weren't far from each other but there was a gap between him and the terraces. He didn't want to startle her, but she looked up sharply, suddenly alert. It was to be expected, he supposed. She stared, then took several steps towards him.

"Do I know you? I think maybe I do. I'm sorry, I don't remember so well these days."

"I'm John Fairchild."

She had spoken Italian, with no trace of accent. He spoke in English. She peered at him with blue eyes, her skin tanned and rosy. An old woman now, but there was recognition in her face.

"John Fairchild! How extraordinary. John Fairchild! That's a name I haven't heard in a long time. Come round, come round!"

She hurried down to let him in, smiling, playing the nice old lady: *what a delightful surprise!* But her smile held a shadow as well. She directed him back out onto the terrace and brought fruit squash for them both: "I can't get used to the tea here, it's not the same." They sat at a table.

"Was it Walter who sent you?" she asked.

"Walter doesn't know I'm here. I found you myself. I have a few contacts."

"So I've heard, so I've heard."

She kept her ear to the ground, then, even in retirement. Fairchild knew his reputation was mixed. Some in the clandestine world valued his information-gathering services, available to almost anyone at a price. Others were less keen, but he was fine with that. For decades he had been trying to trace names from the past using his global network and endless favour-trading. Penny Galloway had proved the most elusive of them all. But here she was, and her name had popped right after the conversation with Rose which made this so much more important. He'd come straight here from Marseille.

"When did we see each other last?" said Penny.

"I think I was about eight or nine," said Fairchild. "You sat in the kitchen with my mother. I remember you laughing."

She blinked a little. "Yes, I remember. That was only a year or two before —"

"Before they were killed."

Her face stilled. "You know that for sure now?"

"Yes. I know that for sure."

"Well, I'm sorry."

"Sorry that it happened? Or sorry that I found out?"

Her jaw tightened. He regretted it instantly. This wasn't Walter he was talking to. "I'm sorry. I didn't come here to pick a fight."

"But you're angry. You feel we held out on you. Well, I can understand that." The tension was still there but she was moving things on. "Walter had good reason to keep things from you. Certainly to start with. You were a child. Later on, well…but it was his call, ultimately. He was the one who was close to it all. He was right there, in Vienna. And Walter didn't know who was behind it. He only suspected."

"Really?"

The stillness remained. The blue of her eyes seemed darker. She would know that he'd come here for a reason, because he'd discovered something or wanted to know more.

"This idea," she said, "that Gregory Sutherland went over to the USSR. They were convinced of it, your mum and dad. People thought they were obsessed. I wanted to believe he was dead. But when your parents disappeared…"

"I met him, Penny."

"He's still alive, then?" She didn't seem too surprised.

"Still alive and still operating. Until a few months ago he worked for the FSB just as he was with the KGB in the Soviet days, with a false Russian ID. But the Kremlin was tipped off about who he really was and he went on the run. The Russians have been going after all his foreign assets. This came to a head recently in Monaco and thereabouts."

"That *fracas* on the French Riviera? Some gang fight in a villa, I read. Something about a painting. Well, well. Gregory Sutherland." She said his name almost dreamily. "You've met him, you say?" There was brightness in her eyes, but she was guarded. A dangerous topic but a compelling one all the same.

"In Russia. I was going to kill him. But…"

"But you didn't. He was always good at talking himself out of a hole. You had reason enough. Either you would try and kill him or he would do it to you."

"He tried it a number of times. He killed others to get to me."

"You see, this is what Walter was afraid of," said Penny. "That if Sutherland found out about you, he'd go after you as well. Not that you had anything to do with your parents exposing him as a double agent. You weren't even alive back then. But he was a vindictive character. And then there was the prospect that you'd go after him."

"Walter should have told me. He should have told me everything." Fairchild could hear the child in his voice. Walter did that to him.

"You were ten years old. The instinct is to protect. That's what he was trying to do. Still is, I'm sure."

"Every time I make some discovery about what happened, I find out he already knew."

She wasn't going to persuade him. She took a sip of squash and moved things on. "So where is Sutherland now?"

"He's in hiding. He lost all his assets. He's gone underground."

"I see. Then why are you here?"

She wasn't afraid of a direct question. And he wasn't here just to reminisce. What sent him was current and mattered now, even if the answers were in the past. "You knew Sutherland. You worked together. You knew my parents, and Walter. What else is there, Penny? What else happened between you all that people aren't telling me?"

There was something more specific, but he'd come on to that later. He'd start with an open question and see where that led. Penny paused, uncertain maybe, then settled back in her chair.

"I'll tell you what matters. There was always something off about Gregory Sutherland. A hardness to him. A lack of empathy, they'd say these days. They do tests, now. Weed out the troublesome personalities. Back then, a lot rode on gut feel. You could talk yourself in, with the right kind of background. If you were a decent sort of chap. And they were almost all chaps back then. He'd been there three or four years by the time I joined. Very strong with cyphers, cracking codes. He should have been in GCHQ really, but that wasn't what interested him. He liked people. Or rather, he liked what he could do with people. Control them, manipulate them. Play them, without them even realising. I know we all do some of that in this business, but he took such pleasure in it. It really was a game to him."

A game, cyphers and codes: it all fitted. What was he trying to remember? *An Aztec religious ritual.* What was the rest of it?

Penny was back in the sixties, trawling through it all. "There was pushback on our operations, information getting out. The Fairchilds were brought in to investigate. I didn't know about it, of course, it was all kept hush-hush. Then Sutherland died. Well, supposedly. A car crash up in Scotland, near the family home. The investigation ended. They could discuss it after that. It didn't surprise me they suspected him. He was given a lot of trust very early. As I said, you could talk yourself in, back then. He had a run of bad luck, let's say. A number of his agents ended up getting killed. I think some people put it down to him not caring enough whether they lived or died. He always had a full explanation, but still. Not a big step to suspecting there was something more organised about it. He must have got wind of it, and disappeared. That should have been the end of it. But they couldn't leave it alone."

"My parents?"

She nodded. "They became very cautious, convinced he was after them. Used to see patterns in things, signals. I didn't think it was real, I have to say. I thought it was their way of caring about you. That was a large part of it. You were born after he left, you see. So he wouldn't have known about you. They worried about that. Sent you away to boarding school as soon as they could. They were always looking over their shoulders. I suppose at times they might have been a little distant. I never thought about it from your point of view."

Fairchild saw a hundred things from back then, scrolling through his mind. Objects and words flooded in. "They took me to the British Museum one time. They set me a test. An Aztec religious ritual. Incense-burning in Yemen." It was coming back word for word. "The birth of ethnography. A stone as precious as gold. What connects them all? My father said that to me. Then they both walked off and left me in the atrium. I had to solve the puzzle to find them again. It took me four hours. I was nine. For a long time, I thought that was normal parenting."

Penny looked pained. "That was your dad. He believed in pure knowledge, the key to understanding everything. He absorbed it all and had this incredible way of drawing on it. He saw connections between things, thought cryptically. It helped them with Sutherland who was very highly educated too. Looked down on anyone who wasn't. Edward was just as erudite but without the snobbery. It must have seemed harsh. They were trying to prepare you, I think."

"I'm not sure how successful they were."

"You survived Sutherland, didn't you? You're not your father but you've taken a different route. More direct, less cerebral, maybe. That's not necessarily a bad thing."

She was perceptive, or she knew more about him than she was letting on. This was getting to him more than he thought it would. He needed more squash. She poured it for him. He drank and carried on.

"When my mother wrote to me in boarding school, it was never in English. French, Russian, Arabic, even in code. If I wanted to know what they were saying to me, I had to figure it out the best I could." He was talking too much but it wanted to come out. There weren't many left who remembered them.

Penny gave a half-smile this time. "She was a natural linguist. I bet you are, too. It's helped you, I'm sure."

She still didn't understand. He had to make her understand. "The night they disappeared, I didn't know what to do. When I came back to the flat and they'd gone, I thought it was another game. A puzzle I had to solve. All those years I was trying to find an answer. But they were already dead. He killed them almost straight away. Took them to some interrogation centre near Moscow. They never came out."

"Oh, you poor thing," said Penny. "What a cruel, cruel thing."

He saw comprehension in her eyes now. He couldn't speak. The wind rustled the geraniums in their pots.

"That's the Ora coming in," said Penny. "The wind is very predictable here. It's to do with the thermals, air temperature over the mountains and the lake. The air over the water heats up quicker than the air over the land. Or is it the other way round? I never remember."

She was chatting to fill a gap, give him time to recover. He stared at the geraniums and listened.

"In the morning it's a northerly. That's called the Pelèr. That dies down, then comes the Ora, the southerly. Every day, like clockwork. Except when a storm is coming. Grom is Russian for thunder, isn't it?"

"He won't come here," said Fairchild, finding his voice again. "Even if he were watching somehow, no one could have tracked me here."

"Oh, that's not what I meant. Don't worry about me. Habits of a lifetime. Nobody creeps up on me."

"I got the impression I startled you earlier."

"Did you?" She smiled. "Did you hear the dog barking when you passed in front of the church? I knew someone was coming, someone new. There are people I can call on."

"MI6 people? Marcus Salisbury looks after old spies, does he?"

She snorted. "Why would Marcus Salisbury care about a faded old flower like me? The Service looks after its own despite people like Salisbury. We don't all end up dead or mad. I lead a regular life here. I get bread and food every morning in the town. I join the *Passegiatta* in the evening. If I don't show up, people will know what to do. What do you think of the geraniums? I suppose they're a bit of a cliché."

He was floored by her question. But she didn't really need an answer. "Truth is, they're hardy. They can take these winds and they don't need much looking after. That's why everyone has them. And what's wrong with that? It's no bad thing to fit in, become a part of a place, part of its routine."

"Like clockwork?"

She sounded content, undamaged by the life she'd led, the dangers she'd been exposed to. "It's not impossible," she said, as if reading his mind. "You don't have to let it destroy you, this life. You can let it go. It's not so bad being normal."

It was good advice. Others had offered it. But too many questions still remained. And now he had Rose to think about too.

"My parents had a Japanese print," he said. "I remember it being on the wall in a number of places we lived. They specifically left it to me. Not just as part of their estate but separately, named. What was special about that print?"

She was looking at the horizon, remembering. Maybe she was sitting in the kitchen again, laughing with his mother. "Cherry blossom? A bridge over a river? I remember. It was just a print."

Fairchild shook his head. "Sutherland had one just like it. I found it in his apartment in Monaco. He had a third one as well. They're part of a set. It's not just a print, Penny."

A bland look. "You think they're sending you some kind of message?" There was no hint of humour, but still, she made it sound ridiculous.

"Those prints must mean something. I thought you might know about it. You were a family friend."

"It's in the past, John. Years in the past and Sutherland's a spent force. Live in the present. Try and fit in somewhere. You could, you know."

She seemed to read his DNA, see his ever-shifting restlessness. He always told himself he didn't want to feel at home, that he liked it this way.

"They wanted you to have a life, you know," she said. "That's why they went to all that trouble. Think about it. But now you're wondering if I'm discouraging you because there's something to find. Well, you'll do what you want."

The words were harsh but the tone light. They'd run out of squash. She didn't offer to get any more.

"I was just asking if you knew anything about it."

"I said I didn't know anything, didn't I?"

"Actually, you didn't. But you've given me something to think about." He stood. "I will be back, Penny."

"Yes, I'm sure you will be." She sounded resigned.

They kissed cheek-to-cheek.

"What was the answer, by the way?" she asked. "The British Museum? What connects them all?"

"Oh! The East Stairs."

She chuckled. "Oh, Edward!"

He walked down the cobbled steps. She knew more than she was saying, and she knew that he knew that. As he'd said to her, he'd be back. But right now he had a plane to catch.

When he glanced back she was staring up at the sky, pulling her cardigan closer around her as the wind grew.

Chapter 4

Fairchild's flight to Tokyo stopped over in Taipei. He made twenty-four hours of it and looked up a few of his contacts there. No particular reason to, but now wasn't a time to neglect any part of his network. Those relationships needed nurturing right across the world, and it had to be done face to face. He had no permanent base; he was constantly on the move. This was what he did. Also, he'd heard that Zack was in Taiwan. So, after getting a few hours' sleep in an overpriced hotel suite, he took to the streets. Taipei was one of his favourite cities, cleaner than Beijing, more down-to-earth than Tokyo, livelier than Seoul, and the island was a mountainous green gem. Its political ambiguity left it partially undiscovered – long may it remain so, was his view.

Eventually, late evening, he headed for the Da'an district. Zack was propping up the bar at Carnegie's. He wasn't as relaxed as he looked. He had a habit of hanging around popular expat haunts to see who was passing through and keep up to speed. He made himself easy to find. Having established Zack was in Taipei, Fairchild knew exactly where to look for him.

"Fairchild, my man! Nice surprise. Sit down. Have a gin. I may even pay for it."

Zack had deep pockets provided by the CIA or some related branch of US security services. He'd given Fairchild a good amount of work over the years, all unofficial of course. Zack was the closest thing Fairchild had to a best friend, though they often went for months without hearing from each other.

"So how are things?" Fairchild asked.

"Tense, is how things are. Getting tenser and tenser."

"South China Sea, is it?"

"Can't confirm or deny." He took a swig of beer.

"Understood."

With a military background Zack often played liaison between civilian and military intelligence. He was at home on a US base as much as anywhere else. It was no surprise to find him in this region of the world. Zack knew it well.

"So you have a reason to be here?" asked Zack. "Other than dropping in to see me, of course."

"Stopping over. I'm on my way to Tokyo."

"Tokyo! Great place. Haven't been in years. What's going on there?"

"Trade Winds is opening there. I'm going for the launch party."

"Trade Winds? You mean that tacky overpriced theme park posing as a cocktail bar is actually expanding?"

"Cocktail bar and restaurant. And yes, it's doing very well. My most successful investment in Asia as of now. Consider yourself invited."

"No thanks. Even if I wanted to, I'm kind of busy here. Mighty big of you to take such an active interest in your business. Mostly you just leave them to it."

"I like to drop in and keep an eye on things. When it suits me."

"Ha! And it suits you to go to Tokyo?" Zack certainly knew him well.

"There may be another reason too."

"Oh yeah?" Zack drew his bar stool closer in a conspiratorial way. Given the size of him it was like conspiring with a wall. Or an aloha-patterned blanket, given Zack's preference for loud shirts.

"Tell me it's not about this woman," he said.

"What woman?" Fairchild sipped a very long gin and tonic.

"Oh, please. Rose Clarke of course. The one who always seems to be bad news. Yet she's always around."

Zack had been wary of Rose since their paths crossed for the first time. And again he'd guessed right that Rose was a part of this. But he'd been sworn to secrecy. Rose had shared her suspicions with no one except him. That was something that made him feel warm inside when he thought about it.

"Last time I saw Rose Clarke she told me she'd resigned," Fairchild said.

"Really?"

"Really." It was actually true. "Though I've heard rumours she's still doing ops with MI6 in Paris."

"Right. So she lied."

"Maybe. Or she changed her mind. Either way, she's not part of this."

And that was true as well, in that she wasn't going to be in Tokyo. He told Zack about the Japanese prints. The American's face, as much of it as he could see around the mirrored shades, registered a distinct lack of interest.

"Your folks had a painting."

"A print."

"Whatever. And this guy had one as well. And you think this means something because Mum and Dad liked to do things the complicated way. They're sending you a message from beyond the grave." For a moment he sounded oddly like Penny Galloway.

"Well, I don't know, Zack. But it seemed to matter to them. I spoke to an old family friend of theirs recently. She said something that I've always wondered about, that they were preparing me for something."

"Preparing you for this guy, Fairchild! This Grom character. And it worked! Because he's now powerless and hiding somewhere. Consider yourself prepared. You won, didn't you? You got your answers. You know why it all happened. What more can there be?"

Logically Zack was right. Fairchild drank instead of responding.

"Look." Zack took on the manner of a sympathetic family doctor. "You're in the habit of finding things out, digging for secrets. It's your job now. You made your life about that. But the reason you did all that doesn't exist any more. You got your answers. You know what happened to your parents. Now keep on doing the work if you like it, you're good enough at it. You're unique. A deniable gun-wielding information mercenary with dubious connections and a death wish. Who could be more employable? But forget the personal stuff. Move on. Oh hell, how many times have I said that to you? Did it ever make any difference?"

"People are still holding out, Zack. There's more to tell."

"What people? MI6 people? That's just the way spies talk. They like to generate mystique. Doesn't mean they know anything. It could all be for nothing. Probably is."

"Yes, probably is," said Fairchild philosophically. "In which case it won't have done any harm. How did it go with Quesada by the way?"

Fairchild's last assignment for Zack was to ensure that a notoriously violent drug baron ended up behind bars. It failed. But Fairchild was hoping a new contact he'd introduced to Zack from the world of offshore financing would help.

"Yeah, I meant to say. Your pal Zoe worked wonders. We tracked down a huge part of his business and the lawyers are now saying we can make a case. Pretty impressive lady you got there."

Zack was right about that. When Fairchild met Zoe she was an administrative assistant in a bank. By the time they parted she was a multi-millionaire, confidently playing the criminals at their own game. That she was now permanently on the wrong side of the law didn't bother him, or Zack. Zack knew when rules mattered and when they didn't. It was one of the reasons Fairchild liked the guy. Fairchild also liked Zoe, but that didn't last. Rose was the only woman who would mean anything to him, he realised that now.

"Sounds like you owe me, then," he said. He got up. Zack would probably be here until the early hours but Fairchild had more people to see. "You're welcome in Trade Winds any time."

"No time, believe me," said Zack. "Hey. Avoid that woman. And forget about the past. What's done is done, right?"

"Sure."

As Fairchild left, Zack gave him a half-wave, half-salute, already looking around to see who else was there. Zack was perfectly correct in assuming that Fairchild wasn't intending to take his advice. At least Rose wasn't going to be in Tokyo. That was one less thing to deal with, at least.

Chapter 5

Not having much of a choice, Rose went home, if you could call her neglected West Ealing flat a home. The streets looked even greyer than she remembered, some half-hearted Christmas glitter rendering everything else even more dull. Her flat was cold, dim and musty, the furniture worn and unloved. London in December. Great.

She phoned her sister-in-law. Realising she didn't even have a mobile number for her, she rang their house landline. Fiona picked up.

"Hi Fiona, it's Rose."

An incredulous pause. "Oh. Hi, Rose."

"How are you?"

"Fine, thanks."

The small talk wasn't taking off. Rose could hear children's voices in the background. "Listen. I got a postcard from James."

Another stunned silence. "Well, aren't you the lucky one."

Rose was prepared for some frostiness. She was probably the worst aunt in the history of aunthood, and with Fiona it was all about the kids. "Well, that's what I'm calling about. Have you heard from him recently? It seems that he's in Japan."

"Yes, it does, doesn't it?"

A pause elicited nothing further. "So, he went there for a conference then decided to stay a few extra days. That's what the postcard said."

"Well, I expect that's what he's doing, then."

"So that's what he's said to you?"

"I wouldn't put it quite like that, no."

"Well, how would you put it, then? You've heard from him, right?"

The next pause was more telling. "Why are you so bothered, Rose? You've never shown this much interest in a postcard from James before."

"I've never had a postcard from James before. Never. In the entire shared history of our lives. Have you?"

"Well – no."

"He works in IT. He had email before anyone had heard of email. He does everything electronically. And then he goes to Japan for no more than a few days and the thought occurs to him to send a postcard. Do you not think there's something strange about that?"

"Well, what would you know, Rose? When did you last see your brother? Or any of us? He could have grown a second head for all you care."

"And has he? I mean, has he been behaving uncharacteristically recently? Has anything changed? Any problems or anything?"

The silence had become hostile. "No. Everything's fine."

By which she meant *none of your business*. Fiona had a point, but this wasn't helping.

"Look, Fiona, I know I haven't been around as much as I might have. It is quite difficult with the overseas—"

"Oh yes, I know all about the job. Diplomatic service, very important. How could we forget?"

"All right, but that's beside the point now. When did you last speak to James, or hear from him?"

She was reluctant, but answered. "He was supposed to come home Saturday, but he didn't show. I got some weird email saying he was going to stay on a few days. He didn't answer his phone or reply to my email. So I left it."

"Fiona, that was almost a week ago!"

30

"He said it was a work thing. They've got an office out there, the firm he works for."

"This email you got, you said it was weird. What was weird about it?"

"I don't know, it just – didn't sound like him."

"So he *is* behaving out of character then."

"I don't know, what's out of character?"

"Well, some might say going to a conference on the other side of the world then not coming home again might fit the bill."

"Look, I'm not going to take lessons in family relationships from you. You've got other priorities, you've made that perfectly clear. I'm sure James is just busy with work and will be on his way home soon. Now, I have to leave. You've phoned in the middle of Sophie's birthday party. Thanks for remembering, by the way. If there's anything else, email." She hung up.

Rose sat and absorbed all this, looking out of a dirty window onto the railway line below. Sophie's birthday! Rose didn't do birthdays, she'd said that before and thought they were okay about it. Well, James was, anyway. Her lifestyle was too unpredictable. If they wanted her to contribute to a present or something, they could ask. How old was Sophie? Seven, eight, nine? Something like that. And the other one? Henry, that was it. Probably eleven or twelve by now.

Fiona wasn't telling her everything, that was clear. Hopefully they weren't having some major bust-up but there were tensions for sure. Fiona was angry, with James as well as Rose. But whatever was going on there, James wouldn't miss his daughter's birthday party for a work junket, even in Japan. At least, the James she knew wouldn't.

Chapter 6

As it seemed that this trip to Tokyo would turn out a bit longer than expected, James felt the need to pop to the shops. His hotel room seemed to be getting smaller by the hour. The phone conversation he'd just had with Fiona made him – well, uneasy didn't quite cover it somehow. He was getting a little short of ideas. A breath of fresh air, now that might get the brain ticking over, mightn't it? Couldn't do any harm, anyway. So he grabbed a few things and took the lift down.

No point asking at the front desk for guidance. He'd tried that once or twice before and came away with nothing but bemused looks and polite laughter. Just have a walk-about, James. See what there is. Find your inner adventurer. Seems like you have a need for him right about now.

He turned off the main road into a side-street. Seemed there was as much going on in the little streets as the big ones – more, even. He looked up. The houses were, how to put it, a bit ramshackle. Not that they were falling down, but compared to the solid brick rectangles at home they seemed more rickety somehow, with their panelled walls and heavy-looking tiled roofs. Telegraph lines looped from one to the other, so low overhead you could almost reach out and touch them. A string of lanterns led the way down the street, glowing in the dusk. Plenty of people, the odd car, but as he tried to say to Mirai, Tokyo didn't roar, like London. Instead it tinkled and beeped and chimed from out of every shop door. And the moon! There was something odd about it, hanging low in a part of the sky he'd never seen it in before. It was all very modern, but at the same time very Asian.

The sliding door of a Seven-Eleven made way for him as he approached. Might as well see what they've got. The hotel room service menu was rather limited. The shop assistants chorused some kind of welcome, at least he assumed that was it, odd they did it without even looking round at him. James browsed. A lot of unfamiliar stuff here. They certainly went for colour and cartoons. He used to love comics when he was a boy. Would he have time to find a manga shop? Probably, the way things were going.

He perused a fridge full of rice balls. Round, square, triangular. Some covered in seaweed. Some with a kind of colour code on the packs, no idea what that was about. May as well go for a couple of triangular ones. Give these things a try when you have the chance. They didn't look very substantial though. A yeasty savoury smell drew him to a counter where all kinds of things floated about in trays of brown liquid. He watched the guy in front point to a few of them and walk off with a polystyrene bowl of noodles and various other bits. If it was a matter of pointing, he could probably manage that.

At the front of the queue the assistant peered up at him and giggled. That happened a lot over here. He tried to enter into the spirit by grinning back and pointing to one or two of the objects that most closely resembled food. Whatever he picked, the assistant seemed to find it hilarious. Then the boy stood there with James' selected oddments in the bowl. Now James had to persuade him to add some noodles and soup and put the lid on, then he could be on his way. He'd rather thought that part of the process was automatic, but clearly not.

"Noodles?" he tried.

"EEeeehhHH?" The boy's voice plumbed the depths then soared, as if James had uttered some cerebral observation that encapsulated the essential mystery of life.

"Noodles. I'll have some noodles, please, and then we're done."

"Eh – tooooooo…." That hum, like Mirai the other day. James wasn't getting himself across at all. Now the young man was calling his colleagues over! Goodness, all he wanted was the same as the last gentleman.

"Noodles!" He repeated his request to the three of them who were there now.

"Ah!" Good! Sounded like one of them had got it. Some muttered words, then: "*Nooduru!*"

"Yes! *Nooduru!*" said James, sounding like a fool, he was sure.

"*Hai! Hai!*" Finally! Celebratory smiles all round. What a sense of achievement.

Balancing the carrier bag with the hot polystyrene noodle bowl, his rice balls, and a couple of other mysterious looking things he'd grabbed on the way, James stepped out of the sliding door and came to a sudden halt when he saw Mirai standing there.

"Mirai! Good heavens!"

"James-san!"

She was all in pink this time, at least the top layer was, as she sported a frilly umbrella-parasol type thing, hard to know which as it was neither sunny nor raining, and a very shiny plastic pink coat which finished somewhere mid-thigh.

"Well, fancy bumping into you like this!" Did he sound forced?

"Yes! Yes!" Mirai nodded energetically, smiling, though perhaps a little sadly. "I think you are home now. Weekend."

"Yes, well." He wasn't sure if he wanted to discuss that. "It's turned into a bit of a longer trip than I thought. Still, plenty to see around here, isn't there? I'm exploring the local food at the moment."

He held up his carrier bag a little too fast, and some noodle soup slopped out of the bowl.

"Oh dear. They must have not put the lid on properly. Let me see if I…" He set it down on the pavement and fiddled around with the lid, achieving little except getting his hands covered in hot soup.

Mirai stood and watched. "You don't want go home to your wife?" she said morosely.

James gave up on the lid and stood up. "Well, you see, I'm afraid there was a bit of a hiccup."

She looked blank.

"My wife, you know, somehow managed to – er – get the wrong end of the stick. About you and me. Struggling to understand how, exactly."

She frowned. "Wrong end?" Clearly it wasn't the right choice of words.

"Well, I mean, Fiona and I never had any secrets. She seemed to think you and I had emailed each other, which is very odd, as of course we haven't. None of this is your fault, naturally. Just some kind of muddle."

Mirai's mouth opened. She held her hand over it, a comic-book expression of shock. "Your wife read your emails?"

"Yes, standard practice chez nous, I'm afraid. As I said, we don't have secrets. Though I don't get to read hers, I have to say. But I've no worries there. If that's the way she wants it, fine by me. Are you all right? You look a little peaky." She'd really gone terribly pale.

"Yes, I'm okay." She shook her whole body like a dog shakes off rainwater, only there was no rain.

James could hear himself jabbering again. "Anyway, the long and the short of it is, she's rather let me know that I'm not currently welcome back right now. Stay out there with her if you like it so much, was the gist of it. And then, unfortunately, she hung up and I haven't been able to speak to her since, although I'm sure it's only a matter of time, but one doesn't want to upset the applecart, if you know what I mean."

Did she? Mirai seemed to have gone into some kind of trance.

"So, I thought, just sit tight for a bit and see how things pan out. And that's it, really. Are you sure you're all right?"

"Yes! Yes!" Such a high-pitched voice she had, sometimes.

"Anyway, I don't want to seem antisocial, but I bought these noodles, you see, and I'd rather like to try them before they get cold." He pointed to his dinner.

This seemed to bring her round. "Ah! Okay!" She gave him a childish kind of wave, although waving seemed redundant as she was standing right in front of him. "Bye, James-san!"

"Yes, bye bye. Take care now."

He headed back to the hotel, or least in the direction he thought the hotel was. How strange, to see Mirai standing right there! And what an odd line of questioning. Her response to what he'd said about emails was decidedly peculiar. This country was getting stranger and stranger. Hopefully he could somehow manage to persuade Fiona to come to her senses before he became a permanent resident. This type of thing hadn't cropped up before, so he was on virgin territory, so to speak. Just going home and showing up at the house was, he sensed, not the right thing to do. Or perhaps he was just scared. Well, it wasn't a bad idea to trust your instincts every now and then. Yes, trust your instincts.

He turned for a moment and saw Mirai standing there pink as blossom, ready for a rain shower, staring down the street after him.

Chapter 7

Rose was in Soho, which was grimy, wet and cold. She wasn't expected by the analysis team at Vauxhall Cross until next week. So she had time to do a little more digging.

Funny James working for a company in the West End. She vaguely remembered on some family visit a few years ago, talk of him ditching his safe job at one of the M4 corridor tech giants to go with some small research and development enterprise. She got the impression her brother's main motivation for the move was that it shaved half an hour off the commute, but Fiona, as she recalled, had some more articulate reasons. Big fish in small pond, along those lines. Of course, with those two, James' career moves were agreed by both of them after much discussion. Rose couldn't imagine anything worse than having to run her career decisions past someone else. But they had little in common, she and her older brother. At the time, she'd imagined some office suite in a business zone somewhere. Croydon, perhaps. But no, here she was, walking past overpriced sandwich shops and late-night bars catering to all tastes, right in the pulsating heart of trendy London, looking for a place with the unlikely name of Viziontecc.

And here it was on a name plate next to a glass door, alongside various other firms: PR companies, architects, content managers. The name gave little away: futuristic and techy with a casual attitude to spelling. It could be anything. Stop being stuck-in-the-mud, Rose. It's probably very important. It was well paid enough, she knew that. James' line of work had provided enough so far to put both kids into private schools. Their incomes had certainly diverged over the years along with everything else. She buzzed.

A man's voice answered: "Viziontecc?"

"Yes, I'm here about my brother, James Clarke."

A pause. "He's not in the office."

"Yes. That's what I'm here about. I'd like to speak to his manager, if I may. Or his colleagues. About his whereabouts. Can I come up?"

"Well, I'm not sure…"

"Look, I've come all the way into central London just for this. I'm concerned about him."

A silence, then the door clicked. "Which floor?" asked Rose through the intercom, but all she got was static.

She went up the stairs and checked each floor. It was on the fourth. They weren't really set up for visitors: no reception area, just a door with a swipe card unit and a bell. She pressed it and heard a "ding-dong!" like a domestic doorbell. Eventually it opened. A young man with messy hair and heavy-rimmed glasses stood aside to let her in. Clearly he'd drawn the short straw with the desk nearest the door. Or maybe they rotated.

"How can I help?" he said.

"Well, my brother went to Japan for a conference, and I don't believe he's come back."

The guy looked blank. "And…?"

"Well, I'd like to know why."

Still blank.

"He does work here, right? I mean, you know he's out there, don't you?"

The man assumed an expression of hesitancy and regret. "I'm afraid I can't discuss any aspect of who works here, data privacy rules and all that."

"Oh, come on. One of your employees doesn't come back from a business trip and that's all you can say? I know my brother works here. We both know that. I also know that he went to Japan, as an employee of yours, and that he was scheduled to return and he hasn't. I don't think it's unreasonable to ask if you, his employer, who presumably paid for him to go out there, and I guess have some expectation that he'll return to the office, have some idea of what's going on?"

The guy looked a little nervous now. Rose looked up at the Viziontecc brand modestly displayed on the wall above them. "What exactly is it that you do, anyway?"

That seemed to galvanise him. "If you'll take a seat, I'll fetch the manager."

He pointed to two colourful but uncomfortable-looking chairs shoved into a corner, and walked off. Rose barely had time to get her phone out and check for messages before a woman appeared in front of her, holding out her hand and introducing herself as Susan.

"And your name is?" Susan asked.

"Rose Clarke. James is my brother."

"And he's been in contact with you, has he?"

"He sent me a postcard."

Susan's face said it all. Rose may as well have said he sent a carrier pigeon. "Was it informative?"

"No, not really. Postcards generally aren't. Listen, what do you think is going on with him? Why is he still out there? The conference finished days ago. He missed his flight, didn't he?"

Susan sat down next to Rose. "His itinerary seems to have changed, yes."

"Seems to have? You mean you don't know what's going on either? Is it to do with what he's working on? The conference was related to his work, I guess?"

"The subject of the conference fell within James' area of expertise. That's all I can say."

"Listen, Susan, what I'm really hoping to hear from you is some recognition that something peculiar is going on, that Viziontecc is aware of this and is doing everything in its power to sort it out."

"Well, you can be assured of that. Our local office in Tokyo has also been making attempts to get in touch with him."

"You can't get in touch with him?"

"I'm sure it's a temporary glitch. James isn't the type to go off-grid."

"He isn't the type to write postcards either. Look, is there any way at all this could be work-related? That's what I'm asking."

"Rose, I don't know what you do for a living, but I'm sure you must appreciate that in some sectors there's a need for a certain discretion."

Discretion? The word slapped her in the face. *She* was being lectured about discretion?

Susan continued. "We carry out high-level cutting-edge research and development into IT applications that may well shape our future. As you can imagine, competition for ideas is fierce, and we would lose the trust of our clients if we discussed our projects with anyone outside the company, or indeed outside of the project team. I appreciate your concern about James' delayed return. But I can't discuss with you any detail of what James is doing. Rest assured we take the welfare of all our employees very seriously."

This may be an alternative-thinking blue-sky enterprise but there was nothing new about Susan's management-speak.

"Delayed return? It sounds to me like you've completely lost contact with him."

"A temporary situation. You're very quick to jump to the conclusion this is to do with work. Have you spoken to his wife at all?"

"Of course I have. And what's that supposed to mean?"

Susan stood. "I appreciate this is frustrating but there isn't anything more I can say to you. As I said, we take the —"

"Yes, yes, the welfare of your employees. That's really it?"

Susan went to the door and opened it. "We're in touch with his family. When we hear something, we'll let them know."

I'm family, Rose thought. But she didn't say it. Susan waited. Rose wasn't getting anywhere. "Thanks for all your help," she said, and left.

Outside, she made for Vauxhall Cross, to see if she could call in a favour. How could James be involved in something sensitive? Was it military? Was Viziontecc a front for something? She could find out if they were on an approved supplier list for secret intelligence work. She racked her brain to try and remember what James actually did. If she were honest, he made it sound so dull it went in one ear and out of the other. But if it had got him into some kind of trouble, maybe it wasn't so dull after all.

On the other hand, Fiona wasn't being forthcoming either. James was meant to be the ordinary one out of the two of them, but suddenly he seemed to have all the secrets.

Chapter 8

Chosen at random, and because it was located conveniently on the main circular subway line, Shinjuku turned out to have a certain buzz to it. James' first sight of the place was of an enormous traffic interchange, billboards flashing on the sides of buildings all around, then when the lights changed a tidal wave of people crossing in all directions. This city certainly heaved with people, and he'd always thought London was hectic. Surely there were other foreigners – it was a pretty international capital city after all – but as the throng passed by on all sides he felt a foot taller than everyone else, quite a bit wider, too, and the only person for miles with blond hair. He sensed one or two shy stares, which he didn't happen to welcome at that time. He'd prefer to stay pretty invisible, truth be told.

He'd done no research before coming here and felt rather naked without his devices, but logic dictated he should leave them behind. He'd heard of these capsule hotels, who hadn't? But here's the thing – what's the Japanese for capsule? Would he even recognise that he'd found one if he stumbled upon it? The mere prospect of trying to ask someone in the street filled him with dread. What kind of pantomime would he have to perform to get that one across? In the end he got lucky and spotted a display next to a doorway. It looked somewhat like a photo of a bank of lockers at a railway station, except that the doors were glass and there were people inside them, lying down or sitting up, although the sitting up part didn't work at all for him, sad to say.

So much concrete! Really, every inch of space was road or pavement or building, and the sky above as well. Seven, eight, nine storeys or more everywhere, it made the West End look a bit stocky, actually. There was nothing here even remotely old. Signs and lights stretched vertically up every available wall space, turning luminous as darkness started to fall. The rounded corner of one such building was decorated with giant animated characters, some kind of king, a warrior, a maid, possibly, with ears like a cat, a couple of punky-looking rabbits.

Manga! He'd almost forgotten. He'd been into manga way back, before they became all the rage, and spent many hours in his local comic shop making long-drawn-out decisions about which highly-priced new edition to spend his pocket money on. He'd made some pretence at understanding them – at least he knew enough to read them back to front – and almost felt inspired enough to try and learn Japanese, but not quite. Languages really weren't his thing, apart form the universal and beautiful language of mathematics of course. Rose was much more the linguist than he was. But manga! how enthusiastic he'd been back then. What was he, nine, ten? Same age Henry was now. Maybe Henry would get into them. Or Sophie, let's not be stereotypical. He realised he'd stopped to stare up at the cartoon figures, causing the river of passing pedestrians to divert round him on both sides. Well, he had nothing else to do. Just twiddling his thumbs, really. So he went in.

They didn't do things by half round here. By the look of what he assumed was a store guide, the place had seven floors. He went all the way up, to get the lay of the land. One and two, books and magazines; three, clothes; four, toys and figurines; five, karaoke maybe; six and seven some kind of cafe bar set-up. He went back down to the bottom. Unable to make any sense of any signage, he wandered, hoping to spot something familiar.

Overwhelming, the scale of it! He found himself looking at boys in red jumpsuits riding futuristic motorbikes through a flooded polluted post-apocalyptic Tokyo. He remembered that one. Sort of *Lord of the Flies*, only not. A whole aisle just on that one. Then things turned into more of a fantasy world, muscular chain-mail-clad warriors with swords and pendants, tales of loyalty and betrayal. He remembered that one, too. Rather bloodthirsty, it was. When he was a kid they weren't even officially translated. You had to rely on someone's precis in a hand-written badly-photocopied fanzine. Technology had certainly moved on since then. And here was Astro Boy! With his quiff and his big brown eyes, not forgetting his ability to fly and do all that superhero stuff, this little chap kicked it all off, back in the fifties it was, probably. Good to see he was as popular as ever, given the quantity of the merchandise.

Moving on, things turned into some kind of fairyland world. This wasn't familiar. A town on a hill, or was it a castle with all those turrets? And a host of creatures with wings and tongues and tails. The women seemed to rule the roost here, wielding all kinds of fearsome tools, long hair and exaggerated bodices. Ah, interesting. Here was one dressed all in yellow. Short dress, strappy sandals, bulging bust, and dancing around her a halo of purple flowers that seemed to have some magical properties, judging from the popping eyes and toothy smiles of the various males in the tableau. Across her front she clasped a sheathed sword that was practically the length of her own body, and she was clearly proclaiming something loud and powerful, though it being in Japanese he couldn't tell what it was.

Very interesting. He was right about the irises, then.

He checked out the prices, thinking of picking some up to take back for the kids, and pursed his lips. Not cheap. It

45

was only cash from now on, he'd decided, and he had a limited supply to last him goodness knows how long. Better not. He'd check them out back home, if he was going home any time soon, that was.

Outside he carried on, time for a turn around the block then back to his kennel again, he supposed. Frankly, these capsule hotels weren't meant for spending any time in, and for someone a bit bigger than the average Japanese they were poky to say the least. Moving about involved an inelegant shuffle that always rucked up the bedding. Besides, time weighed on the hands without a laptop or phone, when it seemed impossible to find an English-speaking channel on those drop-down televisions they had. So he wasn't in a desperate hurry, late though it was.

Half way down a quieter street a glare of fluorescent light caught his eye. Tinny chimes, dinging and rattling, people lined up on bar stools staring into glass screens. This must be pachinko! He'd say something for this city, there was always something to look at. He gazed in at the window for a while, then a chap came to the door.

"Come! Come!" He beckoned James in with a smile of rather brown teeth. There was no hiding here. If you looked foreign, you stuck out like a sore thumb.

"I've no idea how to play!" said James.

"I show! I show!"

Oh, why not, then? He followed the man in. Okay, this was cash as well, but not very much of it, surely. And the man was being so terribly friendly it would be rude not to oblige. A couple of turns or whatever wouldn't do any harm.

The chap took him over to the cash place where he was apparently required to hand over a few hundred yen for some silver balls. The man oversaw this transaction, grinning and nodding encouragingly. He had matching tie and braces in a striking orange colour, and his trousers were somewhat stained. He led James to a machine and sat him down beside him. He put on an energetic display with levers and flippers, not unlike pinball really.

"Now you!" He moved aside.

James' first try was terrible, but things got better after that.

"Ah! You win!" The man seemed quite excited, patting down his greased-back hair. "Where you from?" he asked between games.

"England." No point saying Carshalton or even Surrey – he'd learned that at the conference.

"Ah, England! Beautiful. Island. Like Japan." He beamed, exposing a gap in his teeth.

"Well, it's an island. Britain, anyway."

"You play again." He had little interest in Blighty and its complicated nomenclature. A few games and the balls had gone but it seemed James was quids up somehow. He was presented with a prize, a little box of sweets with a cute cat on it. Sophie might like it, he supposed, but the man beckoned him to the door.

"Come."

"Oh no, I'd better not. Places to be, you know."

Pachinko man raised his finger knowingly. "Not far, not far. Come!" Then the chap actually grabbed James' sleeve and pulled. What happened to all that formality? Well, he'd better go, then. He could always walk away if things felt untoward.

But actually it wasn't far. About ten feet from the entrance they stopped at an unmarked hatch in the wall.

"Here! Here!" The gentleman was pointing to James' prize. "You want cash? Cash prize? Cash better, yes?"

"Oh, I see!" Some exchange was apparently possible. Well, tell the truth, cash was what he needed right now. He pushed the sweets into the hatch, and after a few seconds a pile of yen was deposited there. Somewhat more than he'd paid in the first place. Handy.

"Why you in Japan? Business? Holiday?" The man looked more curious now.

"Business. Well, it was business. Not sure what it is now. Pending further developments, I suppose."

That was all he could say really. He urgently needed to have a chat with Fiona and somehow set all this straight, but the necessary ditching of all his tech gear was rather making that difficult. Still, a solution would no doubt present itself in the fullness of time. No point worrying over-much. Pachinko man looked blank, not surprisingly.

"Well, thank you very much," said James, offering a hand. Time to move on. A bite to eat somewhere then back. Enough excitement for one day. As he wandered off, he glanced back to see pachinko man standing by the parlour door gazing after him curiously.

Chapter 9

Rose got lost on the way to James and Fiona's house from the station. She'd walked it before and thought she could remember it, but one tree-lined residential Carshalton street looked much like another to her. Eventually she showed up at about four thirty, after the school run but before dinner.

Fiona opened the door. Her customary track suit bottoms and sporty top made her look thin and energetic, but there was also a vagueness around her eyes. When she saw Rose she frowned.

"What do you want?"

"We need to talk."

"About what?"

"About the fact that my brother's gone missing. That little matter. You remember, I'm sure."

She sighed and let Rose in. "Come into the kitchen. The kids are in the living room doing their homework."

She led the way and stood the other side of the granite-topped island unit, arms folded.

Rose sat on a stool. "I went to his office. They wouldn't tell me anything. What exactly does he do there, Fiona?"

She shrugged. "I don't know. IT stuff. He doesn't talk about it."

Rose had made some enquiries. Whatever Viziontecc did, it wasn't on behalf of any secret intelligence service, as far as her sources knew.

"They didn't seem to have any idea when he'd be back. Do you?"

A flash of something crossed Fiona's face, haunted and unsettled, evaporating into nonchalance. "What's it to you?"

"You've already played that card. I admit I'm a terrible sister-in-law, but I'm here now, aren't I? In actual fact I seem to be taking this a lot more seriously than you are."

Fiona flicked her head and gazed at the sink, which featured one of those designer taps that probably cost more than most people spent on a holiday.

"Fiona, I can help with this. I work for the Foreign Office, remember? If something's happened to James I can help look into it. But I need to know everything. Is there anything else you can tell me about this?"

In the silence that followed, children's voices drifted in from the living room. It didn't sound like they were doing homework.

Fiona sighed. "I looked at his emails. He's got himself involved with some girl he met at the conference."

Rose almost fell off her stool. "James? James Clarke? Some girl?"

"Well, the emails were pretty conclusive," sniffed Fiona. "They weren't exactly subtle."

"Since when have you been reading his emails?" This aspect of marriage made Rose's flesh creep. No way could she share her life with someone who didn't respect her privacy.

"A while," said Fiona. "It's no big deal."

"Does he read yours?"

"Well – no."

"I see. And you confronted him about this?"

"Absolutely. He denied it, which is pretty silly given I've got it in black and white. I mean, does he think I'm thick or something?"

"This was a phone call, was it?"

"Yes, for what it was worth."

"And how did it end?"

"I told him not to come home."

Rose blinked. "What – never?"

"No, not never! I just said something like, if you find Japanese customs so fascinating why don't you stay on for a while and experience some more?"

"So you were being sarcastic?"

"No! Well, yes, but I meant it as well. I don't want him here, I don't even want to set eyes on him right now. Especially if he's just going to deny it all."

She picked up a couple of plates from the drainer and stacked them. "You probably don't get it, Rose, you probably don't realise how much of a betrayal that is. We have a marriage. We both committed to this, to each other, and for the kids. I gave up my job for the family."

Rose tried to remember what Fiona did for a living. Something medical, that was all she could recall. "So you just throw him off at the first sign of trouble? Fiona, has he ever, I mean ever, done anything like this before?"

"Well, not that I know of! But I can't be sure, now, can I? He could have been sneaking around behind my back for years."

There were tears in the woman's eyes. The plates clattered. The children's conversation seemed to have stopped. Fiona wasn't being rational. But she was so invested in the family that she was touchy, super-sensitive – always had been.

"And you've had no contact with him since that phone call?" Rose asked.

"Nope." She was running water now, with her back to Rose, even though there was nothing to wash. "No email. No text. No call-back."

"No call-back? You mean you called him?"

51

Fiona turned the tap off and faced Rose. "Yes, I did. I left a message saying let's talk. That's what he said he wanted. But he hasn't phoned back, Rose! He hasn't even done that. What am I supposed to make of it?" She turned back to the sink and blew her nose gently.

There was nothing else for it. Either James was in trouble or he'd undergone some kind of personality transformation. There was only one way to find out.

Walking back to the station, Rose dialled Walter's number. Asking for time off didn't come easily to her. But it was the only way. At least she wouldn't be missed in London. She hadn't even started in the analysis team yet.

Japan. Of all places, it had to be Japan.

Chapter 10

Timothy Gardner, Tokyo's MI6 Station head, took Rose to a tiny but crammed noodle bar for lunch. Rose had got off the plane that morning and was feeling very other-worldly.

"Been here before?" Gardner asked.

"Nope." Rose stared at the pictures on the menu of eggs and pickles and seaweed.

"I'll order. It tastes better than it looks. This is one part of the world where you can eat out twice, three times a day and not put the weight on."

He patted his stomach. He was quite trim, admittedly. Gardner had been here a long time, long enough to remember Fukushima. She asked him about it.

He waved a hand. "That! It's the only thing people hear about back home. You know how many people died from radiation-linked effects? One. A couple of thousand died from the evacuation and length of displacement. The tsunami killed fifteen thousand. But the meltdown itself...still, never let the facts get in the way. You worked for Peter Craven, you said. How is he these days?"

"He's okay. I was in Moscow when he got shot. He's recovering well but back in the UK, probably for good now."

"He's a sound man." Gardner's blue eyes looked thoughtful. "You work for Walter Tomlinson, is that right? Not someone I know a lot about. Salisbury I've crossed paths with."

"Yes, well, who hasn't?"

"Not that it's got me anywhere. I've still seen my budget cut year on year for the last ten years. I do say to him, Japan may not be in the news much but it's still the third biggest economy in the world. And it hasn't moved. It's got Korea on one end and Russia on the other, Taiwan bottom left and China top left. Can't get more strategically significant than that. The Americans know it. They're maintaining their presence in the area as much as ever. Me, I'm on a skeleton staff. A couple of decades of economic stagnation and no one wants to know any more. Take a look out of that window. Does that look stagnant to you?"

Dark-haired heads were speeding past on the crowded street in both directions. There wasn't an empty seat inside, either. A shout, and a man in a white chef's hat and apron placed two bowls in front of them. He was wearing wellies, Rose noticed. They all were, in fact, as they rushed around the galley kitchen in a good-natured frenzy.

"They throw themselves into things," observed Gardner. "Quite an endearing feature of the place. The world could do with some more of that innocent enthusiasm." He looked at Rose's face as she stared into her bowl. "Raw egg. It's surprisingly tasty. It has a sweetness to it. Give it a jab and stir it in."

He handed her a pair of chopsticks. Rose did as he suggested and slurped some juice with the spoon. "Not bad."

"Yes, really," said Gardner, demonstrating some innocent enthusiasm himself. "I love the food. Love the whole place, actually. As I said, it gets a bad press. No press at all most of the time. Some people got stung with this slump. All through the eighties Japan was the wonder-kid of the world. All those books on the Japanese economic miracle. Then it devalued, and people assumed what went down would come back up. In other words, that the economy would behave like a western economy. But why would it? This ain't the west."

He sucked a good length of udon noodle into his mouth, the thickness of worms. "You'd think from the commentary these days it's a disaster. It's fine. It's just not growing, that's all. Plenty of places in the world would be envious of a recession that looks like this. There have been changes of course. An ageing population. It's not all salarymen. Getting on forty percent of workers are now 'non-regular', no job for life and so on. Not much has changed for women, unfortunately. Still massively under-represented at senior levels. The 'office lady' is very much at large. Though I have to say, if I had to choose between being a Japanese woman or a Japanese man, I'd be a woman."

"Why?" managed Rose. Her mouthful of noodle turned out bigger than she'd expected.

"In a lot of ways they have more freedom. A salaryman is stuck in a work environment dominated by deference and seniority. You're expected to work long hours even if you don't produce anything worthwhile and your boss is an idiot. Men hand over their salaries to their wives and get a bit of pocket money back. It's the women who manage the household, make all the decisions about the home, spend time with the kids, go on holiday while the man stays behind working in the sweltering Tokyo summer." He shuddered. "Can't say I'm a fan of the summer weather. You came at a good time from that point of view. Anyway. You have a bit of a family situation, you said?"

Rose put down the chopsticks, happy to take a break from the cultural noodle experience. "My brother came here for a conference. He works in IT. Something to do with security."

"Oh yes, well, Japan's often at the forefront of tech innovation. Something else that's overlooked. So what happened?"

"He seems to have disappeared. He didn't go home as planned and wasn't returning any messages. I got a postcard from him. Which is odd, as he never sends postcards. And this one is particularly odd. Here."

She got it out of her bag and handed it to Tim, who scanned the message.

"*The cherry blossom is lovely at this time of year?* It's December. Cherry blossom season's May. It's as far from cherry blossom season as you can get."

"Quite. When I got here this morning I went to his hotel. He stayed an extra four nights beyond what his company had booked, then apparently left without checking out. His laptop and mobile phone were still in the room. Believe me, Tim, that is not normal behaviour for James. He's welded to his gadgets."

"Hmm. I hate to ask, but—"

"Trouble at home? Well, his wife thinks so." Rose told him what Fiona had said about the emails and subsequent conversation. "I tell you, this isn't James. He missed his daughter's birthday party, for goodness' sake!"

"Mid-life crisis?" suggested Gardner. "I hate to probe, but most missing people turn out to want to be missing."

"How does that explain the postcard? Or the gear he left in the hotel? That would only happen if he didn't leave of his own accord. Or he's hiding from something."

Gardner pulled a face. "Are you sure you're not thinking too much like a clandestine? He's just an ordinary chap, isn't he?"

"Well, yes. Although when I went to his workplace I got a seriously frosty reception. I don't know what they do, but they really don't want to talk about it. Viziontecc, they're called. Heard of them?"

Gardner shook his head.

"I've never had any real idea what he does for a living," admitted Rose.

Gardner lifted his bowl and slurped the dregs of his noodle soup directly into his mouth. He put it down. "Excellent. Well, naturally, you'll need to report it at the Embassy through the proper channels. As for anything I can do, of course we're enormously under-staffed…"

"Any way of finding out if his laptop and phone are being traced?"

"We can check for bugs, but you don't necessarily need those to locate a device these days. GCHQ would be a better bet for that."

"Well, if they are being traced, no harm in whoever's doing it knowing his gear's been moved to the British Embassy. It might send a message that he's being looked for. Do you have any way of finding out if he's left the country? I've asked for a flag if he re-enters the UK. Or if he's used a credit card anywhere?"

"Probably, but Japan is still very much a cash society. If he really thinks he's being tracked he could simply pay for everything with cash. Easy to disappear, really, especially in a city this size."

"Even for a foreigner?"

"Well, we are more noticeable, though there are quite a lot of us about."

"If he's using cash, he must have quite a lot of cash on him. Do you have any friends in the Japanese banking system who can see where he's withdrawn cash?"

"I'll give it a try. This isn't going to be easy, though. If he's determined not to be contactable—"

"We don't know that for sure."

Gardner was shaking his head. "There's so little to go on. With a proper network of contacts it would be worth spreading the word, but we're down to a handful now."

A proper network. Fairchild might have exactly that, and it wasn't at all unlikely he'd be in Japan right now. Were things bad enough that she'd approach Fairchild? Talking to anyone in the business about family went right against her instincts, and with Fairchild even more so. Embarrassing if it turned out to be some domestic storm in a teacup.

No, not yet. She'd leave it for now and hope Gardner could come up with something. Maybe it wasn't as hopeless as he made it sound. But she couldn't wait forever. Unpleasant though the idea was, if Gardner came up with nothing she'd have to rethink.

Chapter 11

Fairchild wasn't entirely sure where they were going. Takao, sitting next to him, had instructed the taxi driver by giving him a business card. That was fishy to start with. The driver nodded and set off, his white gloved hands on the wheel manoeuvring them slowly out of the approach to the massive Tokyo Railway Station.

"So, how's business, my friend? You're making money?" Takao, in his suit and tie, may have looked like a typical salaryman but he was anything but. He was a rarity in Japan, a genuine entrepreneur.

"Yes, things are going well," conceded Fairchild. Fairchild was also an entrepreneur, but for other reasons. His global business interests were largely set up to gather intelligence. As long as they were viable and kept him solvent, he was happy. Japan he'd struggled with, though. That was why he needed a fixer, a trusted Japanese citizen to introduce him to potential prospects. He spoke the language reasonably, but the intricacies of its use, more cultural than linguistic, were sometimes a struggle. This was why he needed Takao. The man did come with some down sides, though.

"You said Ueno," said Fairchild.

"Yes, yes, Ueno district!"

Fairchild stared out of the window. "We're going straight there, are we? To this print expert you know?"

Takao gave a good-natured grin Fairchild had come to recognise. "Quick stop on the way. Will be worth your while, Fairchild. Very good opportunity!"

"Ueno is north of Tokyo Station. We're going east. That's not on the way."

"It's not far! You see, it won't take long. Few minutes."

Fairchild sighed. "At least tell me what we're going to."

The sparkle in Takao's eyes was palpable. "Small business, but growing. Good client list. Very good product. Business clients. All over Tokyo, now setting up in Osaka, Yokohama, Kobe."

"What's the product?"

"They need cash to expand. I saw their plans. Very sound, well thought through. They can double their turnover in a year. You get in now, you see real growth."

"Takao, what's the product?" They were crawling through traffic four lanes wide in the wrong direction. He hated not being in control.

"Bento boxes," said Takao.

"Bento boxes? You mean, lunchboxes?"

"Fairchild, there's so much more to a bento box than that! They are works of art, each compartment arranged, all beautifully presented in a lacquer style box. Top of the range! Big price premium, for clients who pay more for quality."

"Takao, I'm grateful that you thought of me, and I know there are limited opportunities for foreign venture capital here, but it doesn't really sound like my kind of thing."

"They hand-deliver." Takao gave him a sly look. "Go right into offices across the city. Banks. Law firms. Big conglomerates. Government departments. They do events, too. Meetings, receptions, seminars."

That made it more interesting. Opportunities there for prying eyes and attentive ears. Fairchild had forgotten how well Takao knew him. "Well, let's see what they have to say, then."

Takao sat back, satisfied. Fairchild sat back too, taking the opportunity to rest. He hadn't slept since arriving in the country that morning. But almost straight away they turned off the main highway, and several turns later came to a halt.

Fairchild had been dragged by Takao on these visits often enough to know the drill. Shoes off, indoor slippers provided, an eager handshake and elaborate business card exchange, then they were led down the aisle of a large communal office with murmurs of "*Irrashaimase!*" following them in a wave. In a modest CEO's office, a long and dull discussion, mainly led by Takao, explored the minutiae of making and delivering high quality bentos on an industrial scale. He mustered the enthusiasm to contribute a couple of questions, which elicited long answers in Japanese which Takao interpreted, at least in summary. Quite accurately for the most part, though occasionally adding a positive spin. Takao knew that Fairchild understood Japanese pretty well; they'd played this game before. Fairchild also peppered the conversation with occasional Japanese phrases, enough to impress their hosts but not to undermine their deeply held belief that it was impossible for any foreigner to learn Japanese.

Eventually, the time came when it would not be impolite to leave. More handshakes and deferential head nodding. Naturally, nothing had been agreed. It would be a long time before any actual progress would be made. These things took time in Japan, particularly when foreigners were involved and trust had to be established. It was one of the difficulties Fairchild had with this country.

Back in the taxi, Takao turned to him, eyes shining. "So, what do you think?"

"Before I answer that, can you please reassure me we're now going to Ueno to see this expert you've found?"

"Yes, of course!" He leaned forward to repeat the address to the driver, who nodded, meeting Fairchild's eye in the rear view mirror. Okay, well, they would see. The taxi slid out into more slow-moving traffic.

"It sounds interesting," Fairchild conceded on the matter of the bento company. "Things are still pretty stagnant here, though, aren't they? I mean, a top-end product like that might be difficult to get off the ground if companies are looking to minimise costs because they're not seeing any growth."

"Don't worry, my friend." Takao placed his arms behind his head in a posture more often seen in New York or London, places where he'd lived in the past, than here in Japan. "We're learning from our mistakes. Economy is set to grow. And when it does, bam! You will wish you acted earlier. You have to anticipate in business."

"In life generally, I've found." Fairchild was keeping a careful eye on their direction of travel.

"Yes. So invest early, before we see growth. Buy when market is low. You know this, Fairchild! You're successful. You can see good opportunity."

"Takao, you've been saying that Japan is about to return to growth for the past ten years."

"Because it's true!"

"Yes, but when? In another ten years?"

"No, my friend, sooner. We're a huge economy. Third biggest in the world. We will take our natural place."

This smacked of jingoism. "And what is your natural place? Second? First? Isn't third good enough? Maybe Japan would do better if it accepted itself the way it is instead of trying to take on other countries."

"Why not be competitive? Other countries are. US, China, UK. But Japan shouldn't be?"

"Well, some people say Japan's post-war bid for global economic dominance was a continuation of the imperialist mindset, a conversion of ambition from political to economic."

"Ah, so because of the war, Japan is not allowed to compete?"

"No, I just wonder if you need to. Why clamour for the top rank? What's wrong with simply being among the strongest? Japan is good at certain things. There's huge creativity here, an originality of approach that you don't see in China or the US or Germany."

"Fairchild, if you aren't trying to move up, you move down. That's how it works. Today third place, yesterday second place. If we don't care, tomorrow we'll be fourth, then after that fifth."

"So what? Will it bring hardship? Have standards of living fallen since the turn of the century? Per capita growth is still in line with the US and the UK, isn't it?"

"Yes, but economy is shrinking because population is declining. And we're all getting older. We're getting older, Fairchild!" He pealed with laughter unexpectedly and slapped Fairchild on the back, or as close as you could in the back of a taxi. "So don't delay! Act while you have the chance. I know you have the money. I know that, my friend. Use it!"

Only Takao could make investing in bento boxes sound like fulfilling your life's destiny. Fairchild moved on. "Tell me again about this print expert. Why has his name never come up before?"

"I heard about him few weeks ago. Through the grapevine, you know. Before, I tried all the universities, art dealers, galleries. Many times you've asked me about this print of yours. Plenty of people have seen it, yes?"

Fairchild nodded an acknowledgement. Takao had even taken custody of the print for periods of time, to trawl round and put it in front of connoisseurs all over Japan. This was Fairchild's own print, the one his parents specifically left him.

"Well, as I said to you before, I don't just have one print now. I have two, which look like part of a set, and I know there was a third but it's now been destroyed. So we need to start again with this. Why have you only just heard about this guy?"

"He's retired. Not been active a long time. Used to be in the trade. Had a shop. Was very well thought of. These days keeps very quiet. But people say, in years gone by, go to Yonemura-san for anything to do with old woodblock prints. He knows them all, they said. So, I got friend of a friend to set up a meeting. Not easy. He's expecting us in, ah" – he looked at his watch – "eh – toooo – we're a little behind schedule…"

Another unusual thing about Takao: in a nation obsessed with punctuality he could often be scandalously late. Fairchild was uncomfortably aware at times that other Japanese people saw Takao as eccentric. But he was also valuable; he could explain Japan to the outsider, a skill as rare as gold dust.

"Exactly how late are we?" he asked.

Takao stared at his watch as if he didn't believe what it was saying. "Ah, well." He shrugged. "Guy's retired. He won't have anything else to do."

"Oh, great."

So an unwanted bento-box diversion might have delayed him in the reason he came to Japan in the first place. There was no point in getting angry with Takao, though; he was who he was, and remained Fairchild's best tool for gaining inroads into Japan. Even the upcoming arrival of Trade Winds in Tokyo owed something to Takao, who had trawled the city for potential premises and secured one in the heart of Roppongi for a just-about-affordable rent. So they'd have to hope that Takao's natural enthusiasm would make up for them being embarrassingly late.

They came off the main highway and turned into smaller and smaller roads. The driver started muttering to himself, staring at doors as they passed. Takao joined in. Fairchild sat back and left them to it. The immense difficulty of finding an address here was one of many Japanese idiosyncrasies he could do without. With no street names, elements of an address referred to smaller and smaller units, but within the smallest unit the numbers followed no logical order. It was like moving round the shell of a snail getting ever closer to the centre, but the centre itself had no spiral pattern and was just a random mess. You knew you were in the right area, but then you just had to hunt for it, which was what they were doing.

The streets were becoming so narrow it was difficult for the taxi to get down them. At one point Takao had to jump out to move a couple of bicycles leaning against a wall. Eventually the taxi stopped. Takao turned to Fairchild.

"It's down there." He nodded down the street. "Not far."

"He knows that for sure, does he?"

Fairchild knew he didn't, but they couldn't get much further like this anyway. They got out and started walking. Away from the traffic it was like stepping back in time. Red lanterns hung outside tiny bars and restaurants. Sounds of chatter and crockery came from behind the dark panelled frontages. There was a smell of teriyaki and wood. A vending machine flashed and chatted to itself on a street corner. Takao was doing a poor job of pretending to know where he was. He stopped and asked a shopkeeper who was standing by the door of his shop. The address yielded no recognition, but when Takao mentioned the man's name, Yonemura, the shopkeeper's eyes widened and he pointed the way with some explanation Fairchild didn't catch.

"It's close! It's close!" said Takao, jogging off down the crowded lane. Fairchild lost sight of him for a moment and sped up to catch him. But Takao was already slowing, approaching a sliding door which to Fairchild looked completely anonymous.

Takao put his hand on the door. "You ready?" he asked.

Fairchild shrugged. "Sure."

Takao swept the door to the side with one confident movement. No need to knock, then. Behind the door was a tiny room laid out with tatami mats. In the centre on a folding chair sat an old man wearing shorts and flip flops. His eyes turned to them but he looked neither surprised nor startled. Takao launched into a long and respectful introduction. Fairchild assumed a deferential expression and gazed round the room. It was piled high on all sides with sacks of what looked like rice.

The man gave the slightest of nods and Takao shed his shoes and stepped inside. Fairchild followed suit and was formally introduced. No handshakes here, just a bow. The man muttered something.

"Yonemura-san says that he's happy to take a look at what you have, though his memory isn't what it was."

Fairchild already had the gist, but waited politely for Takao's interpretation before getting the prints out of his backpack. As he spread them on the floor, he said to Takao "I have to ask. What's with all the rice?"

"He's a seller. Has family in Kyushu who grows it. Very good quality. Very good prices. That's why people round here know him. Makes more money than dealing art!"

"I see." Fairchild had heard about the fiercely protected domestic rice market acting as an informal social security system, the many small acreages providing families with additional income. Another thing Takao would no doubt claim was about to change. He watched Yonemura's expression as he stared at the prints, and his breath caught.

He recognised them. This old man recognised them! Fairchild was about to say something but a small movement of Takao's hand stopped him. This wasn't to be hurried. Silence fell in the room. Outside, footsteps and an occasional voice penetrated as people passed by. Fairchild caught the fresh reedy smell of tatami. Eventually the man spoke. Takao's interpretation didn't add much.

"Ochanomizu." Yonemura pointed to one of the prints, the one featuring a river running through a gorge. Slowly he turned to point at the other one. "Yoshiwara." His finger waggled between them. "Gone. All gone. Fleeting life."

Takao translated it as *floating life*.

"Fleeting or floating?" Fairchild muttered to him. But Yonemura was talking again.

"So long ago now! Barely remembered! Just a name, no physical presence. Just a memory. Only existing inside our heads. Hah!" An unexpected laugh, like a thunderclap. "Then does it exist at all?" He chuckled, enjoying some private joke. Then his face became indescribably sad. "So much change. So much lost. Memories too painful to visit get locked away. The world was so different then! Better? No, not better. More difficult, more arduous. But you felt things. Now it's all so easy. Safe. Enough food, enough warmth. Before, no. Living was a struggle."

He tailed off, looking mournful. A question seemed allowable. Fairchild turned to Takao. "He seemed to recognise the prints. Is there any particular story associated with them?"

Takao paused and launched in. Again it was a very long rendition, the language flowery by Fairchild's ear. The question delivered, Yonemura looked at Fairchild with curiosity before turning back to the prints. "Lots of stories. How many of them true? We will never know."

That seemed to be it. Fairchild tried again. "You mentioned place names. The places these pictures represent. Are they significant? Ochanomizu. That's in Tokyo, isn't it? And Yoshiwara."

Takao obliged. Yonemura lifted a finger and traced the shapes in the pictures. "Ochanomizu. O-cha-no-mizu. Very old name. You know what it means?" He looked directly at Fairchild.

"It means water for tea," replied Fairchild in English. "I guess it was used as a spring. Is there anything of it left?"

Takao interpreted and the man lowered his head. He stayed bowed for a good while. When he looked up his eyes were full of tears.

"Gone," he said again. "All gone."

His face creased and he rocked with silent sobs.

Chapter 12

Rose was feeling as lost as she ever had. Tokyo was reminding her of Beijing, but cleaner and slicker. Back then she'd been sent single-handed on a mission to a country she didn't know at all, and she was feeling the same way about this one now.

Gardner had come through in the end. They'd managed to trace a cashpoint withdrawal in the Shinjuku area within the past forty-eight hours, thanks to a friendly Bank of Japan employee. It took her forty-five minutes from getting off the train to even find the bank where the cash machine was. Now she was circling out from it, combing the streets for places where James might stay. Gardner had written out the Japanese symbols for the word hotel – *hoteru* in Japanese, apparently – but she hadn't seen one yet. She was tired and groggy; she'd fallen asleep on the subway and almost missed the stop. And now it was cold and dark. Every face looked hostile, every sign incomprehensible. How long should she give it? She had all night really, at least nowhere else to be. But an energy boost wouldn't go amiss. She chose a place with window seating looking out onto the busy street, got herself a large coffee and a sugary chocolate donut, and settled in.

Almost as soon as she got comfortable her senses sprang to attention. A blond head bobbed past the window, a foot above the dark-haired heads around it. She rushed to the door but by the time she got outside it had gone. She ran after it, struggling to pass people without colliding with them while trying to catch another glimpse. Nothing.

The road forked into two identical-looking streets curving away in different directions. She picked one at random and raced down it for thirty seconds, then stopped. This was madness. She hadn't even seen a face. There must be thousands of men with blond hair in this city. She walked back to the junction and stood, considering whether to try the other prong of the fork or go back and retrieve her coffee and donut. A door slid open behind her.

"Rose? Is that you?"

She turned. James was standing there in a pair of pyjamas, his hair tousled, clutching a carrier bag and a triangular rice ball.

"James! I thought I saw you!" Her elation at seeing a familiar face in this strange location was real. They did a kind of upper-body hug, James using elbows as his hands were full.

"It's been a long time," said Rose, trying to remember exactly how long.

James looked strangely energised. "I knew you'd show up. Got my postcard, did you? I thought that might tickle your curiosity."

"Yes, it was completely bizarre. I didn't know what to make of it. The fact that you sent one at all is peculiar enough."

"Ah, well," James gave a knowing look. "Sometimes you have to travel back in time to hide, you see?"

"No, I don't see."

"But you're here, aren't you? I didn't know if I was overdoing it, but that's the kind of thing you go in for, isn't it? The cherry blossom in spring, pink carnations, newspaper under the arm and what-not?"

Rose stared at him. "Have you gone completely mad?"

"Oh, yes, right, of course. Very indiscreet of me. Mum's the word, naturally. Anyway, you'll want to know all about it, I suppose."

"Yes, some inkling of what's actually happening would be useful. But first, please tell me there's a good reason why you're walking about in a pair of pyjamas."

"Oh, that! Well, it's completely normal in these parts, you see. Couldn't help but notice other people doing it. When in Rome and all that. I got a craving for one of these rice balls. The ones with the tuna inside or something similar. They have a blue sticker. I'm developing something of an addiction. Maybe they put something in them. I was ready for bed, but I thought I'd just pop out."

Being tall and fairly broad, with pyjamas in a fierce red tartan, the whole effect was of a giant cuddly bear. Worrying that this was James' way of fitting in.

"Right. Well, maybe we can go somewhere and talk."

"Absolutely! I'd invite you back to my hotel room, only it's more of a cupboard than a room."

"There's a coffee place up here." Rose wondered if her donut was still there.

"Lead the way, lead the way!"

The donut was gone but they ordered fresh ones. From the looks they were getting, sitting in a coffee shop in pyjamas was perhaps not as acceptable as dropping into a convenience store, but needs must. Rose encouraged them to a table away from the window in any case.

"Honestly, Rose, you have no idea what's involved in sending a postcard in this country." James described a process in elaborate detail that sounded a lot like how you'd send a postcard in any country.

"I saw Fiona," she said.

James' good spirits deflated as though she'd pricked a balloon with a pin. "How did she seem?" he asked tentatively.

"Well, all right, considering she seems to think you're having an affair."

"Well, this is the problem, Rose. They seem to have got into my mailbox. And if they've got there, where else might they be? It was all terribly fishy right from the start, really."

"Yes, I think it might help if we go back to the beginning. Who's 'they'?"

"She's one of them. Must be. Or else they're using her. She never seemed terribly happy about it, to be honest. Can't say I blame her. Not a very appealing thing to want to do, really."

"What isn't?"

"Well, coming to my hotel room and trying to seduce me. Clearly it wasn't something she did all the time. And obviously I'm a novice, not that I've any intention of taking it up. Quite a bizarre episode, all told, though not as bizarre as her knowing which hotel I was staying in. And the room. That was the thing, you see."

Her head was starting to throb. "James, I really don't see. Who are you talking about?"

"Oh! Mirai, her name was. At least that's what she said it was. But who knows, really?"

"A woman called Mirai tried to seduce you?"

"Yes, although not much more than a girl, actually. Early twenties, though it can be difficult to tell how old people are here, don't you find?"

Rose swallowed her frustration with a slug of coffee, burning her tongue. "But you'd already met before she came to your room?"

"Yes, she was at the conference, you see. The day before. We got chatting in the bar that evening. Well, again, I thought we'd just got chatting, but thinking about it afterwards…"

"And at no point did you tell her where you were staying?"

"No. Well, not that I can recall absolutely everything. We'd had a few drinks. But why would I do that? I mean, it's not the kind of thing I'd do, is it, Rose?" He was frowning, looking as perplexed as she felt.

"Well, I wouldn't have said so, James, but sometimes when men go away on business and they're a long way from home…"

"Rose! Honestly! I would never! Besides, I've never been away on business before. It was Fiona's idea, this. Thought it might improve my career credentials. Me, I'd have been happy without, but I do as I'm told. And now look!"

"Okay," said Rose. "So she came to your room, nothing happened, and then what?"

"Well, then it was the emails. I phoned home for a catch-up as usual and I could tell straight away something was wrong. It took me a while to realise Fiona had seen some emails, and it was only then that I checked my Sent Items folder and sure enough, there they were! A rather lurid exchange between Mirai and myself, apparently. I'm afraid Fiona couldn't be persuaded that I'd never seen them before."

"Did you know she read your emails?"

"Oh, yes."

Rose felt her jaw drop.

"She didn't know I knew, of course, but my password's easy enough to guess. Pretty ironic, really. It won't do any harm, I thought, I don't have anything to hide anyway, and if it makes her feel better, why not?"

Rose shook her head. The complexities of long-term relationships passed her by. "Why ironic?" she asked.

"Pardon?"

"You said it was ironic that Fiona reads your emails."

"Well, I mean, given my line of work. That's the nub of all this, the bottom line, don't you think?"

"Is it? When I dropped in at your place of work they didn't seem massively keen to engage."

"You went there? I'm not surprised. Terribly sensitive they are about privacy. Well, it's the clients really. We do a lot of cutting-edge stuff. They don't want anything getting out there."

"You'd have thought they might prioritise the wellbeing of their staff over some clients trying to protect their copyrights."

"Well, hang on, Rose, actually they're pretty keen to do both, I mean if they can't maintain client confidentiality they wouldn't have any staff. And it isn't just about product releases. It's all about data security. Encryption methods. You know, public keys, private keys? How exactly online transactions are kept safe. If that were ever compromised, it would be the end of e-commerce. You're not the only people with secrets worth keeping."

James looked just about as moody as he ever did, which wasn't very. Bits of a conversation came back to Rose from a post-Sunday-lunch living room a few years ago, the smell of roasted parsnips lingering, children playing with plastic toys strewn across the floor. James, sitting back in his armchair, was espousing the importance of online privacy. Rose had pitched in with some observations about what some people choose to do given absolute privacy, and how many other people might suffer the consequences. It might have got heated had Fiona not intervened to change the subject.

"Listen, I don't know how long you've had this spy obsession, James."

"Don't you? You don't remember, then?" His eyes twinkled.

"Remember what? I work for the diplomatic service. You need to stop watching all those TV shows and come back to reality."

"Of course, of course, whatever you say." He took an enormous bite of donut.

"So you think this has something to do with your work?"

He eyed her, chewing. He'd never talked about what he did at work. Or was it that she'd never asked? It was something pretty mundane, though, unless he'd just given her that impression somehow.

"If it is," she said, "you need to tell me what you actually do. And why it's attracting all this attention."

He wiped his fingers on a napkin. "I'm developing a new kind of cold wallet," he said.

"What's a cold wallet?"

"Seriously? I thought you people were up-to-the-minute with this kind of thing."

"James, enough of this 'you people' thing, okay? I work for the Foreign Office." It was concerning how he suddenly seemed so sure she was more than just a diplomat. And besides, she was itching to add, I'm MI6, not GCHQ. They're the technical people. "Can you please explain to a poorly-informed public servant who's come here to try and help you, what the heck a cold wallet is, please?"

"A cold wallet is the most secure means of storing crypto-currency. You have hot wallets, you see, and cold wallets. Hot wallets sit on the exchange all the time and you don't want that. It's convenient, of course, but terribly dangerous."

"Crypto-currency? You mean Bitcoin? The stuff that criminals use for money laundering?"

"Now, now, Rose, there's no evidence crypto is used illegally any more than regular currencies. And Bitcoin's just one of them. There are dozens of them now. It was all thought up by this chap calling himself Satoshi Nakamoto. He's the one who first described the idea of decentralised ledgers, which of course makes the whole thing so very secure. It may not have been a chap, of course, or even just one person. No one actually knows who it is in real life."

"Hang on," said Rose, trying to piece together this stream of information. "It's secure, but it's also dangerous?"

"Oh, crypto itself is highly secure. The whole point is, you can't have a virtual currency if anyone could just come along and make duplicates of it. You can't fake Bitcoin. That's what gives it its value. That's because the transaction records are stored on a blockchain, which is immutable."

"What makes everyone so sure of this?"

"Because there are multiple records. Something's added to the blockchain and authorised by consensus. It's then effectively copied on all the nodes that are signed up to that system. If you wanted to change something, you'd have to change it on thousands of different drives across the world simultaneously. You can add something, but once it's on the blockchain it's staying there. So you can't copy, and there's a limited supply. That's what maintains its value. One of the key tenets of Bitcoin is that there will never be more than twenty-one million of them. Arguably, that gives Bitcoin more long-term value than fiat currencies, which all lose value in the long term as governments print more money."

"Fiat?"

"Dollars, pounds, Euros. A currency that's controlled by a central authority. Since its inception Bitcoin's value has skyrocketed. Lots of ups and downs on the way, of course.

But someone who invested a hundred dollars in 2010 would be a multi-millionaire by now."

"But what is it really worth? It's not real, is it?"

"Rose!" James was genuinely shocked. "How real is a dollar, if you're going to be like that about it? No currency's been real since they abolished the gold standard. Pieces of paper. Not even that most of the time. Figures on a screen. A currency has value for as long as you can trade with it. A fiat currency could be worth nothing tomorrow if people decided it was worthless. That's happened, hasn't it?"

"I suppose. But if Bitcoin and the others are so safe, why is data security such an issue?"

"The currency itself is secure, but the exchanges where they're traded can be hacked. People have lost millions like that. Whole exchanges have been brought down. Hot wallets sit on the exchange server. Hackers can find vulnerabilities and just go in and empty them. Not good. You don't want to store your crypto fortune online, that's for sure."

"But Bitcoin only exists online! It's a virtual currency. That's the whole point of it."

"Indeed, but it can be stored on something that's not connected to the internet. That's the best way of keeping it away from hackers. The only way, really."

"Then how do you trade it? You just said, it's only worth something if it's tradable."

"That's the thing. Usually a cold wallet is offline, but you need to go online in order to transfer money onto it or off it. You could have a much smaller online wallet for daily trades, for example, but you'd need to transfer back and forth with your cold wallet. Your fortune, your millions now, they're on the cold wallet."

"Okay, but I'm still not sure I understand what it is, exactly."

James did something that looked perilously close to an eye-roll. "Well, they just look something like a standard insertable zip drive. It's when you plug it in to go online that you're vulnerable. Even if it's only for a few minutes, someone who knows what they're looking for could get in. This is what I'm working on. An advanced level of security for cold wallet transactions. It's brand new."

"Would I regret asking how it works?"

James looked doubtful. "Well, you know, all encryption is mathematics at the end of the day. To encrypt something, you need to be able to unencrypt it again, or else it's worthless. But you need to be the only person who can unencrypt it. That's why we talk about public keys and private keys. It's all about multiplying prime numbers, you see. Very big prime numbers. The bigger the better."

"Right." Everything was starting to swim in front of Rose's eyes. "Maybe I can just take it as read that you're working on a way of securing cold wallet transactions."

"Yes, well that's about the long and the short of it. This is all top secret of course. Our client—"

"Yes, who is your client?"

"Rose, I can't tell you that! I've already said enough to get me fired. I just wonder if it might have got out somehow."

"You think that this Mirai and whoever she's with are onto what you're doing for Viziontecc?"

"Well, put it this way, there are billions of dollars' worth of crypto-currency stored in cold wallets across the globe. Whatever the more traditional commentators think, let me tell you, this is real money with real value and a lot of people would be very interested in getting their hands on it."

"You think they're hackers?"

"Well, how did they know where I was staying? Then there was that other time with Mirai."

"Another time?"

"I went to a Seven-Eleven and when I came out she was there. Waiting for me."

"She knew where you were?"

"I took my phone with me, as you do. And I paid with a card. Or maybe she followed me there. Oh, I don't know how but that wasn't normal. And then…"

"What?"

"Yes. I did wonder about that. She was very put out, I think. Yes, put out."

James could really do with a lesson in conciseness. "Put out about what?"

"Well, I told her, you see, that Fiona had jumped to the wrong conclusion about the two of us. That was the thing that seemed to rather upset her."

Then it came together in Rose's mind. "They wanted to blackmail you. This Mirai was a honey-trap. They sent her to the conference, and to your room, to – well – compromise you. Then they'd threaten to tell Fiona and you'd be in their hands. But it didn't work. So, instead they hacked your mailbox and fabricated an affair with some fake emails. What they didn't count on was Fiona reading them straight away. They were going to dangle them over you and threaten to send them to Fiona. So that didn't work either."

James considered. "Well, that would make sense of it all. Yes, indeed it would."

"This really isn't bad, James. You managed to foil two blackmail attempts. Completely unintentionally of course."

"Yes, well, thanks. But I fear Fiona will still take some persuading."

"Go home, James. That's the best place for you right now. Probably the safest as well. If they've tried twice they may be thinking about trying something else. Just get on a plane and sort it all out when you get back."

But James looked troubled.

"James? Just do it! You don't want to stay here, do you? Wandering about in pyjamas and sleeping in a cupboard?"

"Well, it's just – she was very clear, you see. Don't come home. I wouldn't want to risk anything. I mean I'd be doing the exact thing she told me not to do. That could just make everything so much worse, couldn't it?" He looked as mournful as a Labrador.

"James, she's as worried as you are. You know she tried to phone you? She left a message. She doesn't understand why you haven't called back."

James looked pained: an abandoned Labrador. "Well, even so," he said. "A conversation first, I think. I'll call her first, then check the lay of the land. Yes."

"How? You left your phone behind, remember."

"I'll get a burner phone! You, know, a pay-as-you-go. That's what you folk call them, isn't it?"

"James!"

"Sorry. Well, that would work, wouldn't it? I'll call her with that."

"It depends who we're up against. If these people hacked into your phone, they'll have your address book, won't they? All your contacts."

"Goodness. Yes, they might."

"It wouldn't take much to work out which are your primary contacts – Fiona, the house line, and so on. If they monitor who's calling those numbers and you call them from an unidentified phone in Japan…"

"Heavens. You think they'll do that? Track phone numbers back in the UK? But that means they know where we live as well!"

"Wait a minute, James. Let's not get ahead of ourselves. But given what you've said, it may be a precaution not to contact anybody right now. Until we can find out more."

He looked deflated.

"Good idea to get a burner phone, though," she said. "Then give me the number so I can contact you. Don't phone me directly. Call the British Embassy and leave a message there. Tim Gardner's the name you need to use. He'll pass it on and I'll contact you."

"Rose, are these people really dangerous, do you think?"

"No idea. We need to find out. I'll ask around. What did Mirai say about herself? Anything we can use to identify her?"

"Well, hah! You could say that."

"What does that mean?"

"It appears she dresses up as manga characters. Took me a while to realise. I thought she just liked to be flamboyant. But there's a theme to it all, it turns out."

"You're hiding from someone who dresses up as characters out of a comic book?"

"It's quite a big thing, Rose. Especially in these parts. She mentioned some park. What was it? Yogi, something like that. Bit of a shindig every weekend, she said. They all get their togs on and parade about."

"Right. Any way I could pick her out of a crowd of similarly dressed manga nerds?"

He looked doubtful suddenly. "I say, you're not going to – approach her, are you? Not sure about that as a tactic."

"No, I just think it might be useful to find out more about her, that's all. I might get a glimpse of who she hangs out with." She could follow her, as well – was quite good at it, actually, though she couldn't give too much away to her brother.

James described her three outfits, red, yellow and pink, in impressive and slightly disturbing detail. "Of course she may have a different costume for every week of the year," he added.

"Well, I'll take photos, see if we can find her. If you're not going home you should probably stay here for now, out of harm's way. Keep a low profile." She cast an eye over his clothing. "Try and fit in."

"Righty-ho." He sounded like she'd just sent him down to the shop to buy a pint of milk.

"Which particular cupboard are you staying in? It's one of these capsule hotels, is it?"

He told her where it was and they hugged, a little less awkwardly than before.

"Well, thanks and all that," he said. "Appreciate it. Hope I haven't put you to a lot of trouble."

He seemed smaller suddenly. Scared. This was all way outside his comfort zone. More than that – having done nothing out of the ordinary, his life as he knew it seemed in danger of vanishing. Rose hoped she was reassuring enough. But this was outside her comfort zone as well. She needed to focus and get to grips with this place, fast. Her brother needed her.

Chapter 13

An unhappy Takao trailing behind, Fairchild climbed through a hedge, ran across four lanes of traffic (brakes were applied but no horns), scrambled over a wire fence and slid down a concrete embankment to arrive at the rear end of a row of roadside offices and restaurants that backed onto the river.

To say that the river wasn't considered a feature was an understatement. A discoloured concrete wall curved round, lined with air conditioning units and the barred windows of basement rooms. Vents emitted the smell of frying fat. A diagonal railway bridge dived straight into the embankment underneath Ochanomizu station itself, its platform running parallel to the river. Boarded scaffolding and a thin row of green bushes shielded passengers waiting on the platform from any sight of the water. They wouldn't even know there was a river there. A few planters on upper floor balconies did nothing to redeem this sorry scene. In front of him, immense iron girders jutted out of both riverbanks and joined in the middle. Beyond, a squat brick road bridge with thin iron railings, dwarfed by the surrounding infrastructure, may have had some elegance once.

Fairchild took all of this in, then brought up an image of one of his prints on a tablet. He held it up to compare the two scenes. In the print, thin rowboats followed the current of the swirling blue river, rocks rose vertically on either side topped with bushes and spindly trees, a modest wooden bridge traversed the gorge, and white mountains rose in the distance. On one side a wide dirt road curved around the top of the gorge, dotted with figures in kimonos or straw hats.

Apart from something about the curve of the river, it was unrecognisable.

Takao finally caught up, shaking his head. "Fairchild, you're a crazy man!" His hair was ruffled and he'd torn his shirt on something.

"This is what's crazy," said Fairchild. "A major river running through the heart of a city, and it looks like a sewer. I'm surprised someone didn't think of filling it all in and building on top of it."

"Maybe they will." Takao pointed at some plant and rubble on the opposite side. "Building something there, yes?" Fairchild rolled his eyes. "Come, Fairchild! Not enough space in Tokyo, you know that! Every square metre is needed. You want us all to live in slums?"

"What happened to the Japanese love of nature?"

"Nature, of course! But we have to live."

"Water for tea, this place is. You'd be suicidal to drink anything from down there."

"Okay, okay." Takao smoothed his hair down.

Fairchild showed him the screen. "That's what we're looking at. Yonemura told us where this was."

"We know that already. Common subject for prints."

"But he made a point of it. Gone, he said. All gone." Fairchild looked again at the mass of buildings rising on either side. "He was certainly right about that. But what does it mean?"

He turned to Takao. This was why he needed the man. Understanding the words was one thing, making any sense of them quite another. But Takao was looking as blank as Fairchild felt.

"He was making some point about life in the past," tried Fairchild. "Floating life, or fleeting life."

"Floating life. All these scenes from the prints, the geishas and the courtesans, that's what it's called. Kind of like an unreal world."

"But it could also be translated as fleeting, couldn't it? Something that doesn't last, is gone as soon as it starts."

Takao shrugged. "Maybe."

"Should we be looking for something?" Fairchild thought about the British Museum. Was there some connection he'd missed? They'd already been to Yoshiwara. The only thing retained from that era was the name; the streets could have been anywhere in Tokyo.

"I think," said Takao gently, "I think I made a mistake taking you there. Yonemura is an old man. Memory not so good. A bit confused, maybe. Seemed very emotional."

"What do you think upset him so much?"

Takao shook his head. "Maybe nothing. Just reminded him of something. I'm sorry, my friend." He slapped Fairchild on the back. "I keep trying. Now we have two prints, I go back to all the people from before, show them both. We will get there, Fairchild! We don't give up. Now! You want some beers? I meet a few friends. You'll like them. Come join us. Just one beer, even?"

Fairchild didn't want to. It was never just one beer with Takao. He decided to walk back to his flat to clear his head. But after an hour he gave up and ducked into the nearest subway. You could forget how sprawling Tokyo was.

The flat was a tiny one-bedroomed place that Takao had found for him once and which he often requested when he came here. He had long ago become bored of hotel rooms that all looked the same. This was upstairs in a wooden house with outside steps leading up to a separate entrance, tatami mats throughout and a balcony door you could throw open. The air conditioning was under par in the height of summer but it was warm enough in winter. Close enough to the subway to avoid a sweltering ten-minute walk in August, or getting soaked in June. It had what he needed and it was quiet. The people downstairs who owned it did well out of the arrangement.

He dumped his stuff and went straight out again to the baths across the street, another reason he liked staying here. It was a modest place, white tiles and functional pipework, but the water was always scalding hot and it was clean. The stares of the Japanese men no longer unnerved him. Some of them remembered him from previous visits and they exchanged a few words. He stripped and squatted by a shower attachment, sitting on a plastic stool to soap up and wash. He rinsed and scrubbed his body raw, as he'd seen others do. He entered the hottest pool and sat between two other men, losing himself in steam and enjoying the sensation of stinging, tingling skin becoming soft and pink.

He thought about Rose. What if he couldn't solve this puzzle? She was relying on him and him alone. All the education he'd had, the oddball upbringing his parents had given him, it was for a purpose, he was sure of it, but even if he couldn't fathom what it was he had another purpose now and that was Rose. What if it petered out because he didn't get it, couldn't make sense of Yonemura's oracle-like pronouncements, in this country he'd always found confusing and difficult? He'd never forgive himself. Yet, for now, he remained defeated.

There was something else he could try, another contact, one of his own, not Takao's. He didn't want to, but right now he was out of other ideas.

Chapter 14

Sundays in Yoyogi Park seemed to get going around late morning. December in Tokyo appealed to Rose a lot more than December in London. Not warm, but dry, crisp and bright. Glad to escape a cramped hotel room, Rose came up the subway steps at Harajuku hoping to enjoy some open space. But the problem with any open space in Tokyo was that thousands of other people wanted to enjoy it too. Trainloads of Tokyo citizens arrived every five minutes and even in this large space the bottlenecks filled up. Where did the Japanese go to get away from everybody? They didn't, was the impression she got. The cultural norm was to do what everyone else was doing. Which was clearly going to lead to crowd control issues sometimes.

Joining the flow of people, she drifted over to a wide central boulevard. Various groups were positioned along it, with sound systems and big black speakers. Now she could see how much of a big thing dressing up was. A handful of break dancers were doing their thing in baseball caps and fat trainers. Next, a huge group of rockabillies strutted around in leather trousers and black jackets with hair styled like sharks' fins. Further along a band was playing lively pop music and a vocalist in a frilly white dress and wedge heels was dancing enthusiastically. There was plenty to look at in the passers-by as well: two girls dressed identically in burgundy velvet dresses with matching white cloth hats and tiny leather backpacks – sisters, or just friends? Grunge dressers showed off baggy t-shirts and ripped jeans, but they were never dirty – torn and ragged but always laundered.

She got a glimpse of red. A scarlet, flaming red and streaks of it in long hair as well – part of James' description of how Mirai dressed for the conference. Wow, she must have stuck out like a sore thumb. Not here, though. Here it was perfectly normal. Rose followed. The woman was on her own, squeezing her way through the growing crowds, not looking around at the bands or the dancers, intent on something but not moving fast. From a distance between meandering pedestrians Rose made out an old-fashioned style dress with long lacy sleeves yet very short on the leg, lace stockings and pointed boots, all the same shade of red, and long hair with scarlet braids. All exactly as James had described. It didn't mean it was her, though; someone else could share Mirai's cosplay preferences. It must take a lot of time to get these costumes right. The woman made for a grassy patch the other side of some trees where groups were sitting to enjoy what would be fresh air if it weren't for all the smokers. It was noticeable how many there were here compared to Europe, and the smoke hung over the ground.

Rose kept to the trees and watched as the woman sat down next to two young men, the three of them forming a circle. Their muted greeting suggested they knew each other well and that this was a regular meet point. Rose worked her way closer. The woman was sitting with her arms wrapped around her knees, a little-girl pose. The men were both young and skinny. One of them wore a jacket that looked like part of an eighteenth century military uniform, with rows of brass buttons tapering to a thin waist and an ornately embroidered raised collar. The other had hair that was gelled into a 1980's style quiff, and could have been wearing eyeliner. He had enormous boots and tie-dyed baggy trousers. Kind of a New Romantic. Was that a thing? Rose hoped not; it was bad enough first time around.

The three of them had little to say to each other. They looked decidedly glum, in fact, all staring into space or down at the ground. If they came to Yoyogi Park to get into the vibe, it wasn't working for them today. They weren't interacting with their surroundings at all.

Rose passed them from a number of different directions and got photos of all three by pretending to take wide landscape shots of the park. She sat on the grass and sent the photos to James on his new phone. She was now using a burner phone as well. In reply to the photo of the woman: *Yep, that's the girl.* The others he didn't recognise. Then Rose settled down to wait. It didn't take long. Even though visitors were still arriving and things were yet to warm up, the three of them seemed to have very little to say and after no more than half an hour they got up and went their separate ways, giving each other a muted nod as a goodbye. Which of them would she follow? The scarlet, of course.

Mirai plodded back to Harajuku station and got on the platform for the Yamanote Line going south. The platform was tolerably busy. Rose kept a comfortable distance. The train drew up and they got into the same carriage by different doors. It was standing room only. Rose grabbed an overhead strap and gazed at the garish adverts as the train slid off smoothly. She let her eye move down the advertising strip towards Mirai, and her breath caught in her throat. Mirai was staring straight at her.

Had she been spotted? Surely not. She'd stayed well back and Mirai had no reason to pick her out. She was by no means the only westerner in the park, or in the station. She got her phone out and started fiddling with it, as most other people were already doing. When she glanced up again for a second, Mirai was still staring. Her eyes were wide. It was a look of recognition – and not in a good way.

Then she realised. The woman wasn't staring at Rose at all. She was looking beyond Rose, further into the carriage.

Rose turned away as if repositioning herself to get more comfortable. She played with her phone again, and when she looked up, could see everyone behind her in the carriage. It was clear who had caught Mirai's attention. The man wasn't trying to hide his interest. Brown skin, long hollowed-out face, a worn leather jacket: this wasn't one of the players from the park. This was the real thing, a piece of street muscle with a hard look on his face. There was some message in the stare he was giving Mirai, and it wasn't a friendly one. A jolt of the train gave Rose an opportunity to shift and observe more of him. His jeans pockets were bulky. He could even be armed. Violent crime was extremely rare in Japan, but this guy had seen his share, by the look of him.

The train slowed. They were coming into Shibuya station. People shuffled towards the doors. Rose made to get ready, trying to place herself where she could see both of them at once. Neither was moving – but they were both much closer to a door than she was.

They came to a stop. A girly recorded voice announced they were at Shibuya. The doors opened. People streamed off. More people streamed on. Mirai stared out of the door. The guy stared at Mirai. The carriage was more packed than before. Then, somehow, Mirai ducked and squeezed between passengers and was on the platform hurrying away.

The man lost no time. He shoved people aside and jumped off. The manhandled passengers frowned and grimaced but weren't going to confront the guy. Rose made for the door Mirai used. The warning bell sounded. She squeezed through as best she could but some pushing was necessary. A middle-aged woman clicked her tongue and shook her head. It couldn't be helped.

The doors started to close. Rose leaped towards them and stuck out her elbow. The doors closed in on it from both sides. People around her gasped. She got her feet into the gap, grabbed both doors and forced them open. They pushed against her and she almost lost her grip. She fought them apart, squeezed through and stepped onto the platform. The doors slammed shut, trapping a strap of her backpack. She pulled but it wouldn't give. The train started to move. Eyes inside the carriage widened. Someone on the platform was shouting. She gave the strap a mighty pull and it came free, sending her staggering backwards. A man in uniform was running up to her, wagging his finger. She had no time for that. She turned to follow Mirai.

Right at the end of the platform was a set of stairs. She got the briefest glimpse of scarlet at the top and a leather back moving up two steps at a time, as people stepped sideways to get out of his way. She broke into a run, dodging passengers on the platform. She got to the steps five seconds after they'd both disappeared and took them two at a time. Somehow she had to gain on them.

The steps led into a hall with a bank of escalators. People were clustered into a crush at the bottom of them. Up in front, Rose saw scarlet again; whoever Mirai was, she clearly wasn't a member of the clandestine fraternity. Dressed like that she was fully committed, visible to anyone, no get-out. She was on the escalator but there was no pushing her way up; the stairway was completely rammed right to the top. As Mirai ascended, the leather jacket also became visible. Mirai was almost half way up before he got on, and it was several agonising seconds before Rose could set foot on it. As they went up, Mirai turned and stared down at the man. Rose could only see the back of the man's head, but Mirai's face was pale and clenched.

At the top Mirai got off and hurried left. Running wasn't possible in the packed concourse. The man did the same.

Rose was close enough to see which exit they took, and followed. It became a long wide corridor, well lit, not empty but with plenty of space. Now was his chance to catch up with her, if that was his intention. He broke into a run. Mirai turned and saw, then started running herself. But she didn't have the shoes for it.

An unsigned junction came up on the right and she darted into it and disappeared. The man sped up and followed. Rose heard a shout and some shrieks, but could see nothing. She hurried up. The man was sitting on the ground at the bottom of an escalator which led up to the street. He was holding his face. No wonder: it was a down escalator. Two or three people had stopped, holding back, watching him. There was no sign of Mirai. He picked himself up; there was blood on his face. He backed up a few steps and the murmuring intensified as the onlookers realised what he was about to do. Those on the escalator shuffled to one side. He took a run at it. His boots hammered the steps as he ran flat out to keep ahead of the downward momentum. After a long frenzy of movement he made it to the top, leaving sounds of wonder and disapproval in his wake.

Rose sprinted to the next exit which, fortunately, had stairs. She ran up and came out on a wide street next to a vast interchange. At every junction a mass of pedestrians was backed up on the pavement waiting to cross. She started pushing to the front to jump the traffic, but as she did so the lights changed and the whole wave surged into the road. She pressed forward, buried deep in the crowd.

A flash of scarlet. Mirai had just walked straight past her. Rose didn't respond until she'd gone right past, then she turned to look which way the woman was heading. She turned back and walked right into someone. It was the man.

He gave her a nasty look and hurried after Mirai. Rose turned and followed.

Mirai took a smaller road leading diagonally off the main junction. Though she was managing a lot better than Rose could do herself in heels like those, the man was gaining on her. What was he going to do to her? An act of violence right out here in the open would be conspicuous and unusual. But Mirai must have reason to fear the man. He was maybe ten paces behind her now. She darted up some steps and disappeared under an archway into a pink-tiled building. The man followed, but stopped at the top. Rose got closer. The man's progress was being halted by a security guard. An argument was going on. A banner hung on the railings outside the building but it was entirely in Japanese. Another security guard joined the first. The man realised he wasn't going to get in. He stared briefly through the archway where Mirai had disappeared, then turned and walked off.

Rose waited until he and the security guards had gone and took some photos of the building. She needed help now. Walking back to Shibuya, she phoned Tim Gardner and gave him a run-down.

"That sounds like progress," he said. "Listen, I'm tied up now, family, you know."

"Oh yes, of course." Rose had forgotten it was a Sunday.

"But come along this evening. I'm going to an opening night. Some fancy new restaurant. They're meant to be all the rage, these places. Anyway, all kinds of folk will be there. Good place to get out and do the day job. It's a plus one and the wife's not interested. So be my guest."

"Sure, sounds fine," said Rose.

But when Gardner told her the name of the place, her heart sank.

Chapter 15

Trade Winds Tokyo enjoyed pride of place in Roppongi, within staggering distance of the central crossroads where the crowd hanging out was so diverse you could be in any country in the world. The new addition fit well with the numerous other internationally-themed bars, restaurants, clubs and casinos, which all seemed as busy on a Sunday evening as any other day of the week. Rose had never been inside a Trade Winds, but she knew what to expect. She also knew who else she'd find in there, as it was no secret that John Fairchild had a controlling interest in the pan-Asian-going-on-global chain.

Should she have called him to tell him she was coming? Even before Gardner invited her to the opening, she had a pretty good idea that Fairchild was in Japan and why. It was she, after all, who'd told him about the third print, now destroyed, and encouraged him – asked him – to keep digging into it. Someone in MI6 was close to Grom, and these prints, Fairchild and his parents, Walter and possibly Salisbury were all connected in some way with some buried secret that wasn't entirely buried any more. So she had her motivations for encouraging Fairchild in this quest.

He'd agreed, of course. Though she didn't like to admit it, she knew how he felt about her. Was she using him? Yes, probably. But he was the only person from outside the Service who could dig deep enough to unearth this particular body. He would have no idea she was in Japan. So probably she should let him know. She didn't, though. She didn't have time, she told herself. She had to buy something to wear, then get from Shibuya back to the hotel to get ready, then out to Roppongi again. A pretty lame excuse, but never mind.

The clothes shopping turned out to be a bust. She found a couple of dresses that would have been okay but they didn't have them in her size. Being on the small side in Europe, it was a shock to be in a place where she was too huge to find clothes that fit. So she bought a scarf and matching clutch bag, and went back to the hotel to make do with a stretchy little black number she'd thrown into her suitcase at the last minute.

They'd made quite a fuss of the event; there was even a red carpet outside. No sign of Fairchild at the entrance, though. Rose wasn't sure why she felt so nervous. Having to dress up smartly always put her on edge, even though it was often needed for the official part of her job. She was told that Gardner was already inside so she wandered in, grabbed a glass of champagne and went to find him.

It didn't take long. Gardner had felt the need to put on a spotted bowtie, for some reason, and was already circulating.

"Rose! Let me introduce you."

Rose allowed herself to be presented to a senior Japanese couple, but pulled Gardner aside as soon as she could: "I need to show you something." If she didn't prise him away from other guests, the evening would be a waste of time.

In a quiet corner she showed him the photos of Mirai and the other two on her phone. He looked blank. "I don't recognise them, but why should I, really? It's quite common, this cosplay thing. But if they're really obsessed with it, they could be *otaku*."

"*Otaku*? What's that?"

"Well, it's what they're calling it when someone develops a passion or obsession with something like a video game or a manga character. It's more than just dressing up, it's studying every fact to do with them, and dedicating huge amounts of time to knowing all about them and resembling them as best they can. It can be unkind, like calling someone a geek or a nerd. But it can just be a word for people who get into things. And a lot of people in these parts really get into things."

"Yes, I've noticed. Can you tell what this place is?" Rose showed him the photo of the building Mirai had gone into. Gardner frowned, reading the banner.

"It's a university building. Tokyo University of Economics. Shibuya campus."

"So she's a student! They probably all are."

"Well, they certainly look young enough. This *otaku* is something that the youth go for in particular. Most of them grow out of it, but not all by any means."

"Why would three students latch onto my brother?"

"You have me there, I'm afraid. No idea."

"And why did they look so incredibly miserable?"

"Well, I don't think being a teenager in Japan is a lot of fun. Most get through those years walking around in a zombie-like state. It might be all the cramming they have to do to get through their exams. Anyway, it's not a time of great freedoms. You know suicide amongst young people is very common here."

"I'd heard something like that."

"There was one that made the news recently, actually, speaking of *otaku*. The boy was dressed exactly like – oh, what was the name? Cartoon boy, a sort of robot with special powers?"

Rose could only look blank. She hadn't thought to mug up on comics before coming out here.

"Astro Boy!" Gardner exclaimed, loud enough for people to turn round and look. "That's the one. Yes, quite sad really.

He jumped off a tall building. Did it at three in the morning to make sure he didn't take anybody out. Went head first, as if he was doing one of those Astro Boy swoops through the air." Gardner raised his hand in a kind of Superman-flying pose. "Sadly, however much you might want to fly...of course it's only speculation that he was trying to fly. I feel sure it was a suicide myself. Plenty of discussion was had."

"James seems to think they're hackers," said Rose. "He thinks they got into his email and were tracking his location. Any joy with the phone and laptop?"

"Nothing on the devices themselves. But if it's to do with hacking, it's GCHQ you want. You're better off talking to Walter. Ah! Here's the boss himself. I'd introduce you but I hear you already know each other."

She turned, and there was John Fairchild, his grey eyes amused, looking suave in a silk suit and dress shirt, but fortunately no spotted bowtie.

"Welcome," he said. "I heard you were in Tokyo. What a nice surprise."

Chapter 16

Tim Gardner had let Fairchild know who his plus one guest was. So Fairchild was forewarned. Without that he'd have struggled to carry it off. Even so, it was all he could do not to stare. He didn't get to see Rose in a clingy dress very often, but he thought about it a lot.

Last time they met, she'd shocked him with her suspicions and her appeal for help. That was in France. He thought she was still there. Why was she in Japan? Gardner had been circumspect. Fairchild couldn't imagine it had anything to do with him, though a part of him leaped for joy at the mere idea.

Gardner shook him by the hand. "You've done well tonight, Fairchild, getting the great and the good along to this shindig."

"Well, we want to get the word out that we're here. Particularly amongst people such as yourself and those who move in your circles."

Fairchild had used his network to enhance the guest list, and other means; Takao was here, of course, talking to Carmel, the woman he'd moved up to manage the entire chain after meeting her in Manila and deciding to buy the business.

"Yes, yes, well, this event will help, as will the prices, I'm sure." Gardner turned to Rose. "The only place in the world where the popularity of goods increases when the price goes up! Of course I do remember what you said, Fairchild, something about a favour. Flattered, I'm sure."

"Well, if there's anything I can do for you."

"Perhaps so! Maybe you can help out our friend here!" Gardner indicated Rose. "Since you know her already. She's in a bit of a situation, you see, and our resources aren't really up to the job. Maybe you can have a chat, see if you can assist."

It was elegantly done. Gardner was certainly a smooth operator.

"Timothy!" A voice bellowed from behind Fairchild's head. A large American, Tim's equivalent at the US Embassy, Fairchild happened to know, was standing in a huddle nearby.

"Barclay! No need to shout, my good man!" Gardner's response was barely quieter than the American's.

"Come join us! Now!"

Tim turned back to them. "Oops, better go. Have to be nice to our cousins, don't we?"

He went to receive a loud back-slapping greeting, leaving Fairchild and Rose standing. Fairchild remembered a previous occasion a little like this, a reception at the Hermitage Museum in St Petersburg. That was a year ago now, and they knew each other better. A little better, anyway. He started trying to formulate some pleasantry but she got there first.

"This favour from Tim. I suppose it has something to do with woodcut prints?"

He smiled. "Yes, I'm afraid so. I'm yet to make any serious headway, I'm sorry to say. I've known Gardner a while."

"Of course." It was probably irritating that he seemed better connected within MI6 than she was as an officer – but that had taken a lot of work and there were reasons for it. Gardner was a nice fellow, one of the better ones. "So how's Paris?" he asked. "Are you spending a lot of time looking over your shoulder?"

When they last talked, Rose had told him that her team in France had been compromised, lives endangered and the mission very nearly sabotaged, because Grom had somehow been tipped off that she was there. But he and she were the only two people who knew this, a truth that triggered that persistent light-headed mix of elation that she'd trusted only him, and fear that he wouldn't succeed in finding out who the mole was.

"I did," she said. "But I didn't see anything. Whether that means there wasn't anything to see…" She sighed. This situation was affecting her, damaging the foundations that her adult life had been based on, her belief in and loyalty to the Service.

"You saw it last time," he said.

"Because he wanted me to. Because he was playing games. Maybe he's playing a game now. Would I regret asking you how you knew I was in Paris?"

"Yes, you probably would." A waiter was passing with a tray. "May I offer you a themed cocktail?" He grabbed a couple of glasses. "This is a Seven Seas. Invented for this evening. Rum and various other things."

Rose's eyebrows lifted at the decorative fruit and umbrellas that adorned the drink, but she took it after only the slightest hesitation. Would she ever entirely trust him? She was only using him now because she had nobody else. He knew that, but had to hope. She sipped.

"Not bad. It's certainly a colourful place." She nodded at the nautically-themed décor. This was their most dramatic outfitting so far; a full-length window displayed a scale model of a tea clipper, and various Silk Route and Asian-European trade related items graced walls and corners. "Do you really think it will take off as a place for discreet conversations? It's not exactly the Oxford and Cambridge Club."

"This isn't exactly London. It's worked elsewhere. But even if it doesn't, it's profitable. You know I buy these things as going concerns. I'm not really a businessman, though the income's useful."

A pause.

"Seen Zack lately?" asked Rose.

"We crossed paths in Taipei. He's been drawn into the latest South China Sea controversy."

She nodded. "Zoe?"

She said it so casually. He wondered if the name might come up. Zoe was out at sea somewhere, no longer part of Fairchild's life. Rose had no idea the pull she had on him, and what that cost him.

"Somewhere in the Caribbean, I'm told." He managed to sound off-hand. He tried the cocktail. Pretty good, though at that moment he'd have preferred something stronger. "So," he asked. "Am I permitted to know—"

"My brother." She looked almost embarrassed. "Why I'm in Japan. It's my brother." She didn't want to tell him, clearly, but after Tim's introduction wasn't left with much of a choice. "He came here for a conference and thinks he's attracted some unwelcome attention."

Her eyes were dark. She'd never revealed anything personal about herself. She seemed almost angry that this brother of hers had put her in this situation.

"Sounds intriguing," he said. "What kind of attention?"

"Hackers. He has some sensitive R&D role in IT security, so he's just informed me. Crypto currency. Cold wallets. I suppose you're into all of that. Bitcoin and so on?"

The question sounded like an aside, but he could tell it wasn't. Fairchild had a financial advisor who looked after his holdings in a conventional and respectable way. He also had friends in more informal sectors, and a fairly comprehensive understanding of the pros and cons of decentralised finance.

"I have a modest portfolio," he said.

"Of course you do. Worth millions, is it?"

He smiled. It wasn't, but he wouldn't be drawn into that. He'd set himself up with a crypto account to get an understanding of how that world worked. The links with secrecy and the dark web were undeniable, even though crypto trading itself was perfectly legal and above board.

"So, how has this attention affected your brother?" he asked. "It must be pretty serious if you're here."

A flash of annoyance crossed her face, but he hadn't meant it as a criticism. Rose had always been focused, and so was he.

"He's currently hiding away in a capsule hotel from a group of students who dress up as characters from comic books." She sounded incredulous herself.

"How very Japanese."

"And there may be others involved. Less savoury individuals."

"What's stopping him from just going home?"

A pause. "It's complicated."

"Ah. Well, if there's anything—"

"Fairchild!" A hearty thump on the shoulder alerted him to Takao's arrival. "You are keeping your friends a secret from me! Come, come, I must know who this lady is!"

He stepped forward looking unusually dapper in a dark suit, his hair neatly greased back. His wife had a hand in it, Fairchild suspected. He sometimes detected her influence, though he'd never met the woman.

"This is Rose Clarke," Fairchild said dutifully. "Rose works with the UK diplomatic service." Takao looked suitably impressed. "Rose, Takao is my right hand man in Japan. My fixer."

"Good to meet you." She smiled, seeming to find the idea amusing, and turned to Fairchild. "You don't speak Japanese yourself, then?"

"Oh, Fairchild speaks our language very well!" said Takao with the usual Japanese patronising tone. "But Japan, it's not like anywhere else. I help him, you know, with whatever he needs." He was a little obsequious.

"It helps to have someone on the ground," said Fairchild.

"You're based here in Tokyo?" Takao asked Rose.

"No, London, actually." That was news to Fairchild. He thought she was still in Paris. "I'm here for personal reasons."

"Oh?" Takao made no attempt to hide his curiosity.

"Rose's brother," said Fairchild – he saw Rose's look of warning but wasn't going to give anything away – "is staying in a capsule hotel."

Takao's face was a picture of horror. "For how long?"

"A few days so far," said Rose.

"No! No!" Takao shook his finger. "Capsule hotel, yes, for one night! And only when too drunk to get home! More than one night, terrible! I am fixer. I fix this! Plenty of places much better than that!"

"Oh, that's really not necessary," said Rose. "It's a temporary arrangement. Besides, he could share my hotel room if he gets completely fed up of it. It's only a standard double, but—"

"No good! No good!" Takao was laying down the law. "You leave it to me! I find something suitable."

"Yes, but Takao," Fairchild spoke gently, "we must be very discreet in this matter, yes? Very discreet."

Takao understood perfectly, as Fairchild knew he would. He'd done similar things before. Besides, discretion was a Japanese speciality, particularly when it came to hotel rooms.

"Of course. Whatever you need, Takao can help." He gave a little bow. "Tomorrow, right? Don't worry. Tomorrow, I will sort something out."

Fairchild gave Rose an enquiring look. She shrugged. "All right then. Tomorrow."

So Fairchild would have a chance to find out more about her intriguing family problem. He looked forward to it, even if Rose didn't.

Chapter 17

James knew the importance of lying low. Rose had phoned to tell him about this chap who was following Mirai. She was absolutely right that it all sounded a bit dodgy, but really, one couldn't hang around all day in a capsule hotel. There was only the cash desk and the capsules themselves, and they were being cleaned and so on. It really was just a place to kip for the night. Better than a park bench, but not by much, really. So he'd spent the day strolling around getting to know the area and moving from coffee shop to bar to restaurant between times. Slightly concerned that as well as getting to know the area, the area was getting to know him, he tried to vary his route, but didn't want to venture too far or spend too much money although Rose said she'd lend him a wad if need be.

She also said he could come and stay with her if he felt the need. But hopefully this episode would be over before long anyway. He'd like nothing better than to go home, or at the very least try and speak to Fiona. What must she be thinking, him not returning her calls? What was she saying to Henry and Sophie about all this? Were they in any danger on account of this mishap? Was he, come to think of it? Or was he just being overly dramatic? Rose didn't seem to think so.

She'd certainly got rather prickly when he'd suggested she was a spy, though she shouldn't be. He and Fiona had even talked about it, but he'd never before had a particular reason to raise it. He was certainly hoping she could help now, although it had only been a day. She'd found Mirai and those two friends of hers, but this other fellow sounded like a complication. Await further instructions, he'd been told, so here he was, duly awaiting, though time was starting to drag.

He was in a sushi bar this time, not far from the pachinko parlour, trying out a selection from the old conveyor belt. Not bad to be honest, though the wasabi didn't half make his nose run. Looking out at the dark street with the strange lights and noises, he had a sudden ache of homesickness. Oh, to be back in his own house, Sophie and Henry tucked away upstairs in bed, TV on, Fiona busy with something as usual. How had it all gone wrong? His eyes filled with tears. Or maybe it was the wasabi.

He stared blankly outside at the bobbing heads passing, wondering if there might be something like a public library of books in English within striking distance, and how on earth you'd find out without the internet, when he became aware that three heads weren't bobbing past at all but were staring straight in. And that, unfortunately, the one in the middle was Mirai.

How had that happened? He'd been terribly careful, hadn't he? And what did she want? She looked at him morosely for a few minutes then the chap next to her said something to her. In fact, the two chaps were the ones in the photos Rose sent that morning. Now she was coming in, though she didn't look too happy about it. She looked more warrior-like today, in some kind of grey garb and long high-heeled boots. She came and stood next to him.

"Now, Mirai, come on, really, what is this all about?" he asked. He felt in his pocket for his phone but realised it was on the counter in front of him.

"You come with me please, James." She was quiet, but firm.

"What? No, I'm not going with you. I don't know what business you think you have with me, but I'm staying right here. And I really think you should either explain yourself or leave."

She looked up at the window. Her two friends came in and stood either side of her. One of them had golden tasselled epaulettes on his jacket, like some brigadier. The other was in some white silk get-up with black pom-poms, like those Pierrot clown figures. The three of them lined up to stare at him. No one else batted an eyelid. In Carshalton someone would call the police, unless it was Hallowe'en. James reached for his phone, but then, dammit, the brigadier saw what he was going to do and grabbed it off the counter!

"Hey! You can't do that!" James looked around but none of the staff or customers reacted to his shout.

"I'm sorry," said Mirai.

"Well, don't be sorry. Just give it back. It's mine."

"We can't." She looked the picture of misery but James, frankly, didn't care.

"This is just insufferable."

They all stood there. It was getting awkward.

"Well, I'm not prepared to put up with this, I'm afraid." James stood and gathered his things. "I'll be on my way and you can expect to hear from the police about that phone, believe me."

For a moment he thought they would block his path to the door, but they let him through, looking rather shamefaced. James went out, unsure what he'd do after that, but he thought he'd better march off decisively for as long as they could see him.

"James-san!"

He turned. Mirai had run out after him. "You have to help us. Please." She looked pretty desperate, he had to admit.

"Mirai, you know normally I would, but I have my own problems to think about. I can't get mixed up in whatever this is about. I don't know why you think I can help you, anyway."

She really did look terribly agitated.

"Look. If you need help, why not go to the police?"

A tear slipped down her cheek. Oh, deary dear.

"I really am terribly sorry." It went against his instincts to walk away from a lady in distress, but he had to get out of this. He turned and made off down a random street, going as fast as he could without breaking into a run, determined not to look back.

He was vaguely aware that a car was nosing down the street behind him. Something smacked into the side of his head. He lurched diagonally. His face throbbed. The car drew up alongside. Someone came up to him and punched him. He staggered backwards and fell to his knees, right next to the car. Nice wheel hubs. Looked like a BMW. Vintage. A kick in the lower back jarred his spine. They were all round him now. The car door opened and two of them pulled him up. They pushed him inside head first. One of them got in and slammed the door. The car set off.

Another man was already on the seat. James scrambled round to an upright position. He was sandwiched between the two of them, leather jackets and short hair. He wasn't going to stand for this.

"Hey, you can't just grab someone, you know!"

The other chap landed a fist on his cheek, right where it was already aching. He hadn't felt pain like this since school. What else could he do? He tried turning round to look out of the back window, but one of them wrenched his head forward again. Now his neck was sore as well. He could see out of the front but had no idea where they were going and couldn't tell anyone if he did. It seemed he was stuck.

Things were not going at all well.

Chapter 18

On Monday morning Rose tried calling James but he didn't pick up. She'd left three phone messages and three texts when Fairchild called.

"Takao's found some accommodation for your brother. Seems very keen to take him there. It's probably very nice. And it'll be safe."

"Well, that's good to know, Fairchild, but I can't get hold of James today. He's not answering his phone or replying to texts."

A pause. "Are you worried?"

"Yes." She kept thinking about the guy who was after Mirai.

"Well, how about we all get over there, to where he's supposed to be staying?"

She didn't argue; she needed the help. They all drew up in a taxi near Shinjuku Station and Rose led them to where the capsule hotel was. When they got there, Takao looked doubtful.

"Not usually anyone here daytime," he said. "Just for overnight, these places."

Rose was getting more and more concerned. "Can the staff tell us anything?"

"That's not going to be easy," said Fairchild. "I doubt we'll get anything out of them. Especially about guests and their sleeping arrangements."

Takao stepped forward. "I try it," he said. "I have couple of ideas."

Fairchild shrugged. "If you think it's worth it."

Takao disappeared inside.

"Does he know you're pulling his strings?" said Rose.

110

"Probably."

They stood there gazing round for a few moments. The street was quiet. Someone went past on a bicycle. A cat sloped across the road.

"Is this out of character for him?" said Fairchild.

"Completely. He's not the sort to get into trouble. Or do anything out of the ordinary."

"At the reception you said something about unsavoury people being involved."

Rose told him about the guy who was following Mirai.

"Sounds like organised crime," said Fairchild. "Japanese mafia."

"Yakuza? That's what I thought. I don't suppose you have any influence there?"

Fairchild smiled. "I'm afraid not." When he and Rose first met, he'd been trying to get in with a mafia boss based in Hong Kong. Rose didn't think he'd ever really forgiven her for sabotaging his operation. Neither had Zack, whose operation it ultimately was.

"What about Takao?" she said.

"Not really his thing. He's a businessman. Legitimate, more or less. This area, Shinjuku, is quite big for yakuza. A lot of unlicensed sex clubs, places where you can buy drugs, pachinko parlours."

"Pachinko?"

"The mafia pretty much controls the pachinko industry. In theory pachinko is classed as gaming, since gambling is illegal. But they run some kind of prize exchange scheme, which gets around it so you can bet money on your games and claim winnings. It's organised crime outlets that handle the cash and so on. Law enforcement looks the other way. Pachinko is big business after all. And the mafia is semi respectable here."

"Well, I'm not sure the guy tailing Mirai was particularly respectable. She didn't seem to think so."

Takao appeared carrying a bulging carrier bag.

"Any luck?" asked Rose.

"Yes!" He was triumphant. "So, he's been here few days. Paid cash in advance for each night. But last night wasn't here. Even though he already paid. He left some stuff."

Takao held out the bag. Rose took it and emptied it out on the pavement. Some underwear in desperate need of a wash. A couple of shirts and a crumpled jacket and trousers. The pyjamas he'd been wearing when she saw him last. Deodorant, toothbrush, toothpaste. Right at the bottom, a photograph of Fiona and the children, quite recent. She held it up.

"James brought this with him from home. No way would he go off and leave this behind."

"No phone?" asked Fairchild.

"He had a burner phone but it's not here. He left his own phone and laptop at the first hotel before coming here. He thought he was being tracked."

"Maybe he was right," said Takao philosophically.

"I need to escalate this," said Rose. "I'll call Tim."

"Tim said he couldn't help," said Fairchild.

"It's different now. James is missing and he hasn't just wandered off. I need to make it official and get people moving. If this all happened last night, he could be anywhere by now. Tim can't help with hackers, though. I need to call Walter and get him to talk to GCHQ. We have James' devices. Maybe they'll tell us something."

She stuffed everything back into the bag. Stupid, Rose. You should have stuck with him. You didn't take this seriously enough, and now he's gone.

Her feelings must have shown. "I'll try Zack," said Fairchild. "He recently worked with an FBI team that were targeting hackers."

"I call people too," said Takao eagerly. "We find little brother, don't worry."

"Big brother, actually," said Rose. Big brother she took for granted would always be there, always be home, living his ordinary life. But now he was gone. Despite the offers of help the situation seemed hopeless.

Then another terrible thing occurred to her; she'd have to call Fiona.

Chapter 19

There was a spare office in the staff area at Tokyo Trade Winds. Fairchild planned to use it as a base for the next few days. He suggested to Rose that she come back with him so they could work together. She accepted, to his surprise. He thought she'd want to do her own thing; she'd always kept him at arm's length before.

The three of them got in a taxi again. Takao spent the journey calling various people and sounding them out without, as far as Fairchild could tell, saying anything much about what he actually wanted. Indirect would be an understatement. Rose told him what she knew about the three Japanese students, and passed him the photos she'd taken. At Trade Winds, the restaurant area was being prepped to open. Fairchild offered Rose the tiny office and stepped outside to phone Zack.

"I have a favour to ask," he said.

"Huh? Well, I guess I owe you. Seems like I always owe you."

"It does, doesn't it? What do you know about hackers? Japanese hackers in particular?"

"Me? Nothing. But I know people who know quite a bit. What do you have?"

"Some photos. It's a group of three. Young. They may well be *otaku*."

"Ota-what?"

"They're very into manga characters and idols and so on. Obsessively so. Role-playing and the like. I mention it as it may help to identify them. Their online personas might tally with their costume preferences, for example."

114

"Whatever. The Feds are doing a lot on this. Tracking down groups that target organisations in the States. Screwing our economy, amongst other things. I helped them with something a while back."

"Yes, I know."

"Do you?"

"You mentioned it."

"Did I? Don't remember that."

"Well, you did. If you can shed any light, it would be helpful."

"Helpful to who exactly, can I ask?"

Fairchild paused. "The British."

"The British? Any British in particular?"

Another hesitation clinched it.

"It's Clarke, isn't it? Rose Clarke, who's resigned from the Service, or is in Paris, or something?"

Was his life really that predictable? "As it turns out, Zack, she's in Japan."

"You don't say! And I guess she had no idea at all that you were there?"

Another pause.

"She did? Amazing! And already she's roped you into something. You see what I mean with this woman? You're so into the idea you're a freelancer, going around working for whoever you want, but she's got you on a pretty short leash, seems to me."

"Zack, listen."

"Oh, you've got some explanation, have you? How she just happened to be there? You need to wise up, friend."

"It's her brother."

A pause. "Brother? What about him?"

"He came to Japan for a conference. He's not involved in anything, Zack. He isn't one of us. But he thought these hackers were onto him and now he's gone missing."

Zack's bluster evaporated. "Missing?"

"Yes. And right now, Rose is calling his wife to break the news. We don't know where he's gone or what these people want. If it is them. We also think the yakuza is involved."

"Yakuza, huh?"

"And don't think she came running to me for help. Believe me, that was the last thing she wanted."

"Why would hackers be interested in her brother?"

"He works in IT, apparently. Data security. Encryption. Something to do with crypto-currency."

"Crypto?" That got Zack interested. Another long pause. "All right. Send it through and I'll see what I can do."

"Thanks, Zack."

Fairchild hung up. Zack talked the talk but he'd do the right thing, even for Rose. And the resources he could draw on were huge. Even so, identifying online personalities from nothing but offline photos was near-impossible.

He thought a lot before making his next call. There were risks involved, not insubstantial. Mainly to himself, but not exclusively. They needed more leads, though; Zack, Takao, Tim Gardner, none of them had enough. He thought of Rose's pinched face as she stood in the street stuffing James' clothes into a carrier bag. She knew how hopeless it was.

He made the call. It was a Hong Kong number.

Chapter 20

Rose sat in the tiny office, which barely had space for a desk and chair, and stared at the phone. She wasn't sure why she'd agreed to come here with Fairchild, or whether it would turn out to be a good idea. But it beat sitting on her own in her hotel room, and if any of them found something, they could take action more quickly.

Was she being emotional? If she was, she didn't want to make a habit of it. But she needed help with this. Misgivings aside, Fairchild would do what he could, she was sure. And Takao might be useful. She'd already called Tim, who'd promised to escalate it with the Embassy and report James missing, which would alert the Japanese police. He did warn that they may not prioritise tracking down a missing foreigner if no evidence could be presented that a crime had taken place. But it was something, and he had a few sources to try.

Now for the tricky one. She picked up the office phone and dialled.

Fiona answered after five rings. She sounded groggy. It was only then that Rose thought about what time it was in the UK. Japan was eight hours ahead, so it was four in the morning. Maybe she could have waited a couple of hours. It said something that Fiona picked up, though.

"Hello?"

"It's Rose."

"Oh, hello."

"There's been a development."

"Right?"

"I saw James the day before yesterday."

"Oh. He's all right, is he?" Nice of her to ask.

"Well, he was. He thinks some hackers have got onto him. They planted those emails you saw."

"Is that right?"

"Well, actually, Fiona, I think it is. And the same people have been tracking him in some way. He didn't return your calls because he deliberately left his phone behind to try and get them off the scent."

"Well, that all sounds thrilling. And here I was thinking it was a mid-life crisis."

"Fiona, there's no mid-life crisis. He was being set up. Some group put a woman onto him to try and compromise him but it didn't work, because it's James and he wasn't interested. So they fabricated some emails with the intention of blackmailing him, not realising that you're in the habit of reading his emails."

"I see." Talk about the ice queen. "So now what? Is he intending to talk directly to me at some point, or is that too dangerous?"

"I advised him not to until we could find out more."

"Oh. Right. Well, that explains it."

"But he can't now anyway, because he's gone missing."

"What do you mean, missing?"

"We went to the place he was staying, one of these capsule hotels. He wasn't there last night. I can't get in touch with him. He's vanished."

Silence. "I see. And what exactly can be done about it?"

"Well, I'm going to try and find him, Fiona. Because he's my brother and all. I don't know what you're going to do. Sit about and feel abandoned, by the sound of it. I mean, if you cared at all that your husband's disappeared off the face of the earth, there are certain things you could do, like report it to the Foreign Office in the UK, for example. But I don't want to put you to any trouble."

"Okay, okay." Fiona sounded testy, which was the idea. "Look, I really don't know what this is about. It's not like James at all."

"That's exactly my point! James, have a fling with some Japanese girl? But you had no trouble believing it. It's something to do with his work, Fiona. He deals with encryption, crypto currency transactions, security. The Bitcoin world is full of criminals." She still felt James' defence of crypto was a bit of a whitewash. "They tried something on him and it didn't work, so they've taken him. Fiona, are you there?"

"Yes, I'm here." She was sounding vague now. "How sure are you about this?"

"I'm sure. Absolutely. When I saw James on Saturday he was his normal self. He isn't having a mid-life crisis. He just wants to get back to how things were."

"Then why didn't he come home?"

"Because you told him not to, Fiona! He wanted to. But you told him to stay here. So he did, like the dutiful obedient James we know. Look, this is serious. There may be some pretty unpleasant people involved in this."

"What do you mean, unpleasant?"

"I mean, this isn't some game. I've got help here. We're working this from all angles to try and figure out who's behind it. If you want to do something, contact the Foreign Office and follow their advice. Call Viziontecc and sound the alarm there. If that goes nowhere, jump up and down, speak to your MP, journalists, whatever. I've reported it here and I'm doing what I can. Okay?"

A pause. "Okay. If you say it's serious…"

"It's serious, Fiona. Now, do you want your husband back or not?"

"Well, of course I do." She sounded tearful now. It had to be done.

"Okay, then. Let's stay in touch."

Rose hung up. Poor old James. Fiona didn't exactly have his back. Took him for granted all these years. Maybe Rose did, too. Fiona needed waking up and Rose had done that, hopefully. But even so she hadn't told Fiona the worst of it. She hoped she sounded capable and on top of things to her sister-in-law, because she certainly didn't feel that way.

Chapter 21

You'd have thought that extreme stress caused by a singularly unusual circumstance, like being kidnapped, for example, might result in one not being able to sleep too well, but James didn't appear to be having that problem. He'd slept in the car on the way here and he had a pretty good sleep overnight as well. These futons they provided didn't look like much but seemed to do the trick, somehow. Still, the moment he did wake the next day, the enormity of it all did somewhat rush back into his head all of a sudden.

He was in an upstairs bedroom of a small terraced house, quite newly built by the look of it, though that didn't stop it being positively cold inside. A lesson in insulation wouldn't have gone amiss with whoever threw these up. Anyway, he was surrounded on the tatami floor by three sleeping bodies, his sushi bar accosters, who arrived at the same time as he did last night in a similar-looking retro car. At the time, all he could see in the dark was that the row of houses stood on its own with nothing nearby except open space and darkness. Only one of the houses had any lights on, and it was the one they were all prodded into.

It was, he had to say, rather minimal in here with little in the way of creature comforts. Soft furnishings might have helped, some carpet maybe. But it was clear this wasn't anyone's home as such, and he certainly hoped it wasn't going to become his. Anyway, they were all shepherded upstairs, and given the size of the gentleman who settled by the door, with the same kind of theme downstairs as well, they weren't going anywhere. Mirai and her pals huddled in the dark and talked. They occasionally looked over at James but in general terms he was not invited into their worried little cluster, and given it was some ridiculous hour of the morning, he thought he could most usefully spend his time catching up on some sleep.

It was the sun that woke him up. The room didn't have any curtains so it got to a certain angle and shone straight into his face as he lay. There could even have been a little warmth in its rays, but thinking about it, James decided that was just his optimistic imagination. He wriggled about in the smelly sleeping bag they'd given him, and sat up. The three other futons each held a non-moving body. The others didn't seem bothered by the excess of light. It was cold enough to see one's own breath. Was there a radiator or heater of any sort? He could see some contraption, right up at the top of the wall. What good was it there? How were you supposed to even reach it? He was decidedly reluctant to exit his sleeping bag until the room temperature could be improved.

He got to his knees and leaned a shoulder on the wall. Trouble was, he didn't want to get his arms out, as for the sake of hygiene he'd felt it wise last night to undress before going to bed, apart from the essentials on the bottom half, of course. Inside the bag he slid his knee along and got one foot on the ground, but when he tried the other he did a rather undignified roll and ended up back where he started from, only the other way round. He tried again, this time with more success, and ended up standing. It took a fair while to shuffle over to the heater, if that was what it was, and when he got there he established that it was indeed too high to reach. To do this he had to stick his arm out of the sleeping bag, an action which made him even firmer in his resolve to stay inside the bag until the room could somehow be made habitable. Replacing his arm and hugging himself to salvage some of the lost heat, he looked out of the window. Rather beautiful it was out there, he had to admit, a range of rocky snow-covered mountains right across the horizon, looking pristine and golden-white in the morning sun. A layer of snow several inches thick covered the ground right up to the back of the house. Tokyo this was not.

Another shuffle or two and he noticed a white remote control sitting on the windowsill. What was the betting that was for the wall unit? Only one way to find out. He moved forward but in his enthusiasm got a bit carried away and his feet couldn't keep pace with the rest of his body. His lower half remained in the middle of the room while his top half swung forward then down to the floor, far too quickly for him to remove his arms from the sleeping bag and break his fall. He made an involuntary yelping sound on his way down, and that, coupled with the sound of various parts of his body colliding heavily with unyielding tatami, made quite a racket.

The bodies around him sprang up like they'd been electrocuted. Six wide eyes stared at him from dark tousled heads. The door opened. A big guy stood in the doorway and glared. Slicked-back hair, moustache, dark jacket, hairy chest, tattoos. James was glad he didn't get a better look at them last night. He'd never have got any sleep if he had.

"Sorry!" he called out from his prone position. "Fell over! I was trying to put the heater on, you see, up there?"

He tried to nod in the appropriate direction but found it tricky. The man was not impressed. He said something curt in Japanese that made an impression on the others, and left.

Watched by the youngsters, James tried to worm himself into a sitting position back on his futon. "Sorry about that," he said. "I was just trying to get a bit of heat going. Is no one else cold?"

The two boys stared. Mirai eased herself out of her bag and padded over to the window. She picked up the remote

123

control and pressed a few buttons, aiming at the heater. It whirred into life, its ridges opening to emit a warm breeze.

"Oh, well done, Mirai. That'll make a difference."

She replaced the remote and crawled back into her sleeping bag. James couldn't help noticing she had nothing but knickers on her bottom half, and they were a deep burgundy colour. Did she have a burgundy outfit at home to match? She didn't go back to sleep, though. She sat and gathered the bag around her shoulders. So did the others, and James, so they all sat in a circle with only their heads sticking out of sleeping-bag pyramids.

"So, given we all seem to be in the same boat now," said James, "would this be a good time to tell me what on earth is going on?"

She gave him that desperate look again. "So sorry, James-san."

"Yes, yes, but sorry about what? I rather feel like I've earned the right to an explanation. It was you who got into my mailbox and sent those emails. Wasn't it?"

She exchanged looks with the other two and they muttered a few words to each other. The boys shrugged.

"My friends are Tomo and Haruma," said Mirai. James wasn't sure which was which, but didn't think it mattered at that stage. "We like computers."

"You're hackers?"

She looked shocked. "Not hackers. Not. But we know how. We like cosplay and fantasy characters. Manga. Computer games. We go to events. Like Yoyogi Park, but with role play. Many others go also, our friends, other students, but people all ages."

"Okay, yes, I get it." Well, he didn't entirely, but he understood what she was saying.

"A company took over a big event that happens every year. Our favourite. Very popular. But they increased ticket price to ten times amount! Students, young people, couldn't afford to go. So…"

"So?" James encouraged.

"So we hacked their ticket system and made all tickets free. Put out on social media. Thousands got tickets! Only for an hour before they closed it down, but – lots of talk. We were famous!"

"Well, that's impressive, but did you get into any trouble?"

"At start, no. Because online we have different names. Avatars. Nobody know who we are."

"You were anonymous."

"Yes. Everyone knows us online, but nobody offline. You see?"

"Of course. You can be world-famous on the web but no one can connect that to the real you."

"Ah, but…" Mirai put her head on one side, a rather expressive trademark Japanese gesture, James had observed.

"It went wrong?"

"They emailed us. They sent photos of us. They knew our real names. What we did."

"Who?"

"Eh – toooo…"

"You don't know who?"

"A group. Not Japanese. In some other country. Many other countries. They have a leader, we don't know who. But they said they tell police if…"

"If what?"

"We have to do what they say. We have to, James-san! Or they tell police. Everyone know. We bring shame on families, on ancestors."

"Ancestors?" Every time James thought he was getting the hang of this place, it threw him a curveball. He got the general impression, though.

"So to keep your identities a secret you had to do whatever they wanted? And what did they want?"

Mirai's eyes suddenly filled with tears. "You, James-san."

It made sense. The awkwardness of it all. Mirai standing out like a sore thumb at the conference, her gaucheness in the hotel room. As he'd suspected, she didn't want to be there in the first place. A young woman being coerced into throwing herself at someone like him! What an appalling predicament.

"Well, that does rather make sense now you've explained it," he said. "But would it be so terrible if people found out? I mean, knowing something and being able to prove it are two different things. You could become famous! The toast of the cosplay community! The heroic trio!"

She exchanged glances with the others. Though they kept quiet he got the impression they were following the conversation. "Not trio. Hmmm…." It took her a while to grasp the word. "Quartet. We were quartet."

"There were four of you? So where's the other one?"

Mirai was looking in particular at one of the others now, the one dressed as a clown the day before.

"He was Kiyonori. Haruma's brother." Haruma was looking at Mirai intensely. "Kiyonori didn't want to do what they said. He was angry. But also ashamed. So – he jumped."

"Jumped? Jumped where?"

An awkward silence.

"Jumped off a building," said Mirai. It came out as a whisper.

"He took his own life?" What a thick idiot he was. Finally, he'd got it.

There it was again, that morose expression, that sadness which had hung around Mirai like a cloud, despite her forced conviviality. The others had it, too; they were in mourning, these poor people. They'd lost their friend, and one of them had lost a brother. Suddenly James thought of Henry and Sophie, wondered what they were doing now and if he'd ever see them again.

In the silence, a door slammed downstairs. A car started up and drove away. Men talked. Whoever had gone, there were plenty of others left. No one moved.

"Look, I really am terribly sorry," said James inadequately. "These people sound utterly dreadful. We really don't know anything about them?"

Their blank looks confirmed it.

"And the people who brought us here? The chap outside the door? I mean I'm far from an expert in these things, but they look a lot like—"

"Yakuza," whispered Mirai, her eyes flicking to the door. "They work with the other people, the not Japanese people. They told them to bring us here."

"And why here?"

"Here we wait."

"Wait for what?"

Mirai's voice trembled. "They are coming here. The others."

"The ones who emailed you? They're coming to Japan? To see us?"

"To see you."

James sat back. "I see. Well, that's a lot of trouble to go to. Do we know when?"

Mirai shrugged. "Soon."

"Right, right."

So, basically, as he read it, an international group of blackmailing hackers who worked with the mafia were holding him hostage and were on their way to the country specifically to have a word with him. He'd love to think he had no idea what they could possibly want. Unfortunately, he did have a bit of an inkling. And it wasn't a nice thought. Not nice at all.

Chapter 22

Fairchild had spent all day talking on the phone and badgering Takao to call in all possible favours. As a result of the Hong Kong conversation, he'd also booked himself onto the earliest available flight to Hong Kong. Now he was sitting and waiting for something to bite. Rose was out combing the streets of Shinjuku, Yoyogi Park, the conference venue, any place she could think of. It was probably futile but it beat doing nothing. He'd probably do the same. Not that he knew what it was like to have a brother; for the last thirty years he'd had no living relatives at all.

The restaurant was open and doing a steady evening trade, so he drifted into the bar and sat talking to Carmel for a while, sinking a couple of long ones. Then Zack walked in.

"Hey, Fairchild! Surprise!"

Fairchild nearly choked on his gin. "Just a little. What on earth are you doing here? I thought they had you busy in Taipei."

"They did. But something came up that was more important. Hey, Carmel!" He knew the Filipino from Manila. "Any chance of a whisky? Just whisky, not the theme park in a glass?"

"Bourbon?" asked Carmel.

"No, I hate that stuff. Gimme a Scotch."

Carmel did, and floated off.

"So what's more important than the South China Sea stand-off?" asked Fairchild.

"Your hackers."

"My hackers? The people who've taken James?"

"I spoke to some people. The FBI runs a special cross-agency team dedicated to finding and neutralising hackers across the world who attack US targets. They have a broad remit to operate internationally. Your Japanese group rang a bell. They're trying to trace a group that calls itself Fire Sappers. These people are slippery. Because there are so many of them and they're all over, they're mighty hard to identify. Their attacks could be made from anywhere in the world."

"What kind of attacks are we talking about?"

"Ransomware, most often. The hackers paralyse a firm's critical systems and copy their databases, then demand a payment to restore them. Usually in crypto. Many companies just pay up and keep quiet. That's a problem."

"I wouldn't blame them though. Particularly if the ransom payment's covered by insurance."

"Yeah, but then the hackers get what they want so they keep on doing it. They're more and more confident all the time. This is why it's a priority now."

"So what do they know about these people? Presumably they try and trace the money."

"Yeah, they spend a lot of time doing that, but the methods to hide transactions are pretty sophisticated. They must be cashing the ransom money in somewhere, but it just disappears. That's why they're jumping on this. They're desperate and they think they've caught a break."

"With this Japanese group?"

"Yeah. They intercepted something that gave them the online identities of a group in Japan who pulled off some event ticketing scam. They think three of them are a match with the people whose photos you sent."

"Based on what?"

"Their avatars. One of them calls herself something like the Scarlet Sorceress, but in Japanese. It's a character from one of those manga, apparently. The others in the group match up as well. Though there's one missing."

"How do you mean?"

"The team thinks there were four of them. You only sent three."

"We only know of three."

"Well, the fourth one models himself on some boy robot who has his hair in a quiff and can fly. So if you spot anything like that, could be our fourth guy."

"I'll keep an eye out. So this group is into some serious stuff?"

"Fire Sappers? For sure. They've got away with millions in ransomware demands and filched a load of credit card details that they can sell on to anyone who wants them."

"And the Japanese group?"

"Only this one hack that we know of. But there's a connection. They're linked. Fire Sappers is global, like I said. They have people using pre-written code to carry out ransomware attacks in their own regions."

"Which they get a cut from."

"Yeah. Like licensed software."

"They must have methods of enforcing that. In case any of their licensees feel like not paying. Rose spotted someone tailing the Japanese scarlet woman who looked like mafia."

"Wouldn't surprise me. We're talking massive sums of money. All crypto, but still."

"You can spend crypto. It's accepted more widely all the time. That ought to make it easier to trace."

"Well, this team isn't in the mood to sit around and wait for someone to mess up. A sniff of a chance to get to Fire Sappers and they're all over it. There's a bunch of them arriving tomorrow. Headed by a hard-ass by the name of Agent Alice Rapp. I'm seconded onto it, as liaison."

"You're going to introduce us?"

"Yeah. And make sure we all work together. Whether you like it or not. That's how it was put to me."

"Why would we not want to work with the FBI? We're all after the same people, aren't we?"

"Kind of."

"Only kind of?"

"You're helping Rose Clarke get her brother back. Agent Rapp doesn't give a rat's ass about Rose Clarke's brother. Or anyone else except getting to the heart of this hacking network. She has a reputation, Fairchild. For not being too bothered about collateral damage. If you were being nice, you'd say she was focused."

He drained his Scotch. "That's why I'm here now. I'm giving you a heads-up. I'm meeting them tomorrow morning and bringing them here." He looked regretful. "You don't have a lot of choice about this."

"Well, not being a US citizen, I don't feel the need to accept the authority of the FBI on foreign soil. And I'm pretty sure Rose Clarke will feel likewise."

"The Feds have already been onto MI6 and okayed it all with them. If she's using MI6 resources, she's now part of the team, period."

"Well, we'll see about that." Zack must be seriously worried if he showed up in advance to warn him. Usually he was pretty adept at US agency power games. "Thanks for the heads-up. Sounds like I owe you now."

"I like the sound of that." Zack gave him a cheesy smile underneath his shades. "How about another drink?"

Chapter 23

Twenty-four hours was pretty much enough for the terraced house to showcase all its characteristics. The main one was that it defied comfort in every way. It was all but impossible to warm up a room with one of those ceiling heaters, with all the draughts and inadequate glazing, and in any case it was no good getting the ceiling lovely and warm when folk here were in the habit of sitting on the floor. James took to carrying his sleeping bag downstairs and draping it over himself where they sat, but it was really the wrong shape for that, and he was getting a little fed up of the fact that it was far too small for him. He asked for a blanket, but that didn't seem to be an option. And if there'd been something to do in the place to take your mind off things, that would help. Time really did drag along very sluggishly when there was nothing to do but stare out of the same two windows.

Occasionally the men brought food, cold rice cakes and noodle pots from a convenience store. It was okay but inadequate for a western appetite, and while James unashamedly hoovered up everything left by the other three – who didn't seem to want anything very much – he was getting hungrier all the time. Of course they had it easy compared with some kidnap victims that you read about, but it was starting to get oppressive now, and the thought of how much worse it might be when these mysterious hackers arrived filled him with dread.

The only item in the house designed to provide comfort was the heated toilet seat. Odd set of priorities, it seemed to him. A hot water bottle would have made much more of a difference, but he'd take what was on offer, and when cold or boredom got the better of him he'd wander off and plonk himself on the throne for a few minutes. He explained this by inventing a dicky tummy, patting his abdomen and looking pained. No one seemed to want to question him about it.

None of the captors had any devices of course, but there was a laptop in the house which was kept locked away. Judging from the stickers all over it and its knocked-about state, it probably belonged to one of the Japanese youngsters. After getting a phone call, one of the guards retrieved the thing out of a locked cupboard and passed it with some terse instruction to whichever of them was the nearest. It was Tomo who led, the brigadier, who'd donned his snazzy jacket for warmth although the epaulettes were looking sad. The three of them huddled round as the machine booted up, and the guard stood behind them glaring at the screen. Tomo did some tapping then stopped, and they read what was in front of them. It didn't cheer them, whatever it was. They exchanged glances then nodded to the guard who grabbed the laptop and stowed it again, putting the key in his jeans pocket.

"What was that about?" asked James when they were done. "A message from those hackers?"

Mirai nodded forlornly.

"Does it change their plans at all?"

She shook her head.

"Not nice. Not nice people." That was all she would say.

The next day they were sitting around in the downstairs room – it didn't deserve the title of living room – and the same thing happened again. This time James watched the opening of the cupboard very carefully, and timed a visit to the heated toilet seat precisely, so as to see Tomo's hands dance over the keyboard to enter the password. On the way back he didn't even glance over at the huddle. It wouldn't do any good to demonstrate an interest, but an idea was forming in his head. A rather desperate one, he had to admit, but one borne of the heaviness slowly accumulating in his gut at the prospect of these unpleasant people arriving and making their demands.

In the middle of the night when all were quietly sleeping, James got up to go to the loo. Well, you did, didn't you, if you had a dodgy tummy? The guard let him past and he padded down the carpetless stairs to the downstairs toilet, just as he did the previous night, which was when he noticed that there was no guard in the main room. By the front door, maybe, and upstairs, but not here as well. Any others must be asleep on some rota system, he'd guess. Anyway, that wasn't his concern. He paused, then flushed the loo to cover the sound of him opening the door and creeping to the cupboard. It was locked, with a key that was probably in the pocket of a gently sleeping gangster. So that wasn't an option, but the cupboard itself, like most things in this house, was a flimsy insubstantial thing and while the cistern was still filling, the noise echoing off all the hard surfaces, James got out a chopstick he'd kept earlier, inserted it into the gap between frame and door, and ripped the thing open.

The lock came away from the inside of the cupboard, taking a big chunk of chipboard with it. So much for Japanese quality. Unfortunately, the door kept swinging open so he couldn't push it shut and hide the fact that it was broken, but at least he had the laptop in his hands. He scurried back and locked the door. Sitting on the loo he opened it and powered up. The keyboard was littered with Japanese characters but luckily the old QWERTY was there as usual. What he'd noticed passing by before was that Tomo's password wasn't a BIOS password. It was a password to the operating system of the machine, not one that you needed to boot up the device itself. You'd need Tomo's password to get into his files, but that wasn't necessary. What he needed was to get connected. James hit the function keys to bypass the default start-up. Ah! This brought it all back. Good old command prompts. Like riding a bicycle, this. You only needed a few lines of text. That was the easy part. And he'd had plenty of time to decide what the message would say. The problem was that they'd see it, if he didn't cover his tracks, and that was trickier. But he was still composing the email when he heard footsteps. The guard was coming down the stairs.

Done! He sent the email. It wouldn't mean much at first glance, but if Rose was who he thought she was, she'd know people who could make sense of it. The guard let out a cry. He'd seen the open cupboard door. Oh dear, he didn't have long at all! Now for the cover-up. He worked quickly, fingers flying. The guard was pulling on the door and others were running to join him. A few more keystrokes and he'd be done.

The door crashed inward and banged against the wall. The mafia guy was standing there with his foot in the air. He grabbed the laptop from James' hands and kicked him in the shin. James tried not to cry out, but it damn well hurt. Another guard pulled him by the shoulders and dragged him out into the main room. He pushed James onto the floor and kicked him in the ribs. James couldn't breathe. He clenched as much as he could. More was coming, he knew that. The next kick was to his abdomen but it caught his hand as well and might even have broken a finger. He was a soft vulnerable mess, lying on that floor with those big boots looking to inflict the most pain.

Somewhere else in the room a conversation was going on. The three Japanese had been herded in from upstairs and ordered to look at the laptop. The moment of truth. Would they be able to figure out what he'd done? He saw Tomo log in, before a kick to his lower back sent a jarring pain through him. He felt sick. These people certainly knew their anatomy. He hoped he wasn't going to wet himself or something embarrassing like that.

One of them said something sharp.

"Ahh, James-san." It was Mirai's timid voice. "They want to know what you did."

Of course they did. "I didn't do anything. I couldn't get past the password."

An interchange between Mirai and the thugs. This was followed by another kick. James closed his eyes and focused on his own shallow breathing. He felt the cold laminated floor under his cheek. The youngsters conferred quietly. Someone was tapping the keyboard. Did he tidy it all away properly? These people were hackers, despite what Mirai said. James wasn't, though he spent a lot of time thinking from a hacker's mindset. Was that enough?

The guards were getting impatient. It was a problem for them, he supposed, if they failed in their task. Who were these absent people that everyone was so scared of? One of the men barked at the students again. They didn't respond. Even with the adrenaline James was starting to shiver. At least he'd put a t-shirt on before coming downstairs, but that was practically it. Various parts of his body were starting to throb, and his nose felt mushy.

"James-san," wavered Mirai's voice again. Bless them, they were as scared as he was. "You send email? Message?"

His heart plummeted. Had they found it? All he could do was stick to his story and hope.

"No! Like I said, I couldn't get past the password. I didn't do anything."

A few words between Mirai and the guards. He braced himself but it didn't help. The big-booted guy went for the back of his thigh this time, leather on bare skin. It felt like the boot connected directly with his bone. That was going to leave a heck of a bruise. He could taste the sick in his mouth. Though that was the least of his worries. If he chose to, this guy could stick that boot in the right place and kill him. What a spot to be in. He thought of Rose. Had she ever been in a situation like this? She'd know what to do, James was convinced of it.

One of the guards mumbled and strode across the room. Mirai shrieked. James strained to look round. The thug had her on her feet, holding her by the hair, his other hand on her neck. He was shouting at her. James didn't know what, but got the general idea.

"Now look! There's no need for that!" he said. "She didn't do anything! None of them did."

The boys were staring wide-eyed at Mirai.

"Have a go at me if you want to take it out on someone!" James added, but no one seemed to be paying any attention to him. The thug slammed Mirai against the wall. The other one pointed at the laptop and barked some order at the two boys. They scrambled forward and Tomo resumed his keyboard tapping.

"You can access my mailbox yourselves, anyway," said James. "You did it before, didn't you? Take a look. I didn't send anything. I didn't get a chance."

He could tell from Tomo's alert expression that the boy understood what he was saying. He looked back at the screen and typed some more. Odd, to think he was in the process of hacking James' email. He thought about asking if there was anything in there from Fiona, but it didn't seem the right time.

Mirai uttered some muted noise. The animal was pressing on her throat again, and her head was jammed up against the wall. Had he misjudged this? No point getting a message out there if they didn't survive the experience anyway. But clearly they were wanted alive for something. Though what kind of state they'd be in, who knew? Both youngsters were looking at the screen conferring. They were shaking their heads. Good, good. They looked up at the guards. The hand gestures and everything said what he was hoping, that they didn't find anything. Nice to know he hadn't completely lost his touch. Unless of course it occurred to them how he might have done it.

Mirai was released and the three of them trudged upstairs. The laptop was taken away somewhere. When James tried to get up, a fat hand slapped the back of his head and he collapsed back on the floor.

"Can't I at least have a sleeping bag?"

That drew another kick in the gut. The one with the biggest boots drew up a chair and sat directly in front of him. James wasn't going anywhere. He curled up as much as he could, and lay there shivering.

Did he do enough? He'd just have to wait and see.

Chapter 24

By evening, Rose had been walking the streets of Shinjuku for hours. She'd have claimed to be carrying out a rational plan, checking everywhere James could be within a fifteen-minute radius of the capsule hotel, but it felt more like an aimless walk. What was she even looking for? He wasn't sitting in some bar, she knew that. She passed the cafe where they'd eaten donuts together, and felt tearful. She wasn't usually like this, but it was different when family was involved. She'd known James her whole life, and even though he'd turned out to be a boring, bumbling buffoon, there was still something of her in him and vice versa. Dangerous situations she could cope with, but when the threat was aimed directly at a part of her life she'd always kept separate, something inside seemed to seize up. It shouldn't be happening to James. James should be back in Carshalton leading a life of unspeakable dullness. She was the one who should be out there. This kind of thing happened to her, not him.

She'd noticed the huge manga store, and checked out every floor of the place. It would be amazing if James hadn't been in there. He used to go mad for Japanese comics when he was a kid. She also clocked the pachinko parlour nearby. As she walked past, a man with slicked-back hair stood outside smoking. Tanned face, grimy clothing, tattoos on his chunky arms. She could feel his eyes following her. They must have tracked James to this location somehow. If he'd ambled this way at some point, looking very foreign and very lost, he'd have been noticeable.

It was around then that Fairchild called. "Zack just came in to the bar," he said.

"Zack? He's in Tokyo?"

"Yes. He's been assigned to this now. They're bringing in a special FBI team focused on international hackers." Fairchild explained the purpose of the team and Zack's role.

"So they think our Japanese people are part of a bigger group?"

"They're hoping so."

"Hoping so? It's not very good news for James if they are."

"No, but this team desperately wants a way in to this group. The agent in charge has something of a reputation. Alice Rapp, her name is. Zack wasn't complimentary."

"Yes, well." Zack wasn't exactly complimentary about Rose, either. Maybe he had a problem with women in positions of power, like so many men did.

"It's just a heads-up," said Fairchild. "Can you get here first thing tomorrow? That's when the whole gang will arrive and we'll get some idea of the lie of the land."

"Sure. And thanks."

"No problem."

All very understated, but it was decent of Fairchild to warn her. She hadn't heard anything about this yet from Gardner or Walter. Being on Fairchild's inside track certainly paid off sometimes. It should be good news having the FBI on the case, but somehow it wasn't, exactly.

Eventually, too tired to think or even walk straight, she went back to the hotel and tried to sleep. But then of course the jet lag set in and she couldn't. The manga store, the pachinko parlour, FBI suits showing up *en masse,* they all danced around inside her head. Then her phone dinged. Someone had emailed, to her personal email address. Not many people did that.

She reached out for her phone, and when she saw the screen she sat bolt upright. It was from James. But what a weird email. The subject and the content were made up entirely of numbers. Was it genuine? She had to assume so. The guy was a mathematician after all.

She called Walter, checking the time as she did so. One in the morning. Mid-evening in the UK.

"How's it going with GCHQ? Is there anyone who can help?" she asked.

"I've made some progress. What's the hurry?"

"I've just had a really odd-looking email from James. Strings of numbers everywhere. If it's really him, he could have managed to get a message out somehow, but I can't make sense of it. Any chance of pushing this through urgently? It could be a lead."

"Forward it to me and I'll get onto them straight away. I'll tell the analyst to contact you directly. It shouldn't be a problem now this has been prioritised. I take it Tim has updated you about the involvement of our FBI colleagues?"

"I've heard something about it."

"Yes, well," Walter was choosing his words carefully. "This is good news, of course. A joined-up international response to global hacking makes sense. And the additional resources and urgency are very timely."

"Of course." All very political and on message. "Walter, that analyst will come straight to me, won't they? Nobody else first?"

"Absolutely. Of course we will be sharing everything with our FBI colleagues. But you'll know first. You have my word."

At about five am, her phone rang. She was asked for some protocols to establish a secure line, then a woman come on introducing herself as Amy. She sounded very young. She started straight in with an explanation of the email.

"It was sent using code, not via a web browser. Quite clever actually. He's included the IP address in the email header. He wasn't trying to hide where it was coming from."

"No, he wants us to know where he is. Can you get that from the IP address?"

"That takes us to the general area. Somewhere in central Honshu, outside of Tokyo."

"That's as close as we can get?"

"From the IP address, yes. What I'm more intrigued by is the long string of numbers in the body of the email itself. It looks like a one-way function to me. I think it's a number he's got by multiplying together two prime numbers, one of which at least we're supposed to know."

This was perplexing. "Why would he do such a thing?"

"Well, he's a mathematician, isn't he? Into encryption. This is the fundamental principle behind standard RSA encryption which is used, basically, everywhere on the internet."

"Right."

Amy sounded like she thought she was talking to an idiot. Clearly GCHQ officers were used to working in a rarefied atmosphere.

"It's easy to multiply two numbers together, but not that easy to divide them again. Like mixing red and yellow paint to make orange. It's irreversible. But obviously an encryption no one can decrypt is useless. You want something that can be decrypted, but only by someone who has the right information. In this case the private key. The function is the public key, but you need a private key to unlock it."

Public keys, private keys. Rose remembered James' enthusiasm about it last time they met – and how she'd cut him short.

"And how are we supposed to know what it is?"

"Well, I suppose he thinks you'll figure it out. I reckon it's an eight-digit number we're after."

"Why do you think that?"

"Well, firstly because if you divide this number by an eight-digit number, you'll get something that's about the right length to be a set of map co-ordinates. He's trying to tell us where he is, right?"

"Well, why didn't he just email me the address of the place?"

"That's outside of my remit, but what would happen if his captors knew he'd disclosed the address?"

The penny dropped. "They'd move him. So by the time anyone got there they'd be gone."

"It's a long shot, but if he's managed to hide this message or just keep them guessing for a few hours, they may stay put long enough for you to find them."

"Okay. That works." Rose had no idea James was so devious. "But how sure are you about the eight digits?"

"I think the subject of the email is a clue. The number is 16,777,216. That's eight to the power of eight. Eight multiplied by itself eight times."

"Woah. This is complicated."

"Not to a mathematician. It's kind of like a times table, one to the power of one, two to the power of two, and so on."

"Whatever you say. So how do we figure out this eight-digit number?"

"I was hoping you could tell me."

"Really?"

"Is there a memorable number that would mean something to you and him but no one else?"

"A secret number? We didn't play number games. He was the mathmo, not me."

Amy sounded like she was trying really hard to be patient. "Eight digits could well be a date. Two digits for the day, two for the month, four for the year. That's a standard UK date format. Can you think of a date that has a special meaning?"

A long pause. "No."

"Oh." Amy sounded disappointed.

"I really can't think of anything. We didn't really…" We didn't have private jokes, or shared experiences or things that only meant something to us, she could have said. James was a geek, and Rose spent most of their time growing up just ignoring him, basically. She was starting to have a little more respect for him now.

"Couldn't it just be something really simple like his date of birth?" Rose asked.

"What's his date of birth? I'll try it."

Rose told her. Amy typed it in and waited. "No, that's miles off. We know the latitude and longitude have to be within a certain range to correspond with the IP address."

"What about my date of birth?"

"Go on, then."

Rose told her. She came back straight away. "No, that won't work."

"You haven't even tried it."

"It's not a prime number."

"Why does it have to be a prime number?"

"Well, strictly speaking it doesn't, if I'm right and we're only trying to find one number by dividing the big number by another one. But, the whole principle of one-way functions and factoring is based on prime numbers. I just think he'll be in that mindset."

Multiplying prime numbers together. James had said something about that.

"So, I'm looking for a date that means something to us both and is also a prime number?"

"Yeah." As if it was obvious.

"And how am I supposed to know if it's a prime number or not?"

"There are loads of places on the internet where you can type it in and it will tell you. But for starters it has to end with a one, three, seven or nine."

"Oh, right. That narrows down the field."

"Yes. You still can't think of anything?"

"Sorry. I mean, if it was his wife…" There were loads of possibilities there, surely, first dates, anniversaries, anything to do with the kids. "I'll get Walter to send someone round there. They may come up with something, especially if they're at the house."

"Get them to pass any possibilities straight to me and I'll check them. But he sent this email to you, didn't he?"

"Amy, honestly, I can't think what he had in mind. Can't you just check every possibility? Put in every eight-digit number and try them all until something bites?"

"That would take a very long time. I mean if it were all eight-digit primes, of which there are over five million… but of course it isn't every prime, it's only the ones that work as a date, and if it's personal it'll probably be within his living memory which dramatically reduces the years…" She was thinking out loud. "But we're assuming he's using the standard UK date format and he might not be. Also, we could get multiple hits. And it would still take a very long time. But I could set up a program. It's better than nothing. It would be a lot easier to start with suggestions, though."

"I'll see what I can do."

After the call Rose phoned Walter, who undertook to get someone local to go to her brother's home and quiz Fiona directly about dates. Then she sat and reviewed her life as far back as she could remember, at least all the events that fell within years ending with a one, three, seven or nine. What a weird way of thinking. Had he always been like this? Probably, and she'd never noticed. The most uncomfortable idea circling in her head was that James might have memories of them that he held more dear than she did. She'd always assumed that they shared a common indifference to each other. Two very distinct people leading very different lives who happened to be brother and sister, she'd always thought. And it wasn't as if they argued, exactly. They just weren't close. So what was this thing she was supposed to guess?

Of course it could be that Amy was on completely the wrong tack. The woman was certainly reading a lot into some strings of numbers. Running the whole thing by someone else wouldn't do any harm. Someone who'd bring a fresh perspective, with a cryptic mind that saw connections between things, a puzzle-solver.

Oh, hell.

She phoned Fairchild. He picked up. She'd never known him not to, in fact. She described the situation as briefly as she could.

"Maths isn't really my forte," she said.

"Nor mine. But I know about factoring and one-way functions and how a lot of encryption is based on it."

Of course he did. Fairchild's ability to absorb information from so many eclectic sources was impressive, though annoying. The reason behind it was poignant; he'd spent most of his life studying everything he could to equip himself to resolve the puzzle of his parents' disappearance. Which he'd done, at least in part, but old habits died hard.

"What she's saying makes sense to me," he said. "They have some powerful processers at GCHQ and entering all those parameters should reduce the task considerably."

Rose wondered exactly how much Fairchild knew about the strength of the processors at GCHQ.

"How much does your brother know about your role?" Fairchild asked her.

"Nothing. At least I thought nothing. I've certainly never said anything. You know how much of a no-no that is. But he did drop a few hints when we met, like he suspected something."

"It may be that there is no significant date, and he's assuming you have access to code-breakers. He might just have the idea you can click your fingers and do any kind of hacking job you want."

"Well, to be fair, people are working on it as we speak."

"But do you think they would be if the FBI hadn't got involved and upped the stakes?"

Rose didn't want to think about that. "I don't know what else to do," she said, sounding rather helpless.

"I don't think there's anything else you can do. Try to think about something else. Empty your mind. How much sleep have you had?"

Not enough. "I can't even think about sleep right now."

There was a pause, quite a long one. "Well. Don't think about it then. Take a step back somehow. It might just come to you. It's only a few hours until we meet with the cousins anyway."

"Cousins? You spend more time in the pay of the Americans than anyone else. You are a cousin, Fairchild."

He laughed softly. "That's true of me and Zack, maybe. I'm not sure about the rest of them."

She thanked him and hung up. His endorsement of the whole GCHQ approach was useful, but the rest sounded like platitudes. She went back to bed and spent some time lying there wondering what Fairchild was going to say during that long pause. Whatever it was, he'd thought better of it. Was he going to suggest something? And if he had, would she have taken him up on it?

That one was still spinning around somewhere in her head when she did, unexpectedly in the end, fall asleep.

Chapter 25

Fairchild thought Rose looked tired when she arrived at Trade Winds, but she was still early for the meeting, as was everyone else. Earliest of them all was Agent Alice Rapp, who'd walked in half an hour before the agreed start time and wasn't prone to small talk. She brought a guy with her and they sat at a table in the empty restaurant, closed at that time in the morning. After a brief introduction, they both worked their mobile phones in silence. They were dressed in standard issue FBI uniform: suit and tie, skirt and jacket. Rapp's long dark hair and heavy-rimmed glasses took the edge off her muscularity a little, but she could handle herself, Fairchild could see that. He wondered if she was carrying, even here on foreign soil. It wouldn't surprise him.

Zack came separately. That lifted the mood a little. At least they could sustain a conversation, if only small talk about hotels and traffic. Next to arrive was Barclay, the booming CIA head who came to the opening.

"Fairchild! Hey! Didn't expect to be back here so soon. Great party. Any chance of one of those cocktails? Only joking, it's a little early even for me."

Then came Tim Gardner – more greetings and introductions – then finally Rose. Fairchild didn't have the chance to ask her about the conversation they'd had last night but she gave no indication things had moved forward. He remembered with some self-consciousness a long pause, during which he'd toyed with the idea of suggesting that they get together to discuss the matter face to face. He was glad he hadn't in the end, and hoped that Rose hadn't read too much into that awkward silence.

Not being privy to the full invite list, Fairchild wasn't expecting to host such a large group, and they had to engage in some table-moving to accommodate everyone. Rapp stood with her arms folded and watched.

"How secure is this place?" she said to Zack, who'd suggested it.

"It's clean," said Fairchild. "I sweep it for bugs regularly."

"Yeah," said Zack. "If anyone's going to be listening in here, it'll be Fairchild."

Rapp was unimpressed. "Well, if you can vouch for it."

"Sure." Zack met her gaze.

As soon as they were seated, Rapp got started. "Right. It seems we all know each other now, so let's get to business." No one questioned her authority to lead. "You all have the background, but let me tell you more about these scumbags and why we want them. You know that ransomware attacks are surging. Over two thousand organisations reported an attack to the FBI last year but that's a gross understatement because most firms simply pay the ransom. It's quick, it's low-profile, they get an insurance pay-out and it's becoming seen more and more as just another cost of doing business. But that just sets it up as a successful activity, puts money into the pockets of cyber-criminals and encourages more of it. The criminals will go wherever the pay-outs are bigger and come easier. That's why they target organisations, not individuals. More recently we're seeing a surge in attacks on public sector bodies, government of different levels, and in particular healthcare."

"Because their defences are less up to date?" asked Rose.

Rapp gave her a hostile look. "No. Because there's more at stake. A hospital that has patients on life support or being prepped for vital operations can't just stop. If they do, people will die. In one twenty-four hour period, six US hospitals were targeted by the same group. This group. Some of those places were out of commission for weeks with patients having to move elsewhere. Others just paid the ransom, despite the FBI directing them otherwise."

"What can you tell us about this group in particular?" asked Gardner.

"Fire Sappers are all over the dark web. They appear on industry advisory lists worldwide now. They're getting more and more daring, and they're clever. The striking thing about those hospital attacks is that all the hospitals were in the same area. That's a lot more serious because you could have a situation where no emergency room for hundreds of miles is able to take patients. Online, their branding is aggressive and triumphalist. They just love what they do." She drew out the word love – *lurve*. "They big themselves up like wrestlers or prize fighters. It's part of the intimidation process. The message that comes up on screen when they've broken in is kind of like, look what we did, stupid!"

Whatever else Rapp was, she was passionate about the task for all the right reasons.

"Is it directed at the west?" asked Gardner. "I'm just wondering if they're tied in with Islamic extremists or anyone else who has a problem with western so-called imperialism."

"We can't rule it out, but their messages haven't been political so far. All kinds of people can turn to hacking for all kinds of reasons, but the Fire Sappers brand isn't about that. It's more, hey, we're more clever than you, so pay up! Nothing too idealistic there."

"So where are they based?" asked Rose.

"That's exactly what we don't know. We've identified individuals all over the place, although we don't know who they are in real life. Russia of course, China, India and southern Asia, right across Europe and plenty on home turf. But the uniformity of the attacks, how they're co-ordinated and their consistency, demonstrate that there's central control. Someone somewhere is running this show. It's far from random. Hackers generally are becoming more networked. Some of them sell ransomware software on a franchise basis to other hackers to widen their footprint and increase the number of attacks. Just like a regular franchise, they'll impose rules about how the software is used and will claim a cut. This group takes it a step further. They co-ordinate their attacks to make them more powerful. The participants are not franchises so much as military units. But we have no idea where to locate their commanding officer."

"There's more to that as well," said Fairchild. "How do they impose discipline? How do they get disparate rebels and criminals the world over to march to their tune?"

"Enforcement," put in Zack. "Or coercion. They have muscle on the ground."

Rapp was nodding. "There's every chance they're working in league with traditional organised crime. We could try infiltrating mafia groups but we'd need to know where to start."

"The yakuza is involved here," said Rose. "I saw one of them tailing one of the hackers."

"From our point of view, the more people involved the better," said Rapp. "The more likely we'll be able to get to them."

Fairchild could read Rose's face. Clearly she didn't think yakuza involvement was a good thing.

"What about the money?" asked Gardner. "Where does it go?"

"They invariably demand Bitcoin, and currently they use an encryption product that prevents anyone from being able to trace where the payments are going. The US government and others are in negotiation with the people running that little outfit to put pressure on them to close it down."

"So it's above board, the product?" asked Fairchild.

"It's not classed as illegal. Loads of crypto investors use it for so-called privacy. Unfortunately, that kind of complete privacy attracts cyber criminals in large number."

"So if tracing the money isn't possible, what else are you doing?" asked Rose.

"Identifying the hackers," said Rapp. "But it's slow going. It's virtually impossible to connect an online identity with a real person, unless someone messes up or is outed in some way. We spend a lot of time reviewing code to see if we can spot habits or idiosyncrasies in code writing that might lead back to specific people."

"Like bomb-makers," said Gardner. "They have their own traits."

"Exactly. It helps, but doesn't give us their physical ID or location."

"So what's the Japanese connection?" asked Rose. Fairchild could tell she was getting impatient.

"We found a connection between Fire Sappers and a bunch of Japanese hackers that seem to match up to your group," said Rapp. "Details about their avatars seem to tally with what you sent. How they look, how they dress. Whoever they are, they're not pros. A pro would be way more careful than that. For months now we've been working in the dark, going round in circles, tying things back to figures in the ether but with no way of connecting them with actual people you can arrest. This is a good break. A weakness in the chain. We need to get right onto these people and use them to take us into the Fire Sappers network."

"We also need to rescue my brother," said Rose. "Who's gone missing. And I don't know about anyone else, but I'm pretty sure that those Japanese hackers, who are no more than students by the way, must have had some help. Tracking him down half way across Tokyo without the aid of any tech and bundling him off somewhere has mob written all over it."

"Yes, maybe it would help," prompted Gardner, "to take everyone through how your brother got caught up in all this. It was rather unfortunate."

Rose did so. Rapp's man took detailed notes. Rose took them right up to the current time including James' email, but glossed over Amy's theory that Rose (or someone else) was supposed to know what the key was.

"The computing is being done right now," she said. "They're systematically working through every possible combination and when they get a hit, we'll have our location."

"Do we know when?" asked Rapp.

"No. It could be hours, it could be days."

"Well, we can use the time to prepare," said Rapp.

"Yes, what exactly is going to happen when we get the location?" asked Rose.

Rapp stared, as if she'd asked a stupid question. "We will use all possible means to get hold of these people and persuade them to help us."

"Help us how? They may not know themselves who the Fire Sappers ringleaders are."

"They're inside, we know that. They're in contact with the people we want. We can work with them to utilise that and get the info we need."

"We don't even know that the Japanese hackers are with them," said Rose. "They could be safe at home in Tokyo. It could just be my brother who's being held by a bunch of thugs."

"You don't have these Japanese guys under surveillance?" asked Barclay, the first contribution from him.

"Sorry, old man," said Gardner. "We don't have those kinds of resources. Rose here tailed one of them for a while, but once this became about a missing citizen, our priorities changed somewhat."

"*My* priorities," said Rose. "I'm the only resource working on this. It's James I'm interested in, not the others."

"I really feel that given the vital importance of a British national in all this, we need a role in planning operations," said Gardner.

"Of course, Tim," said Barclay. "We're all working together on this. We'll do everything we can to get your man out."

"Even if he's the only captive?" asked Rose.

"Sure," said Barclay.

Rose clearly wasn't convinced. "Let me make something clear. Whatever the circumstances, my brother is not to be used to try and access this group. Even if he's the only option. James was caught up in this accidentally. The number one priority of any mission to locate him is to ensure his personal safety. He is not getting involved in any FBI cyber operation. He needs to be on a plane on his way back home to his wife and children. It's the Japanese hackers you want. Not James."

"Absolutely," said Gardner. "This is a rescue mission. An extraction. Once James is out of harm's way, I'm sure he'll happily supply you with any information he has about these people."

"Now, Timothy," said Barclay. "You can rest assured that we will do everything we can to ensure the safety of your man. But you need to understand that the resources we're bringing to this are part of a high-priority mission to nail some of the world's bad guys, people who don't care who's about to die in a hospital bed as long as they get their money. These lowlifes are threatening our freedom and way of life, and we will pursue them any way we can."

Here we go again, thought Fairchild. An ideology waved about to justify how cheaply a single life can be valued. Rose wouldn't be fooled by any of this. As an agent runner herself, she'd used the same justification often enough. But this was family.

"The priority right now," Barclay was saying, "is to find these people. We have a possible location from this email. We can also see if these hackers are still in Tokyo. You can help us with where they might be?"

"Sure." Rose relayed what she saw of them at Yoyogi Park and Mirai's journey to the Shibuya campus. "And you have their descriptions already. The conference organisers might be persuaded to give up Mirai's registration details as well." Rapp and her man took all of this on board. "But we need to plan the rescue together."

That last comment seemed to fall on deaf ears.

"Who will be running the op on the ground?" asked Fairchild.

"We have our people for that," said Rapp shortly.

"The reason I ask is that Zack has considerable experience with lightning-fast raids." Fairchild had been extracted himself in that manner from tricky situations more than once. "He might be a good person to head it up given his liaison role."

"Happy to," said Zack. Rose and Gardner nodded. Rose had her moments with Zack but she could see he'd be a better choice than Rapp and her team.

"We have our people for that," repeated Rapp.

"Good thought, guys, but it isn't necessary," said Barclay, weighing in with a shade more diplomacy. "We're all set up for this. Don't worry. We're on the same side here. We make sure your boy is safe then we take it from there. In any case, we'll need to run this by the Ministry of Internal Affairs, and that's best done as a joint effort."

"Now, Barclay, can you give me every assurance we'll be totally in the loop on this?" asked Gardner. "Remember, we're supplying the intelligence here so we're very much a part of the team."

"Of course you are!" Some of Barclay's bluster was returning. "Want to shake on it?" Come on, we all want what's best for our people."

He held out his hand. While Gardner shook, looking dubious, the expression on Rose's face changed. Her eyes widened but she wasn't looking at anything. She'd thought of something – but she was keeping it to herself.

The conversation continued, arrangements for follow-up and so on. Rose took no part in it. Fairchild was watching her. At one point she got out her phone, idly tapped something into it then put it away again. People got up, more hand-shaking. Despite the warm words, the overall story was that all intelligence would be passed to Rapp who would then do whatever she liked. The British seemed to have little to bargain with. Unless of course they didn't pass the information on.

Fairchild got caught in a side conversation with Zack and Barclay. When he broke free, Rose was gone. He went to the door. No sign of her in the street either. But he knew her well enough to have an idea of what was going on.

She'd realised what the key was. She could get the location, and she was going after James herself.

Chapter 26

Rose was on the bullet train before she stopped to draw breath. It was clear how things were panning out in the meeting. The FBI were the only people in the room with any clout, and they were exclusively focused on getting into Fire Sappers. The Americans stopped short of even saying that this was a rescue mission. What they wanted was to use anyone they could to try and gain access to the group. She knew how this game worked and they weren't going to do it to James.

It was the handshake that did it. Big red-faced CIA man Barclay holding his hand out to Gardner took her right back to a slightly drunken evening years ago, sitting on a grassy bank with James, both of them staring at the sky and putting the world to rights. Then she just had to recall the date. When she had it, she called Amy. But she'd already left the meeting by then. No way was she going to share this. Not straight away.

Amy had called back almost immediately. "Bingo! It checks out perfectly. It's in a village in the mountains. I can get you to within the block."

"Best way of getting there in a hurry?"

Amy had that too, bless her. "If you don't have a helicopter, that would be the bullet train. Then a taxi, probably."

"Which train?"

Amy offered to send her the details. Rose went back to her hotel room to kit up. A hurried subway journey to Tokyo Station got her on the next train. Only then did she look at her texts. Several from Fairchild. Nothing from anyone else. She called him.

"You know it, don't you?" he said on answering.

"Where are you?"

"I'm on my own. Everyone's gone. What was it?"

"It was nothing. Just a conversation I had with him years ago. I'd forgotten about it. But the date checked out."

"You're on your way there now, aren't you?"

She didn't reply.

"You're going to have to pass on that information, Rose."

"But I don't have to do it now."

"No." In that one word she knew he understood perfectly why she was doing this. He'd probably do the same. "I can join you. Zack might, as well, if he can think of an excuse. Are you armed?"

She wasn't, and was tempted to accept his help. But even in the rush to get the train, she'd thought about this.

"If either of you join me, that scuppers the whole partnership. If it's just me, I can be dismissed as going rogue for personal reasons. We might still need the FBI. We've no idea where this will lead. It's better if it's me taking a hit, not the whole arrangement falling apart."

There was a silence while he thought about it. He wasn't giving much away.

"What do you think you'll find there?"

"It's a house just outside a village, quite remote. I think I'll find James and some street thugs. Beyond that, no idea."

"And what's your plan?"

"Go in and get James out of the picture. After that they can have what they like."

"But James *is* the picture. He's right at the heart of all this, somehow."

"Well, he won't be. He'll be gone, and so will I, and Rapp can scrape up the crumbs and do what she wants with them. No way is she getting her hands on my brother."

Another pause. The train was gathering speed, rocking slightly as it made its way through the urban sprawl of Greater Tokyo.

"If we want to keep the Americans on board," said Fairchild, "we have to share this. There's no way of avoiding it."

"Give me a head start, Fairchild. Then pass it on. Tell them you only just got it from me."

"How long do you need?"

She thought. "Three hours."

"Okay. I'll give you three hours. If there's anything more I can do…"

"Sure. Thanks"

She hung up and texted him the location. The Americans would of course find out there was a delay, but it would all come back on her and frankly she'd be happy to argue her corner. Was Rapp a safer custodian than the Japanese mafia? Rose had her doubts.

Outside, they were still passing through industrial hinterland, but further ahead the land started to rise up. Rose went back in her mind to that day, the 10th of May, 1997. It was a Saturday and some kind of family celebration: wedding anniversary, big birthday, something. The weather had been unseasonably hot, like July. There'd been a garden party, trestle tables with sausage rolls and mini onion bhajis and crumbly slices of quiche and awkward conversations with relatives, and warm orange juice, at least for Rose because she was only seventeen. James on the other hand was nineteen and back from university for the occasion, looking more like a man than when he left, though Rose couldn't have said exactly how. As the gathering started to diminish the two of them wandered out of the garden into the fields at the back where a hollow invisible from the house used to catch the evening sun. They lay on the grass.

"Hope I'm not corrupting you with this," James had said, pulling a hip flask out of his jacket. "I doubt it, somehow."

"Hardly." Rose took a swig. It was pure vodka. The heat of it made her cough. "Gross."

"Yes, well, needs must." He took a generous swig himself. One day Rose would remind him of some of this in front of his children. They chatted about this and that; she didn't remember it all. She remembered slipping her shoes off, feeling the warm earth under her feet, lying back, the sun in her face, the smell of spring grass, birds singing. James was going on about the internet.

"People could do all their shopping online. All of it, why not?"

"Why would they want to do that? People like going to the shops."

"Because it's easier. There could be a lot more choice. Cheaper, cuts out the middleman. It's going to change the world, Rose."

"Right. That's what you're going to do with your life, is it? Figure out how people can buy dining room chairs and frilly knickers from their couch with the aid of a computer?"

"Well, I could do a lot worse. Now's the time to get in with some killer app that will change everything."

"Such as?"

"Hmm. Need more time to think about that. And more vodka." He took another swig.

"So what are you going to do with your life, Rosie-Posie?"

She leaned across and poked him in the ribs, making him choke all over his hip flask. "Don't call me that."

"You made me spill it!"

"It's your fault. I'm going to travel the world."

"Ah! Hence the enthusiasm for languages. Yours would take you to France and Russia, anyway, unless you've changed your mind again."

"I haven't. And lots of places speak French and Russian. Well, French, anyway. People don't get the importance of languages. They think everyone in the world speaks English, but they don't. Languages are a key. They unlock doors. They tell you a lot about the people who speak them."

She didn't normally take her big brother seriously enough to bother lecturing him, but here he was now, all grown up and away from home while she was still a child.

"Well, that's true of maths as well," he said. "It's a key that unlocks the world."

"Yeah, right."

"Well, yes, actually. The way we live our lives is dependent on maths. Everything we do, all human activity is in some way reliant on our understanding of maths."

"You know, university hasn't made you any less pompous."

He was typically unconcerned. "It happens to be true."

"Can you order a beer with maths?"

"So that's what you'll be doing going round the world? Guzzling beer?"

"Maybe."

"What else?"

Rose reached for the hip flask. "Something important. Something that matters. Something interesting. More interesting than Surrey suburban *bleugh*." She necked the vodka.

"Hey! Leave some for me!"

She handed it over, wiping her mouth. "Sorry, not much left."

"Great." He shook the bottle. "You could be a diplomat. That's important."

"I'm not very diplomatic."

"I think there's more to it than that. Hey! You could be a spy! Go on special missions to defeat wealthy megalomaniacs who want to blow up cities in peculiar ways."

"You've read too many comics, James."

"It would certainly be interesting! You'd be good at that. I'd be happy for you to rescue me from certain death, if it came to it."

She made a show of thinking about it. "All right. It does sound cool. I'll be a spy. You make a fortune doing internet something-or-other, and I'll save civilisation as we know it."

"And to think that to everyone here we're just two ordinary Surrey teenagers. Pah! What do they know?"

"You're sounding drunk, James. You'll have to learn how to hold your liquor if you're going to get anywhere in the world."

"Never!" He belched. "You're a bottle a day girl, I suppose, even with your tender years."

"I wouldn't tell you if I were."

He sat up, red-faced with the sun and the booze, and stuck his hand out.

"Shake on it!"

She raised her head off the grass. "Are you okay?"

"Yes, I'm fine. Come on. Shake on it."

"Shake on what?"

"On not being ordinary. Whatever we do, not ordinary."

"All right. Agreed. Not ordinary."

They shook.

The train was in full pelt now, driving through thick forest towards distant icy peaks. She hadn't realised how mountainous Japan was; they went from cutting to bridge back to cutting again, concrete banks and huge spans of steel betraying the massive engineering costs of infrastructure projects like this railway line. It bothered her that James had remembered that conversation and she hadn't. It meant more to him than it did to her. He had such a jovial, easy-going manner. Had he been using it all this time to hide a hurt?

Having finally remembered, her first emotion was panic; she'd never recall the date. How on earth did James? But then she thought back to earlier in the day in the overheating garden, Dad in a sun hat complaining: *Now the Socialists are in, we'll be stocking up on candles again. Power cuts, inflation, all our money gone in taxes, this country's gone mad.* Of course; there'd been a change of government, a Labour landslide victory. This was easy then. That election was the 1st of May, 1997. She recalled being put out she was still too young to vote. So this family event, whatever it was, must have been a Saturday shortly after that. It couldn't be May 3rd, since 03051997, according to that wonderful thing the internet, wasn't a prime number. But 10051997 was.

James, what a mind. Definitely not ordinary.

At the town she got a taxi and eventually conveyed to the driver the name of the village. The taxi dropped her at a crossroads by some shops. It was some way from Amy's coordinates but she walked the rest, snow crunching underfoot. She was glad of the thick quilted jacket she'd brought with her, partly because of the cold but also because she could put up the hood and from a passing vehicle it wouldn't be obvious she was foreign. A foreigner would be more of a talking point in these parts, she imagined. The jacket also had pockets hidden deep within its generous padding in which she'd secreted some tools of the trade:

lock-picking kit, torch, lightweight monocular and even a few poppers. She had to be prepared for anything.

Approaching the coordinates – she had the map on her phone – she skirted round, finding some tree cover on the lower slopes around the back. She could see the row of houses and two old-looking cars parked out front. Old enough to hotwire, if their security hadn't been upgraded. Would they have bothered upgrading? Who'd be fool enough to hotwire a mafia car?

The situation was not ideal. It was mid-afternoon but if she waited for darkness she'd be overtaken by Rapp. Everything showed up against snow, and it left footprints. No gun. Two cars' worth of mobsters and she had no idea who else was inside. She crouched, rubbing her hands to stay warm.

This was going to be tricky.

Chapter 27

It didn't make a lot of sense, James knew, to stand at the front window and stare out, as if that in itself might summon some kind of rescue team. But he did seem to be the only person who had any expectation of something like that. A good thing, of course, and besides, if anyone had any suspicions, they wouldn't all still be here. Clearly he'd persuaded them that he was some kind of blundering incompetent. Amazing how easy it was. Even now you might have thought someone would consider it odd that he kept gazing out of the window. But no, they probably just assumed he was staring into space for no reason, or becoming fond of the scenery.

They could be right about the incompetence. He'd had too much time on his hands, that was the problem. Enough time to invent some ridiculous puzzle that only a geek like him would understand, and which relied on Rose remembering a rather inconsequential conversation they'd had some years earlier. It was only because they'd talked about spying that he'd settled on it. How touchy was she, really? If she were, she might remember it. But that would only work if he were right about her in the first place. But then, the whole thing would only work if he were right about her in the first place. Oh, stop going round in circles, James! What he wouldn't give for something to read.

The sleek black vintage BMWs looked particularly elegant set against the snow, as if posing for an advertisement feature. Strange, they weren't the most practical cars for these conditions, or indeed any conditions, but maybe that was the point. Like a peacock's tail feathers, they said that gangsters were tough enough to defy even loss of traction and ice, they were that powerful. What utter drivel was going through his head. He'd hoped to get used to the cold but he hadn't. At least they'd let him sleep on the futon again. And the slow starvation was affecting his brain. He kept thinking about bread and butter pudding and custard. Then telling himself not to. Bread and butter pudding and custard belonged in a different universe right now. His stomach rumbled. Enough, James!

Something moved and caught his eye. But he didn't see what it was. Something to do with the cars. He stared, barely breathing. What was it? Probably nothing. No, there it was again! The passenger door on the car furthest away was slowly opening. But no one was there! No one he could see, anyway. It was definitely moving, though. He watched the frame angle away from the car and stop. And then, slowly, it closed again, but not quite. It was slightly ajar, he thought. Still he couldn't see anyone. The other car was parked in front of it, shielding it partly from view. What did this mean? Part of a stealth mission, or was he just going mad? He didn't dare move but was desperate to know if anyone else had seen. He pictured all the goons lined up behind his shoulders watching. Should he turn round and check, or would that draw attention to himself? What to do? His heart was pumping like a piston engine.

He risked a casual look round the room behind him. The three youngsters all appeared to be asleep, sitting or lying in various poses. An incredible capacity they had for dropping off whenever they pleased. One of the guards sat on a hard-backed chair with his arms folded staring at the ceiling. No one paid the slightest attention to what James was doing. Nothing new there. But don't complain, James – that's exactly what you want right now! He turned back to the window, feeling the tension in his shoulders. Something was going to happen, but what? Gunfire, grenades, a helicopter, sirens and squad cars? Right now everything seemed terribly, terribly quiet.

Wait! The door was opening again. Don't look round, James, and don't be too intense. Just stay exactly how you are. Once again, a slow opening, a pause, a slow closing with the door left just ajar. Then nothing, except, a few seconds later, in the small gap between the front car and the building line, a figure passed, too quick to recognise. There and then gone. Every muscle in James' body was tensed. Surely someone would notice. But there wasn't a sound. Then, in the silence, a heavy click came from the front door. He let his gaze drift round the room. Unbelievably, no one had heard.

He turned back to the window and blinked. The white space between the house and the car was occupied by a figure in a dark padded jacket, looking straight at him, a finger at her lips. It was Rose! Good God, he was right after all and here she was! It was all he could do not to wave frantically, but clearly she'd already seen him and he got the message of course: keep a lid on it! They'd barely exchanged looks before she turned and disappeared. Well, all he could do was wait and follow instructions. Strange, he wasn't expecting to see Rose in the flesh. He had the idea that her people had folk to do this kind of thing for them, and that she'd be off somewhere giving instructions. But what did he know?

He half-turned into the room and looked down at himself. He should be ready for a quick getaway. But here was a thing; in these parts it was a big deal to take your shoes off indoors. He looked down at a pair of old and somewhat crusty brown socks. Was he going to be called upon to dash about through the snow in his stockinged feet? He'd really rather not; he quite liked the number of toes he currently had. Would it be noticeable if he slid off into the hallway and retrieved his shoes from the cluster by the front door? Yes, was the answer. Decidedly so. None of them had worn shoes since they got there. Even the thugs took their boots off for the tatami mats. Damn! Well, maybe Rose's contingent would have a plan for this. They were professionals after all.

His shoe worry was brought to a sudden end by the eruption of an extraordinary popping sound from the kitchen. The Japanese sleepers awoke, their heads jerking up as if some master puppeteer had yanked all their strings at once. The guard ran to the kitchen, knocking his chair over in the process. A door slammed, then came a kind of ripping sound and a volley of shouting. Something was giving off a lot of smoke. The thugs in the kitchen were hammering on the door.

Rose appeared in the doorway.

"Get out," she said. He'd never seen her look like this — sinewy, fast, on fire.

"Through there?" He pointed behind her.

"No! Through the front door! I picked the lock. The door's open. Get in the car!"

A hammering on the stairs. One of the guards was coming down.

"Now, James!" Rose turned and some kind of altercation with the guard resulted in a yelp and something heavy landing on the stairs. Well, he should obey orders. But when he turned, Mirai was directly in front of the door, holding an arm out towards him.

"No, James." Her hand was shaking, but her gaze was straight. "You must not. You must stay."

"Now, Mirai. This really won't do."

"Push her out of the way," said Rose.

171

"Mirai, we really do have to get past." But she wouldn't budge. The two boys were hovering on either side, rather, it had to be said, like a triptych, two angels ranking the evangelist, or whatever.

"James! Knock her out of the way! We have no time!"

The kitchen door gave way with a crunch and the burliest of the guards ran into the room. Rose stepped up and her foot came out, then a hand or two, heavens, it all happened so fast but this huge man was on the floor and his sister, his little sister, was standing over him.

"Move, James!" she shouted. James realised all four of them were gazing with their mouths open. "Get out of the door! I can take one at a time but not all at once!"

The other guards were coming into the room. James turned and made some effort to reach for the door, hoping the girl would sense his innate determination.

"Mirai, really, I can't be staying here, I have family to think of, you know."

"We too," she said, and her hand was as steady now as her eyes.

The room was full of men. Rose lashed out at one of them, who staggered into the wall, but two others were behind him and they grabbed her on either side. Now the one from the stairs was up again and headed directly for James, placing himself firmly in front of the door.

Someone gasped for air; one of the others had punched Rose in the stomach.

"I say! Is that really necessary?" said James, and ended up getting a similar punch himself. Goodness, these people knew how to hurt. One of the guards spoke harshly. Mirai interpreted.

"They want to know who else is coming."

"Nobody," said Rose, from where she was kneeling on the floor. "It was just me. I came myself."

The men seemed sceptical. So was James, he had to admit. The thugs briefly discussed the matter and one of them produced heavy duty duct tape. Poor old Rose got her hands tied behind her. Then it turned out poor old James got the same treatment. They were pushed onto the floor and the Japanese ordered to sit while the men moved in and out talking to each other, and on their phones.

James couldn't even bear to look at Mirai. He shuffled closer to Rose. "Looks like they're going to move us, doesn't it?"

She didn't say anything but he recognised the fury in her face.

"Is it really true there's no backup? I'd have thought you'd have some kind of crew, you know."

"I was getting you out before the backup arrived." That made no sense but Rose carried on before he could query it. "All you had to do was get through the door, James! There was a clear exit. The car was hotwired ready to go. You even got a warning. We just had to move quickly and we'd have been away. But no, you had to stop and play the gentleman."

"I've never hit a woman in my life."

"This woman is the reason you're here! She was part of a blackmail plot to entrap you! You just needed to give her a shove, that's all."

"Well, look, this kind of thing may be second nature to you, Rose, but all this fisticuffs is not in my nature. And anyway…" There was no anyway. He just wasn't ready to back down. The scheme did seem very seat-of-the-pants, though. "They'd have come after us in the other car," he finished lamely.

"I let the air out of the tyres."

"Oh. That was clever."

"Yes, it was pretty clever. The whole thing was, actually. But completely wasted, because you couldn't manage to get yourself out of a doorway! For heaven's sake, James! Have you any idea how much trouble you're in, or what these people could do to you? To both of us, now! I took a massive risk coming here like this, and it would have worked, if only you had even the vaguest sense of urgency about you!"

"Right, well, I'm terribly sorry," said James. "As I said, I'm not the expert in all this. But are there really no others coming at all?" He felt a little confused.

"Yes, there are others coming. But we'll have gone by then and they won't know where we are."

"I see." This all seemed like a bit of a disaster. "Wouldn't it have been better to wait for them before—"

"Long story." Rose cut him off.

"So what do we do now?"

"I've no idea. We'll just have to think of something as we go along. But next time, do as you're told, okay?"

He shrugged. "Well, okay."

The men came in from outside. They'd discovered what Rose had done to the cars. As you'd expect, they weren't the type of folk who'd take kindly to people messing about with their rides. He and Rose both got a kicking as the youngsters looked on silently. It would have been much worse if they weren't in such a hurry to leave, but one of them came in with a curt order, he and Rose were pulled to their feet and they were all bundled into the back seats of the BMWs.

They drove off. James was squeezed in next to Rose, but she stared tight-lipped out of the window. He wasn't sorry to see the last of that little house, but suspected where they were going might be even worse.

Chapter 28

Three hours on the dot after receiving the text from Rose, Fairchild alerted Zack, who alerted Rapp. She was certainly ready. Three vehicles were already loaded and the logistical planning was done in the vehicles *en route*. Satellite imagery showed a row of houses away from the rest of the village. Rapp had requested a live satellite feed, but it took two hours to kick in. So they were in the back of a jeep, Fairchild on one side of Rapp and Zack on the other, when the feed started. Fairchild hadn't even put Zack in the loop; as instructed, he was going to point the finger entirely at Rose.

"Here we go," said Rapp. The screen on her device flickered on and they got a bird's eye view of a row of houses looking insubstantial at the foot of a sweep of mountains. Two cars outside. No movement. "How far are we?"

The navigator up front checked. "Forty-five minutes."

"All right then. You just sit tight." Rapp appeared to be talking to the screen. But they didn't sit tight. Two heads appeared from the door of the house, dark figures against the snow.

"What's this?" The tension in Rapp's voice made everyone sit up. "You seeing this, Two?" She was talking to another of the jeeps.

"Yeah. A number of people are exiting the building."

A steady stream, in fact. A pair, one of whom was stumbling and being held up by the other. Another similar pair. Then three people walking freely followed by another two.

"They're on the move. All of them, by the look of it."

"Agree. They're securing the house and loading the cars. We got five detainees and four guards."

"Five? Who's five? There should be four, Clarke and the hackers. Who's the other?"

They were expecting the three Japanese students to be there, as they'd discovered that none had been seen in Tokyo for days. They all peered at the screen. The figures were only out in the open a few seconds before getting in the cars, and none of them looked up. But they didn't really have to; it didn't take much to figure out.

"Where did you say Rose Clarke was?" asked Zack.

"Making her own way there," said Fairchild.

"How?" That was Rapp.

"She didn't say."

"Didn't you ask?"

"I didn't get the chance."

"How about why? Why isn't she with us?"

"I didn't get that either."

On screen, the cars had driven off.

"That was her, wasn't it?" said Rapp. "In that car. Somehow she had a head start on us by, what? Three, four hours? Which she used to conduct some half-assed ambush that achieved nothing except tip them off and get them to move."

"I guess she must have held onto the location for a few hours," conceded Fairchild.

"Great," said Zack. "And you knew nothing about this, I suppose."

"I passed it on as soon as I got it."

"Yeah, right."

"I'd have tried to talk her out of it if I'd known. All she's done is put herself into their hands and get them on the defensive."

Some of that was at least approaching the truth. Going in alone was a risky venture and clearly it had gone wrong.

"We had a good lead and now it's wasted," said Rapp. "Her bosses are going to hear about this, for sure."

"We can follow the cars, can't we?" said Fairchild.

"By satellite? We can try but it's not as good as a tracker on the vehicle. Which we'd have done as soon as we'd got there."

"It's still worth going to the house to see what's there. They could have left something useful behind."

"Yeah, since we're almost there anyway."

They carried on with few words. At the house they found very little. Walking around outside, Fairchild found footprints coming from woodland at the back and circling the perimeter of the block, all of which now seemed to be empty. Rapp wandered away and spent some time being angry with someone on her phone. Zack came over and gave him a baleful look.

"Don't try and tell me you weren't in on it. I know you, and I know her and you."

"Well, what could I do, Zack? You heard them in the meeting. They don't care about James. They'd gun him down in cold blood if he got between them and those hackers. Tell me you wouldn't have done the same."

"Yeah, maybe. But I'd have told you. We go back, Fairchild."

"Fair enough. She wanted it to all stop with her, though."

"Huh."

That word said a lot from one of his oldest friends. Helping Rose out never seemed to be easy. Zack wandered off and walked about kicking up snow.

"More good news," said Rapp, coming over. "The cars were heading back to Tokyo but we lost them. They went into an underpass and didn't come out again. We're right back to where we started. Going great, isn't it?"

No one argued with her.

Chapter 29

The next morning Fairchild flew in to Hong Kong and got a train to Central District, where he went into a quiet, run-down restaurant and sat for four hours without ordering anything. Eventually a car drew up, almost blocking the narrow street, and he was invited to get in. The driver, exchanging no words, took him to a building site along the harbour and directed him towards the base of a half-built tower, its skeletal structure topped with cranes. There he was given a hard hat in line with site health and safety regulations, and escorted into a cage lift that climbed the outside of the building and slowed to a halt. The construction worker who got in with him pulled up the bar and they stepped over a gap into the open ribs of the building. They were thirty, maybe forty, floors up. On the far side, with a group of men who were all taller than her, was a neatly turned out woman, in her sixties maybe, wearing a skirt suit and a pearl necklace and with impeccable grey hair.

"Lovely spot for a meeting," he said as he walked over. "What an incredible view."

Two of the men stepped forward and frisked him, finding nothing.

"I apologise for the wait," said Darcy Tang. "I wanted to know how serious you were. Last time we met, things didn't go too well." They were speaking in Cantonese.

"Last time we met it was a disaster and I apologised for that." It was only then that he noticed another man standing with his back to them all staring out across Hong Kong harbour at the view of the Chinese mainland. The man turned round.

"My nephew. You remember," said Darcy Tang.

"I'm afraid I do." It was in the Hong Kong Famous Central Golden Palace, where he'd just spent four long hours of his life, that Fairchild had first met Rose Clarke, whose unfortunate intervention had caused Fairchild to shoot Tang's nephew in the shoulder. "I hope you made a full recovery."

This did nothing to neutralise the man's hostility. He took a step nearer. Fairchild gave passing thought to the distance down to the ground and the general lack of walls. You could step out between any of the concrete joists, and just fall. "You do realise it was an accident, I hope?" he said mildly.

"Accidents happen," said the nephew. "Especially on building sites."

"That's enough," said Tang. "Mr Fairchild is a potential investor." This was news to Fairchild. "I will show him around. You can wait here."

She led Fairchild away from the others through the bones of the building.

"Office or residential?" he asked, trying to get a feel for the layout.

"Residential. Top-of-the-market apartments. People don't want tiny places any more. Space, best facilities, and of course a view."

The views were heart-stoppingly spectacular, uninhibited as they were by walls or glass. A fresh wind gusted straight through the structure. The boats and traffic below looked tiny and unreal. The sounds of the city barely reached them at all. Fairchild pointed at the high-rise directly to landward.

"I can't think that the owners there were very pleased. They must have lost their views practically overnight."

"We dealt with that," said Tang. Fairchild wondered how, exactly. The Wong Kai clan was known for its ruthlessness, especially under its current leadership. "No one can stand in the way of progress," she added. "If Hong Kong needs homes, we build homes. Harbour is very popular."

"There won't be a harbour for much longer if progress continues at this pace." Fairchild nodded towards the Kowloon side where a land reclamation site mirrored this one. "You'll be able to walk across soon."

She laughed briefly. "Not in my lifetime. And I intend to live long. I've outlived a husband and two sons so far. How else would someone like me get to run the Wong Kai? It's the only way. But I'm careful. I have to be."

Fairchild heard the warning in her words. "I appreciate that. I hope we squared things off after the unfortunate incident last time. I did give you the identity of the associate who was passing your secrets to the Chinese police. That checked out, I trust."

"It did. I am grateful for that. He did not cause any further trouble. That went some way towards repairing the damage between you and me, Mr Fairchild. What I never established is the reason for your approach last time."

"I had a business offer. But that was a while ago and things have moved on. Now I need some information. Maybe there's something I can offer you in return."

Her eyes rested on him, then she walked over to the other side of what would later become a room. "View of the Peak from here, too." She nodded upwards. Sure enough, the green tips of the Peak were visible over the top of the packed-in high-rises of downtown Hong Kong and the Mid Levels apartments rising up behind.

"Until someone builds in front of this one."

"Let them try. These views are here to stay, Mr Fairchild. Our name is on this development."

"It certainly sounds like an interesting investment. Are you taking down-payments already? It seems a little early."

"Not too early. We have plenty of interest. Mostly from mainland China. I will bear your enthusiasm in mind."

They were some distance away now from the others. The wind was ruffling Tang's hair. She wasn't wearing a hard hat. In fact, Fairchild was the only one who was. He didn't think it would help him much.

"There was a woman with you," Tang said suddenly. "The last time. British, I think."

"She wasn't with me. Actually she'd been sent to find me. But I didn't want to be found."

"You lost her, then?"

"Yes. Although our paths have crossed since."

She frowned. "You see, this is the kind of thing that makes me wonder about you. I saw the way that woman handled herself. She was no tourist."

"No, she wasn't."

"Then what did she want with you? I don't like the British." She strode off into another room-to-be, this one looking westwards along the coast. "Patronising, paternalistic, controlling, they think because they were great the century before last they can still tell everyone what's good and what's bad."

"I don't have much time for them either."

"You're British descent, aren't you?"

"I haven't been there for twenty years. I'm stateless. By choice. I have interests across the world. Sure, I know people in governments, influential people. They take an interest in me from time to time, but I'm my own person."

"You're a businessman. Just that."

"Just that." Nothing else. True, when he first walked into the Golden Palace two years ago he was on a job working for Zack, whose paymasters wanted inroads into the Wong Kai – but Tang would never know that. He was an entrepreneur, that was all. An entrepreneur with a need for information.

"I'm not precious about who I do business with," he said. "But sometimes you get a bad feeling. I've been approached by a group of anonymous hackers known as Fire Sappers."

Her face changed. She knew the name.

"They've made me an offer," he said.

"I've heard that's what they do."

"It's not a ransom demand. It's a genuine offer. Quite an attractive one. But I've been told a few things about the way they operate. I understand they work with – organisations like yours."

"Criminal gangs, Mr Fairchild. Wong Kai is a criminal gang. We can speak honestly to each other, can we not?"

"Of course." But her eyes still narrowed when she looked at him.

They'd walked around now to the harbour side again. She stepped up to the edge and stood looking out, arms folded. Fairchild hung back. A tight sensation pinched the base of his spine. She wasn't even that close to the edge, he told himself. There were maybe eighteen inches in front of her before the floor ended. Beyond that, a sickening drop down to the rubble-lined blue sea. He glanced round. The men were watching, arms loose by their sides. Tang started talking.

"We don't work with Fire Sappers. On the contrary. They stole from us."

"What did they steal?"

"Power."

"Power?"

"Electricity. We control some power generation plants in southern China. Mainly coal fired. We supply the Chinese government. Fire Sappers broke into our systems and tapped power away. They were clever. It took months for us to notice. We lost millions in revenue."

"Was it a hack, or a physical intervention?"

"Both. They made changes in the plants, broke in somehow, maybe paid people, then covered it up by changing our security protocols."

"What did they do with the electricity?"

"They mined with it."

"Mined?"

"Bitcoin. They have a huge operation. Banks of servers all over China, Asia, Eastern Europe. Making a fortune. Plus all the ransom money. But it takes power. You know, I think."

Fairchild did. Mining Bitcoin was how the currency was created from scratch. It involved a huge amount of processing power to generate the multi-digit numbers needed to bid for winning lots out of the limited supply. The methodology was designed to be the online equivalent of panning for gold in the Yukon, but it had turned into a mass-scale energy-guzzling race to harvest as much as possible.

"So what happened?" he asked.

"We got to work." An enigmatic answer.

"Did you get your money back?"

"Some."

"But not all?"

She looked at him. "No, not all. What's your problem with them really, Mr Fairchild? You come all this way and sit for hours in my restaurant to ask me about a business offer? Fire Sappers doesn't make business offers. They have a hold on you for something. What do they have? Tell me."

"All right," said Fairchild. "They have a person. They've kidnapped someone. At least, some branch of the yakuza has, under their orders. This person is being held somewhere in the Tokyo area."

"Tokyo? That's all you know?"

"At this time, yes."

She was intrigued but her face clouded with suspicion. "Who are you working with on this? The authorities?"

"The authorities are involved but they're not getting anywhere. My interest in this is personal. Whatever you tell me, no one will know where it came from."

She was looking closely at him again. Behind her the sky was a thin December blue and the Kowloon skyscrapers twinkled in sunlight.

"I know the name of the boss," she said. "The guy who runs the whole empire. Online he calls himself Milo. Nationality, Hungarian. We know his real name, identity, address, everything."

"Can you prove they're the same person?"

"Yes."

"You're not tempted to pass that information to the authorities? If the FBI had it, Fire Sappers would be a lot less powerful."

"That's not how we do things. We have our own way of settling scores."

"Would you be willing to share this information with me?"

"Maybe. For a price."

"How will it help me find the hostage, though? That's my interest in this. I'm not the FBI."

"This person is important to you. Very interesting. But I'm not sure I can help with that. I know the firm they work with in Japan. They have premises everywhere. They could hold someone in any part of Tokyo. You cannot search for them that way. Impossible."

"What if they wanted to hide someone on a more permanent basis, but keep them alive? Or get them out of the country?"

Tang considered. "They have some interests in shipping. Out of the Port of Tokyo. Freight. Useful for stolen goods, contraband. That's what I'd do."

"Can you give me the details? The shipping companies they deal with, a name maybe?"

He sounded too eager and she picked up on it. She smiled a little.

"I could." A pause. "You know, I don't really believe your story." The air seemed thinner suddenly. Tang started walking around the outside edge. "Oh, I believe some friend of yours is kidnapped. But the other part. You came to me two years ago with a business opportunity which has now passed? No, Mr Fairchild. There was more to it than that. I got curious about you after last time. I did some research. You're an extremely well connected man. Very useful to a lot of people. You could be very useful to me, too. I have an idea how. If you're in agreement, we could help each other."

Her tone was so even, her offer so politely made. But in reality he had no choice. Descending in the cage lift, he looked down and felt light-headed. But it wasn't the height. It was a gradual dawning of what it meant, the bargain he'd just struck with Darcy Tang. He didn't know how he was going to do it. But he had to do it, and it changed everything.

Chapter 30

Landing back at Narita, Fairchild had a message from Tim Gardner asking him to call back urgently. Strange, as he'd already spoken to Gardner earlier. He'd phoned both him and Zack from Hong Kong with the name of the shipping company Tang had given him.

Tim picked up after one ring. "Fairchild! You're back?"

"Just landed."

"Listen. Bit of a situation. Can you come straight to the Embassy?"

"Why? What's happened?"

Gardner expelled air in a noise of frustration. "Well, it turns out that Clarke's wife has shown up. With kids in tow."

"James' wife? From the UK?"

"They came straight here from the airport and marched into reception. She's been there for hours. Won't budge until she gets some news. Eventually it filtered through to me and I went down. Of course she was expecting Rose, so it's all rather difficult."

"I see. And what are you expecting me to do?"

"Well, a little bit of hand-holding is really what they need. You know, some mild reassurance. Obviously we can't tell them a lot, but I thought, perhaps…?"

"Me? I need to be with the team. Get up to speed with the plan and keep an eye on Rapp. Zack can't control her on his own."

"And I have to play nicely with the Japanese Internal Affairs minister."

"Can't you play nicely some other time? We have a situation unfolding."

"That's precisely why I need to speak to Internal Affairs. We need their approval for an op. Particularly if it's likely to involve guns. It's the Ambassador's Christmas Ball tonight, the minister in question will be there, as will Barclay, and we'll both be taking him to one side during the course of the evening and talking him through a number of scenarios. It's politics but it's important."

"Did we have approval before we went after them at the house?"

"The ministry was aware, Fairchild, but not entirely happy about it. More work is needed. Otherwise we could fall over our own feet here. Besides, I need to try and smooth things over with Barclay after the actions of our friend Rose. So, I really need to hand this family situation off to someone I can trust, old chap."

Old chap. Tim was overdoing it. But it didn't sound like Fairchild had much choice. So much for being his own man. Some days he didn't feel independent at all.

"All right. I'll be there as soon as I can."

A stressed spouse and her children in a foreign country? How to deal with that when there was nothing much to tell her? There was someone who would know what to do with them. He phoned the person he always phoned when he didn't know what to do in Japan: Takao.

Takao's taxi pulled up at the Embassy at the same time as Fairchild's. Gardner was waiting by the door and came out. He was wearing a tuxedo.

"Have to let you in myself. The day staff have all gone home." He used his pass to take them through to a small interview room, desk and four chairs, picture of the River Thames on the wall. Gardner introduced Fairchild and Takao to Fiona as 'part of the team' although that was a stretch as far as Takao was concerned. At least they knew each other; they'd met at the Trade Winds launch.

"So, I'll leave you in John's capable hands," said Gardner, as he left. "You have my details, Fiona, so please don't hesitate." Gardner's business card was sitting on the desk in front of a very unimpressed Fiona.

"I don't think we've all been introduced," said Fairchild, looking at the children.

"Henry and Sophie," said Fiona listlessly. Henry was staring into space. Sophie was leaning against her mother, her eyes closed. "So who are you?" Fiona asked. "I don't see a badge."

"I don't work here."

A flash of annoyance crossed her face. "Then what?"

"I'm a friend of Rose."

"Ah." He wasn't sure how Fiona had taken that. "So where's Rose, then?"

"What have they told you?"

"Nothing."

"What have they said, then? About James and his whereabouts?"

"The pompous one who just left said that he wasn't able to provide more details but that everything was being done, blah blah blah."

"I see." There were lines under her eyes. "You came straight here from the airport, is that right? It's a long flight, isn't it?"

"Listen, don't try and fob me off. I know there's something going on. A bunch of people came to my house asking all kinds of weird questions about dates and birthdays and anniversaries. What was that all about? Them I'm just told to sit tight. The more I ask, the more people clam up.

His company won't even take my calls any more. What am I supposed to do? And where the heck is Rose?"

"Honestly? We don't know."

Her eyes widened.

"And James?"

"We don't know that either."

Takao was starting to look nervous.

"The thing is," said Fairchild, "the fact that I'm not employed by the Embassy is in some ways quite a good thing. You see, I've never signed the Official Secrets Act."

"Really?"

"Really."

"Does that mean you're planning to tell me what's actually going on?"

"Yes. But some of it might not be what you want to hear."

"Look, I don't want it sugar-coated. If he's in trouble I need to know how bad."

Her gaze was steady. Fairchild glanced down at Sophie, who was wrapping her mother's cardigan over her head. Henry was fingering a scratch on the edge of the table. She got his meaning and hesitated.

"Listen," he said. "You've had a long day and so have I. I've just got off a flight myself. Do you have somewhere to stay?"

"Yes, I booked a room," she said absently.

"Well, how about we all go and get some dinner and I'll put you in the picture?" He could feel the children's eyes on him at the mention of food.

Fiona crumpled a little. "Well…"

Fairchild turned to Takao, whose face came alive. "I know perfect place!"

Takao took them to Akihabara, Tokyo's high-tech hub. From the taxi, he pointed out sights such as the massive Sega

World and cutting-edge games and video arcades. The children seemed mesmerised. They stopped at a restaurant with a mass of blue fluorescent lighting and video screens. Fairchild was starting to question Takao's judgement.

"This is it?"

"Trust me, it's good place!" insisted Takao.

A woman with cat ears and huge painted eyelashes took them to a table. Henry and Sophie stared. Each table had its own monitor, and a massive screen opposite the bar was showing an animated movie featuring outsized robotic suits.

"So, it's anime and game themed place," beamed Takao.

The menu was a colourful mass of manga characters and large-print Japanese. "Perhaps you can order for us, Takao," said Fairchild, wondering if he needed to find a new fixer. "I think the priority is getting a square meal inside everyone."

"Sure! Sure! Eh, toooo…"

He called the waitress over and they left him to it. The kids were gazing round at the weirdly costumed staff and some of the even more weirdly dressed patrons. Fiona asked Fairchild some questions about himself. She'd perhaps got the wrong impression about the relationship between him and Rose. He'd have to put her straight at some point.

Takao finished ordering. "Okay, so we play game?" he said to the kids. "Nothing violent." That was to reassure Fiona. The children registered only mild interest but Takao was on a mission, calling over the waitress and getting hold of a remote control for their screen. He flicked frantically. "Eh, toooo…..must be…Ah! Food is here already."

Takao put the remote aside to focus on the food. He was in full ambassadorial flow now. "Miso soup! Very hot. Very nice. Stir it with your chopsticks then drink out of the bowl. Easy, yes? Go on – try!"

He demonstrated and the children cautiously imitated.

"We also have edamame, green beans, very tasty. Very healthy." He gave Fiona a reassuring look. "Try a little sauce. Not too much! Now here, some pickles. Maybe a bit sour. Careful! This is seaweed. Yes, really! But it's tasty. Tastes like fish. Try it!"

It kept them busy until something more substantial arrived, yakitori chicken on sticks with rice. The kids dug in. Fairchild wondered how long it was since he'd asked after Takao's family. He couldn't even remember how old Takao's children were. While they were eating Takao cued up the game and the waitress brought brightly coloured headphones and consoles. It was only then that Fairchild noticed quite a lot of other diners, especially the younger ones, plugged in to headphones and busy on the screens.

"So! You ready to play?" said Takao. The game looked suitably tame, knights on horseback and a forest of mythical creatures. He talked Sophie and Henry through it and pretty soon they were all on their headphones battling away. Fairchild and Fiona were free to talk.

"Okay," said Fiona. "Hit me with it."

"Well, first of all," said Fairchild, "James was subject to a blackmail attempt. He didn't have an affair with anyone. That was fabricated to try and get control of him."

"Yes, I realise that." In response to his look, she said: "I don't think six people would have come to my house asking when our wedding anniversary is if he'd just gone off with some woman. So who's really behind this?"

Fairchild told her everything he knew himself, including Rose's disappearance, what they knew about Fire Sappers and the shipping lead. She looked stunned. "All this for James? Why?"

"His encryption work. He holds the key that unlocks vast amounts of money. They want the money. It's probably as simple as that. It's good news in that they want him alive. And there's a lot of effort going into tracing them. I'm standing by right now for news." He patted his phone.

"And why are you doing all this, if you're just a businessman?" said Fiona. "It's Rose, isn't it?"

"Maybe," he said, feeling a little warm in the face. "We go back some way. But it isn't what you think."

As if on cue, his phone beeped. It was Zack. Fairchild moved away from the table to take the call.

"We've found something," said Zack. "And we're moving. So get over here if you want to be a part of it. And hurry. They won't wait."

Back at the table, Fairchild didn't even sit. "I've got to go."

Takao paused the game and they all removed headphones and looked round.

Fiona's eyes were wide. "What's going on?"

"Not sure yet. They think they might have found them. When I know more I'll tell you."

"Is that a promise?" The children were looking upset as well.

"Yes, that's a promise." Fairchild turned to Takao.

"Well," said the Japanese man with exaggerated regret. "Fairchild, it sounds like you are going to miss dessert!"

As the children's eyes lit up and they turned to their mother, Fairchild slipped away. They'd be okay with Takao.

Chapter 31

From the house in the mountains the hostages were driven back to Tokyo, right through the city to the port. There, in darkness, they were led onto an immense ship and locked in a crew cabin, a tiny room with four bunk beds and one window overlooking a vast container deck. They remained in there the whole of the next day, getting hot and stuffy while the ship sat. Their old yakuza friends brought occasional food. No freight was moving on or off. They were waiting.

Rose was still furious with James. But after about eighteen hours she relented and climbed up to sit next to him on the top bunk. It was dark again, and the others were asleep.

"What do you think we're waiting here for?" she asked.

"Well, it's these people, Rose. They're on their way here, apparently."

"The hackers? They're coming to Japan?"

"So I believe. They're the real enemy. Not these folk." He nodded towards the Japanese students. "They were being blackmailed. This international group, whoever they are, were going to betray their identities and get them into trouble with the law, and, you know, their ancestors and such like."

"Ancestors?"

"Yes, bringing shame on your ancestors is a terribly bad thing, apparently. You know Haruma's brother killed himself because of this?"

"Really?"

"Jumped off a building. It's very real, even if we don't exactly get it."

"Even so, James, they're the people who got you into this. There's a time to do the right thing and a time to just do what you have to do to survive. You want to get back to Fiona and the kids, don't you?" She saw pain on his face. "I could have got you out of there. It would have worked. Now we're in even more trouble. No one knows where we are and these Fire Sappers are coming here."

"Fire Sappers? That's the group?"

She frowned. "You didn't know?"

"The youngsters said they didn't know who was blackmailing them. If they knew the name they never said it."

"You've heard of them?"

"Oh, I've heard of them. They're pretty renowned in the IT security world. They're not good news, generally. I was a fool, I suppose, getting chatting to Mirai in the first place. Or even coming to the conference." He looked incredibly glum all of a sudden.

"They were onto you before that, James. How could you have known? And you got a message out. I found you. That's pretty good going."

"Yes!" He perked up at that. "Glad you were able to decipher it. I was worried I'd overdone it a bit. Did you get the date or did someone have to run a search program? I wasn't sure."

"I got the date. But it took a while. Do you really have all this off by heart somewhere in your mind, James?"

He gave a little giggle. "Not really, but I thought, you know, first mention of your possible future career, it might have stuck in the mind."

"James, enough already of this spy obsession of yours."

"Oh yes, sorry, keep schtum and all that. Anyway, it was easy to remember given Father having a good old rant about a return to Socialism, so that gives the year, and it must have been the second Saturday in May, the first as you know—"

"Isn't a prime number. Your mind really does work in a very peculiar way, James. It was pretty brave as well. Did they take it out on you?" Rose had noticed some bruising on various parts of her brother's skin.

"Oh yes, caught me red-handed. Gave me a bit of a kicking. Never mind, we're all here to tell the tale. I say, these other people, the backup, they're not just going to give up on us, are they? When they find we're not at the house any more?"

"No, they're not going to give up. They want the hackers, James. They want Fire Sappers. This is the closest they've got to them. So they'll keep looking."

"Well, that's something, I suppose." James was probably still curious about why Rose came on her own. Fortunately he seemed to decide not to ask about it again.

A long, tedious silence was interrupted when the door was unlocked. The ever-present yakuza took them down one flight into a living area with sofas, carpeting and a few framed pictures on the walls. They sat and waited, the guards standing arms folded at the doorway. A deep, low vibration started up. Rose and James exchanged glances. The ship's engine was going.

Eventually the door opened at speed. The man who walked in was not yakuza. Western features, dark hair, young, skinny, wide brown eyes and a dark goatee, dressed in jeans and a casual shirt. Out of the window the perspective was shifting; the ship was starting to move. This was the man they'd been waiting for.

The door slammed behind him and he stopped abruptly, hands in his pockets.

"So this is what I've come all this way for." There was an angry, impatient air to him, as if he had better things to do with his time. He spoke English with a European accent Rose couldn't place. His eye roved over them all.

"I can see the mess-ups here. Mirai. Of course that's you." Mirai looked up sulkily. Then to the other students he said "So you're Tomo, Haruma or Kiyonori. Don't tell me which is which. I don't care. Sorry about the other one, by the way. I guess if he thought he could fly away from this, he learned his lesson. You learn it too. You can't get away. I can always find you."

He sat in an armchair, crossed his legs and sighed wearily. "Unbelievable I had to come to Japan to sort this out. I was tempted to get our yakuza friends here to write you all off as a bad mistake, but I was persuaded it was worth the effort of coming here. Looking at you all, I'm not so sure. Such a simple task you had to do." He shook his head. "What a bunch of incompetents."

"Now, wait a minute," interrupted James. "They never wanted to be a part of your grubby little enterprise anyway. You coerced them!"

The man looked amused. "How sweet! They got you into all this but you still feel protective." He put his hand on his chest. "My heart is warmed by that. You're James, of course. I know a lot about you. Who's this?" He nodded towards Rose.

"I'm his sister," said Rose. "And who are you?"

"Most people know me as Milo," he said. "What do most people know you as?" That question had an uncomfortable edge.

"Rose."

"Thanks for joining us, Rose. Of course you didn't mean to come along for the ride. Seems that incompetence is

197

everyone's game here." He turned to the students again. "I mean, really, a simple piece of blackmail. How many times can one thing go wrong?"

"Well, as James says, you can always let them go if they're not up to your usual standard of criminal," said Rose.

"No, no. Nobody is let go. Once you are in our web, you stay there. Fire Sappers chooses its victims. They don't choose us. The mistake these amateurs made was to try some hacking themselves. They were ours after that. I think you say, in your language, a little knowledge is a dangerous thing."

"And what do you say in your language?" asked Rose.

He laughed silently, showing a lot of teeth. It was worth a try.

"I know you, but you don't know me," he said. "That's how it works. You're a diplomat, I believe. Or something like that." So he did already know who she was. She thought so. But what else did he know? "Could be useful if your bosses discover you're here."

"They won't trade. They don't make deals with criminals."

"We'll see. One thing I've learned is that all kinds of people who don't trade, trade. When it's all laid out. When the arguments are made clear."

"Not in this case."

He leaned forward. "They'd let you die?" The word charged the atmosphere. He was telling them what was at stake.

"Yes. They would. And a good thing too. Better that than you get rewarded for what you do."

Milo turned to James. "She's brave, isn't she, your sister? Are you brave, James? You know it's you we really want. I think you know it. Because you're quite clever, aren't you? You act like a fool but you're not."

James opened his eyes wide in innocence. "I'm terribly sorry, but I have no idea at all what you could possibly want with me."

"Oh, really?" Milo rolled his eyes. "Maybe you are a fool after all then."

"You know," said James, "talking like that really isn't going to help—"

"The cold wallet." Milo cut across him like a knife. "It wouldn't be difficult, would it? With your years of encryption experience? To place vulnerability inside, a hidden key that only we can access. Something embedded so deep that it wouldn't be detected."

It was clear from James' expression that this was exactly what he was expecting. Everyone was looking at him. "I have a team of coders working for me. I can't pull the wool over their eyes like that."

"You could find a way. Or give us the encryption codes and we'll do it if you really can't manage."

"That's not the way it works. It's completely new. It's—" James was almost visibly biting his tongue.

"Yes! I know, that's what we've heard. Very new, much safer than anything that's come before. Likely to take off and be widely adopted. People will trust it with their millions, their billions! Which is why we want a secret way in. That you will give just to us. Don't tell me you can't. I know you can."

"I'd get fired," said James. "They'll cancel the project, stop the development. I'd be out of a job. Out of the industry."

"They won't know it's there. Our back door will be a secret back door."

"That's not the way you usually operate. You like the publicity, the fireworks and all that. You'll do some enormous hack a few weeks after launch, millions' worth of coin will go missing and you'll be jumping up and down all over the dark web shouting about how great you are. That's your usual gambit, isn't it?"

Milo blinked with mock shame. "You don't like us very much, do you?"

"No, I don't. And once that happens they'll go back and analyse how you got in, and it will come back to me. Sooner or later, it will come back to me."

"They'll never prove it, though. You just have to keep denying it and say we got lucky."

"Lucky? The odds of you stumbling on the right key are astronomical! That's the whole point!"

"Don't worry so much, James!" Milo raised his hands casually. "Even if they do point at you, there's always a living to be made with Fire Sappers. We can find openings for you. Get you out of sticky situations. As long as you're loyal."

"I'll keep my life the way it is, thank you very much."

"Your life the way it is? But that's over. You're with us now. Whether you like it or not. Perhaps I need to show you. Which one of these children is your favourite?"

He turned in his chair to examine the Japanese trio. "Mirai? But you didn't like her, did you? You rejected her! Interesting. Maybe one of the others, then." He nodded at one of the mobsters. "The little one, bring him over here."

"I have to say, I really do think—"

But James' disgusted voice was drowned out by the Japanese man's hasty interpretation, which prompted two of the guards forward to grab Tomo from the sofa. He gave an "Eyy Yayy!" sound, and Mirai breathed a soft "No!", barely audible. Haruma sat staring, face pale, sweat beading on his brow.

The thugs dragged Tomo to the middle of the room. Milo turned to the one who interpreted. "Let's give him something to think about."

A flurry of words then the goons set upon the small Japanese guy, repeatedly kicking his curled-up body. They could easily kill him that way, Rose knew. Milo stood up and peered, arms folded, as if watching some vaguely interesting spectacle. Haruma rose slowly to his feet.

"For heaven's sake, Milo," James said. "It's got nothing to do with him. This is really very unfair!"

"Fair has nothing to do with it," said Milo lightly. "And if Fire Sappers decides it's his problem, it's his problem."

The next thing happened so lightning fast no one could have stopped it. Haruma took a sharp breath as if bracing himself, and ran straight into Milo. Milo staggered backwards. Rose was on her feet. It may be she was the only one who saw the flash of steel. But when Milo fell to his knees, everyone saw the blood seeping through the fingers clutching his abdomen, and the knife in Haruma's hand.

The room was a blur. Tomo lay forgotten as the guards grouped around Milo, trying to staunch the blood flow and running for first aid. Two of them were on Haruma, who dropped the knife and raised his arms, his eyes skywards. He didn't even try to fight or run. Between the two goons he crumpled while they battered him. On the sofa, Mirai sat forward, one arm outstretched in some kind of silent entreaty. James' mouth was open, literally. No one was looking at Rose, who silently stooped to pick something up.

The men beat Haruma until he didn't move. Bandages and tape were brought and applied to Milo's stab wound. Lying on his back, Milo lifted his head. His attendees took a step back. He sat up on his elbows and looked at Haruma, who was moving a little, face down.

"Get him up," said Milo. The command was passed on and two of them pulled Haruma onto his feet. Through bloated eyes and over a broken nose, he looked at Milo defiantly. Milo tried to get up. They jumped forward to help but he waved them off. He turned and pulled himself up on the armchair, climbing to his knees and then his feet, breathing heavily. He was soaked in blood but the bandages were holding. He met Haruma's defiance with a look of his own.

"You people, you just can't manage to do anything, can you?" he said. He held his hand out. "Pass me a gun."

Words were exchanged between the Japanese men — followed by a look. Slowly, one of them got a gun from his belt and passed it to Milo. Swaying slightly, Milo checked the barrel and clicked off the safety catch. He aimed at Haruma.

No one moved. Mirai breathed a word, too quiet to make out. Milo fired three times at Haruma's chest. The sound in the confined cabin was deafening. Haruma fell to the floor as the noise still echoed. Milo threw the gun down.

"Lock them up. I don't want to see any of them."

He sank into the side of the armchair as they were led away, past Haruma's still body.

Chapter 32

The planning meeting was in a room inside the vast US Embassy, which seemed to reflect who was in charge now. When Fairchild arrived, Zack came down to let him in and updated him on the way to the room.

"We've done a complete analysis of ships leaving or arriving at Tokyo or Yokohama that belong to the company in question. One of them was due to leave for Busan in South Korea, but didn't. Just sat there for a day. No freight on or off. They claimed a mechanical problem but there wasn't much evidence of anything getting fixed. We got a satellite feed up and running but the conditions aren't ideal. Sporadic cloud cover."

"Don't you have satellites that can penetrate cloud?"

"We do. But they don't give us a live feed. There's a delay of at least an hour."

"So what's happened now?" They were at the room.

"We'll cover that. If you're holding something back, Fairchild, bargain hard."

Zack opened the door and they went in. A dozen people at least were sitting around a table. Fairchild didn't know any of them. The room was airless and smelled of the half-eaten food all over the table. They'd clearly been in here for hours. The screen on the wall was showing the satellite feed, winking lights on a wide dark channel lined both sides with city lights. Patches of darkness obscured some of it. Other screens on the desk were showing schemas of cargo ships and detailed maps of the area.

Rapp was speaking but she stopped when Fairchild came in. "Glad you could make it," she said, not sounding as though she meant it.

"We have eyes on the ship?" he asked.

Zack stepped in. "A car rolled up a few minutes ago. One passenger boarded, a male. Then they prepped for leaving and set off."

"They were waiting for him," said Fairchild. "He must be a key player."

"Which is why we're going in now," said Rapp. "The task force is scrambling. You can watch from here if you like."

"I don't think so," said Fairchild.

"Excuse me?"

"That's not how it's going to work." He drew out a chair and sat. He'd certainly managed to get everyone's attention.

"That is exactly how it's going to work," said Rapp. "Whoever this guy is, this is a huge opportunity. They're sitting ducks out there right now. We're going in while we have the chance."

"Good. But I'm coming too."

Rapp's lips were thin. "We don't need you. What we need is that guy, before he disappears underground again."

"And what if you don't get him?" said Fairchild. "What if he slips away somehow? What if he's caught in the crossfire and killed? What will you have then?"

"We'll have the others, the Japanese students and Clarke. That's a lot better than nothing."

"Well, I have something even better than that."

Rapp stared at him. "Like what?"

"My source in Hong Kong told me more than just the name of the shipping company. I know the real name of the Fire Sappers leader, and his nationality. What's the betting it's the guy who just stepped onto that ship?"

"Well, you'd better tell us, then."

"Sure I will. Just as soon as I have both feet on the deck of that ship. And you'd better keep looking out for me, because I have the actual evidence linking the guy to Fire Sappers. If this plan goes up the creek, that could be the only lead you have left."

Rapp pointed a finger at him. "Now you'd better cooperate with this mission."

"Or what? You'll get me fired? You can try that with Rose Clarke but it won't work with me."

"Do you have any idea how long we've waited for an opportunity like this?"

"And we need to use it. Fast. So don't argue. Here's how it will work. Zack will head up the extraction force. The top priority is the rescue of the captors alive. The next priority is to apprehend the guy who just boarded. Minimal casualties. I will be a part of the team. If things go as agreed, I will share the information I have with you. If they don't, I won't. It's as simple as that."

They stared at each other across the table, two people who wanted something equally badly. Rapp wanted it all, she wanted the intelligence and the firepower, but she wasn't going to have them both, at least not yet. If it pissed her off, too bad.

"All right." She nodded at one of the men. "Tell the squad to stand by." The guy got on the phone and relayed the message.

Rapp rolled her eyes. "Zack, it's your show. Get to the muster point. Take your friend here. And I'm coming too. Now you listen!" Her voice rose to cut Fairchild off as he started to protest. "You want teamwork, you got teamwork. Without me, we don't have an extraction at all, and you know it. I'm coming, and I'm not letting you out of my sight. You will tell me what you know. You will tell me everything."

"Like I said, as long as you keep your side of the bargain."

Fairchild looked round at Zack who was carefully retaining a neutral expression. "Well, we'd better get moving, then, hadn't we?" he said.

Chapter 33

Rose wasted little time once they were back in the cabin. The ship was now moving at a steady pace some distance from shore, making everything more difficult. Wherever Milo planned to take them, she didn't want to go there. Now she knew what they were up against, bigger risks were called for. And there was no sign of any rescue mission.

While the others fell silently into the bunks, she washed and cleaned off Haruma's knife, which she'd picked up from the floor earlier. It was a folding penknife, usefully sharp but not a killing weapon, as they'd seen. Who knew where he'd got it from or how long he'd been harbouring it, along with his plans for it? What they witnessed was shocking, tragic, but she had no space to process it now; time was critical and she was the only person here who seemed to realise that.

She stepped up to the window and ran the knife along the rubber seal. It cut open nicely. This would work, but she needed help.

"Listen, all of you," she said. "I don't know what Milo has in mind for us, but I for one don't want to be part of it. So I'm going to take a look around."

She showed them the progress with the window seal. James peered out of the window. "That's quite a drop. How are you going to get down there?"

"Bedsheets. There are four beds in here. So there ought to be enough sheets tied together to reach the deck."

"Bedsheets? Seriously? That actually works, does it?"

"It actually does. And it'll get me back up again. This is a recce, not a one way journey."

She started working the window seal with the knife. "We need to think of a way of fixing this back in place once I'm out, in case anyone comes in."

"Okey-dokey, then." James seemed unsure but was probably too shellshocked to argue. He started hunting around in the cabin.

"Mirai and Tomo," said Rose. "Can you make me a rope from the bedsheets? Put the bed clothes back again so no one can see the sheets are gone."

After only a slight hesitation they got up and started pulling everything off the beds. It felt right to be doing something and not sitting and thinking.

Rose worked the seal. As the knife became blunter the job got harder and she had to dig in deep to reach the edge of the pane. James took over for a while, having found sticking plasters in a first aid box that might work okay if enough of them were used. A load of questions hung over them that no one wanted to ask. What could this achieve when they were away from shore on a bleak December night, on this huge hulk of a ship full of armed mafia with a ruthless killer of a leader? But still they worked, each of them, lost in their own thoughts.

The seal was cut all round; Rose and James worked the window loose and pulled it into the room, bringing a blast of cold air into the musty cabin. The door rattled. Tomo shoved a towel along the bottom of it to stop the noise. Rose stuck her head out. On deck, the stacks of containers loomed. No one was down there. With one end fastened around a bed leg, Rose threw out the other end. It dangled below, within three or four feet of the deck.

"Should we pull it up again when you're down?" whispered James.

"No. I'll have no way to get you to drop it when I'm ready to come back. We'll just have to hope no one sees it. It's the same colour as the tower at least."

She checked her coat was loaded up with her gear. At the last minute she went to grab a glass bottle from the bathroom and stuffed that into a pocket too. She clambered out, lowering herself down the sheet rope with hands and feet. It was slippery, but she managed to grip hard enough. On deck, she wrapped the glass bottle in the bottom of the rope and hung it. The weight stopped the rope from moving around too much in the wind. That would have to do.

The containers loomed over her, packed tightly on the raised deck. She moved over to the outer deck on the starboard side, making for the bow, using her torch sparingly. The deck was unlit and clouds obscured the moon. There was a cold steady wind; the speed of the ship was much more noticeable here.

She heard voices. She killed the torch and ducked into a passageway beneath the container stacks. Two guys were walking along, flashing their torches and chatting. Rose held her breath, but they didn't even look her way. They were crew, not mafia, smaller guys, not the big beefcakes looking after them, and not Japanese. Filipino, maybe. It was almost reassuring to see some evidence that life was going on as normal at least for some people on board. What did these crew make of their visitors? They must know that the ship's movements were determined by who was coming and going and not by cargo requirements. Did any of them hear the gunshots? Were they completely unaware of what was happening? Or just paid extra not to see or hear those things?

The men gone, Rose continued towards the bow, not looking for anything in particular, just ideas for a way off the thing. At the bow she leaned over the side and watched the hull cutting through the water. It wasn't obvious looking at the shoreline how fast they were moving. There was no time to waste. Right out at sea this would be much more difficult. She made her way round and down the port side back to the stern, crossing the base of the tower with care. She looked up at the lifeboat suspended above, a huge covered cylinder attached with thick wires and hooks to a crane. How to even get it into the water? And then what?

She continued her circuit, pausing to look down at the roiling water around the stern and picturing the size of the propellor that could move a ship like this. Passing the tower on the other side, she looked up. On a raised dock was another craft, also held with wires and winches, but smaller than the lifeboat. There was no one about and the windows facing this way were dark. She climbed up a set of steps onto the dock, praying that none of the windows would light up, loosened the canvas cover and took a brief look inside the boat. Then she replaced it and returned to deck.

At the base of the tower she tugged the sheet-rope twice and got two tugs back: all clear. As she climbed she saw the window pane come out above her, angled awkwardly. For a moment she thought it was going to fall and hit her, but instead it disappeared inside. James and Tomo pulled her into the room, and they hurried to get the rope in and replace the window. Then they gathered round her expectantly.

"Well," she said, "how desperate are you to get off this ship?"

There was a pause. "It's that bad?" said James.

"It won't be easy. It's a risk. Is it worth taking?"

"Well, let's think about this. How sure are we that any friends of ours know where we are?"

"We can't be sure at all. And if they don't know we're on this ship we could end up anywhere in the world. James, you have the most to lose. Milo will happily kill the rest of us, but he'll hang onto you out of sheer greed. If you agree to what he wants you can survive this."

"It's not much of a life if you ask me," said James grimly.

Mirai and Tomo exchanged words briefly. Mirai looked at Rose. Her face had a hardness that wasn't there before. "We want to leave. We try it," she said quietly.

"Well, it's dangerous," said Rose. "Some might say better to wait for the possibility of rescue. But that's an unknown. And we know what Milo is like, now. We all want to take the risk?"

All three nodded.

"All right, then. Well, the way I see it – the only plan that will work involves one of us going overboard."

Six shocked eyes looked at her.

"And, I'm sorry, James," she said, turning to her brother, "but it has to be you."

She outlined her idea. They absorbed it in silence.

"You know, that's probably a step away from absolutely crazy," said James.

"It should work if we plan it well enough," said Rose. Of course James was right, but someone had to be positive.

"Eh, toooo…" ventured Mirai. "Problem, maybe. Tomo can't swim."

The young man reddened.

"Oh," said Rose. "Was he going to mention that at all?"

That made Mirai redden also, for some reason.

"Well, we'll have to amend the plan, then. A bigger role for you, Mirai. Can you manage it?"

She looked, frankly, terrified. "I try," she said faintly.

Chapter 34

At some ungodly hour the night shift was roused into action by the piercing scream of a woman, coming from the deck. Especially shocking, as the crew had no idea there was a woman on board. What was anyone doing on deck at this time of night? And the area was restricted anyway. Even with the strange assortment of passengers they got on these lines, not to mention the freight with the missing paperwork and the unexplained changes to schedules that seemed to have nothing to do with cargo, the captain did manage to lay down the law there. Do what you want in the private cabins, was his rule, but stay out of the crew areas and keep away from the cargo. Well, not tonight.

The first ones there noticed a window pane missing from one of the cabins on the superstructure, and some kind of rope hanging down. Was there something wrong with the stairs? Then they heard what the screaming woman was actually saying; they had enough Japanese for that.

Man overboard! Man overboard! They ran to the side and stared down into the blackness of the water. Of course they couldn't see anything. How many knots were they doing? He was probably done for, to be honest, but they followed the procedure and sounded the alarm. The bridge reacted fast; the engine rumble fell away.

Then came an oddity – the captain wanted to know who was overboard. What difference did it make? But orders were orders, so they asked her.

"James-san!" screamed the lady, pointing with a horrified look on her face. "James-san! Fast! Fast, please!"

This was relayed back, and they were told to proceed. Made you wonder what would have happened if it had been someone else, but that was just another question you didn't ask. The crew ran out of the superstructure like ants from an anthill. Up to the rescue boat! Regulation said this had to be launchable in five minutes. Was the captain timing it? Wouldn't put it past him. Lights were trained all over the wake of the ship as far as their beams would reach, but there was no sign of James-san or anyone else down there. The cover was off, the launch crew was in place, the crane came out and the winches whirred. Down the RIB went until it hit the water. Nicely done. Just like the drills. The next bit wasn't, though.

The rescue boat powered up – but then it died. How's this? There should be two people on that boat, but somehow there were four! No – five! Now wait – their two crew were in the water and the boat was powering away from them! What on earth was going on down there?

People clustered round to get the jettisoned crew out of the water fast. Lifesavers went down, and ropes. Meantime the rescue boat circled towards the bow. Now the screaming woman was silent, and standing the wrong side of the railings staring down at the water. You don't want to do that, lady. It's a long way down and a shock when you get there. A shout came from the launch: *Mirai, jump!* A woman's voice. There were two women aboard? Well, there would soon be none because this Mirai was steeling herself to jump, though she was clearly petrified. She didn't look like she could do it. But then, two of those great lumps who were staying in the guest cabins came lumbering up. Anybody would jump to get away from those animals. She turned and saw them, turned back, took a breath, and was gone.

Over the side, a splash and a scream, or maybe it was the other way round. But the launch was already alongside and they were pulling her in. Now one of those goons pulled out a gun. A gun! The things you saw. The other stopped him, though, putting out his hand and shaking his head. That thug was all set to fire until then.

The RIB raced off, back towards Tokyo. The searchlights followed, turning their wake a huge white scar on the water, but what can you do? The affairs of the passengers were nothing to do with the crew, but the captain wouldn't be pleased they'd stolen his rescue boat.

Never mind, though. They had another.

Chapter 35

While Rose steered the boat at full pelt back up Tokyo Bay, the others dried off the shivering Mirai as best they could and wrapped her in the towels they'd brought from the room.

"Is she still shivering?" asked Rose, intent on the horizon.

"A little," said James.

"Get her clothes off if you have to." She sensed him looking round at her. "Well, it's her clothes that are making her cold."

"We don't have anything for her to change into. All we have is our own clothes. We're keeping her wrapped up."

"Get something over her hair."

The two of them manhandled a towel, practically smothering the woman. Mirai ended up taking it off them and wrapping it herself. She was okay.

"You did brilliantly," James said.

"Yes you did, Mirai. Well done," said Rose.

Whatever Tomo said in Mirai's ear put some colour in her cheeks as well.

"Where exactly are we heading?" James asked Rose.

"The nearest bit of land that isn't the port we just came from," said Rose. "All this bay area is built-up – roads, trains – we should be able to get somewhere from anywhere along the shore."

James gazed anxiously behind.

"See anything?" asked Rose.

"No. You think they'll come after us?"

"If they can, but they'd need something fast enough. They might call the authorities and claim that we're pirates or something, but I doubt it. Not with a dead body on board."

"So we're probably okay?"

"Probably. Unless they have access to something like a drone or a helicopter. Didn't see anything like that. Or…"

She felt James stiffen next to her.

"What?"

"I think I see a light."

"Could it be another ship?"

"It's a white light, not green or red. Or what?"

"Sorry?"

"You were going to say something."

"Or, they could have another rescue boat stashed away somewhere. A spare. That might be a problem."

She glanced behind. It was a long way off, but the light was steady, pointing their way.

"Is it getting closer?" she asked.

All three of them were looking back now. James waited a while before answering. "Yes. Slowly. Can we go any faster?"

"I don't think so. That doesn't help." Rose pointed to a section of the inflatable bow that was flapping in the headwind. "The knife caught it when we sprung the crew."

James stared at it. "We're not going to sink, are we?"

"No. But it's slowing us down." She pushed the gear to try and get more speed. The bow tipped up sideways. Mirai gasped and James reached out to grab something. Rose pulled back on the gear and they straightened. "This is as fast as we can go. We just have to hope we get to land before they catch us."

They carried on. The engine was whining. The rigid underside of the boat thumped on the swell. In the distance, a trail of lights along the horizon emerged.

"Land up ahead," she said. "It's not far."

"Well, it had better not be," said James. "They won't be shy about using a gun out here."

"I don't think they were shy before," said Rose. She'd wondered if anyone else had noticed the yakuza drawing his gun on the deck of the ship. "They don't want to accidentally hit you. You're our ticket out of here, golden boy."

"Golden boy? You used to call me that when you were twelve years old!"

"Well, you always were the favourite child."

"No I wasn't! You just told yourself that. It was an excuse to act up."

"No, it was real. Mum preferred you."

A pause. "Well, maybe. But Dad preferred you. I think he saw you as the man of the family."

They briefly exchanged glances. Rose had forgotten about all this shared history, decided years ago that it was unimportant.

"How close are they now?" she asked.

He glanced back. "Oh, hell. Closer."

"Compared to the shore we're heading for?"

He looked back and forth. "They're further away than that. But they're gaining on us. It'll be tight."

The lights in front became more distinctive – street lights along a highway. It was flat; all the land surrounding the harbour was reclaimed. In front of the road was a concrete drop and a uniform line of boulders, too narrow to form a beach. Her best play was to drive the boat as far up onto land as possible so they could jump out. As the rocks got larger in front of them, she kept going towards them full throttle. She glanced behind. They were close enough now that you could see a boat, not just a light. Possibly within firing range but they weren't trying that, at least not yet.

James kept looking across at her. "You are planning on slowing down at some point, aren't you?" he said.

"You want them to catch us?"

"No, but we can't just plough through a bank of rocks."

"Not through them. Onto them."

"Without flipping over, or some such thing?"

"Ideally not. But you'd better hang on. All of you. Twenty seconds."

They all reached for the rope grabs around the inflatable layer.

"Ten seconds," said Rose. She risked a glance over her shoulder. "Shit." They were close.

"This is too fast, Rose." James sounded stressed.

"Five seconds."

"Slow down, for God's sake!"

Two seconds out she slammed into reverse. The engine howled. They lurched forward and jolted to a complete stop with enough force to cause a whiplash injury. Something snapped at the back: the rudder, probably. But they were on the rocks, not pansying around in the water trying to wade in.

"Go! Go!" she shouted, jumping out and clambering up to the concrete wall. She looked back. They had about a minute before the other boat made land. The wall was no more than three feet high. They hoisted themselves up. Then came a boardwalk, a line of grass and the highway. There was no traffic. Rose ran across, trusting that the others were right behind. Now they had a problem – a wire fence. She fished in her coat for wire cutters – they were only the size of nail clippers but with a ratchet grip that made them surprisingly powerful. She attacked the fence from the bottom up. As the others ran up she'd cut about eight inches.

"It's enough." They pulled the wire up and twisted it out of the way. She dropped and slid under on her belly. As the others followed she looked back. The other boat was now on the shore. Four or five figures were getting out, one of them looking like Milo. That might slow them down a bit, she hoped.

They climbed up to a raised railway line that looked like a monorail, then across another road. A steep drop took them down to a promenade and more water. On one side was a building made of stone with battlements along the top like a castle. Directly opposite was some kind of dome, in front of which futuristic catamaran-like craft sat on the water. Off to the right was a ship, but it looked small, somehow, and old-fashioned.

Mirai put her hand in front of her mouth. At first Rose thought it was shock, but it wasn't. It was a delighted recognition. Tomo was looking at her, smiling. It was the first time she'd seen either of them look remotely happy.

"Mirai, what is it? Tomo? Where are we?"

Mirai turned, looking suddenly elated like a little girl. "Disneyland! This is Disneyland!"

"Oh, golly!" That was James.

"Tell me this is good news," said Rose.

"It's good news. I know Disneyland. I *know* Disneyland! This way!"

Mirai ran along the promenade. The others followed.

Chapter 36

In the early hours of the morning, a helicopter navigating with night vision entered airspace over Tokyo Bay and hovered over a cargo ship that was previously heading away from port but for some time had been sitting with its engines idle. A number of figures dropped from ropes onto the top of the superstructure. The copter withdrew but stayed close, a constant background thrum. The running and shouting on the ship was brief, and not witnessed by anyone else. It was soon over.

Considering Zack was in charge, it was a very restrained, low-key affair. The lead team went straight for the bridge and took control. Others worked systematically down the superstructure, taking everyone they found to the galley, the biggest room in the tower. Fairchild and Rapp were sent to the bridge. Fairchild intended to stick to the woman like glue, and she seemed to feel just as untrusting towards him. So while the cabin doors were booted open one by one, all Fairchild could do was monitor what was going on via his radio earpiece.

The bridge crew was secured and under guard. The captain was offering no resistance. How could he? This was a civilian cargo ship being raided by an armed group. Without the blessing of the Japanese government, this could be considered piracy. Did they have such a blessing? They could only hope Gardner and Barclay's work that evening would ensure continued ministerial support. There were Japanese hostages too, after all. The crew, on the other hand, seemed to be mainly Filipino. The captain was; he spoke very good English.

Rapp drew Fairchild away. "Okay, you got what you wanted," she said. "Now spill."

"He calls himself Milo," said Fairchild. "He's Hungarian. I've got his real life ID as well. I'll share it with you at some point."

Rapp radioed that to Zack.

"Roger that. Hungarian." Zack was in the galley looking over whoever was being taken there.

"That's it?" said Rapp to Fairchild. "An online name? Big deal."

"That's not it. Like I said, I have the proof of who he really is. We can use that when we talk to him. We have him in the palm of our hands."

She didn't look impressed. Fairchild walked away from her to look down onto the cargo deck. Soldiers were working their way over it, torches flashing. He turned to the captain.

"Does the deck have floodlights?"

The captain nodded towards the control panels which he couldn't reach from the chair he was tied to.

Fairchild radioed Zack. "Do you want more light on deck? They have floodlights."

"Sure."

"Show me," he said to the captain, walking over to the console.

"On the right," said the captain. "The white switches." Fairchild flicked them all, and the deck burst into light.

The captain's face was showing fear or anger, it was hard to tell which.

"We're not here to hurt anyone," said Fairchild.

"Who are you?"

"Americans. FBI."

He didn't seem overly impressed. "What do you want with us?"

"With the crew, nothing. It's your passengers we're interested in. Some of them aren't here of their own free will."

"You're not American."

"You're not a hostage-taker. But I guess we have our roles to play."

His earpiece exploded with shouting. Stressed voices yelling orders. *On the ground! Now!*

"Update," said Zack from the galley.

"Weapons found in a cabin. Handguns. They've been disarmed."

"Everybody heard that," said Zack.

Fairchild turned to the captain. "You have guns aboard this ship."

The captain shook his head.

"Well, you do. We just found them. They were pointing at us, it seems."

"I wasn't aware."

The next sound in his ear was like a punch in the gut.

"We have a body. Confirmed. Not breathing. Body on the third floor."

He took a look at the captain. "I don't suppose you were aware of the dead body, either."

He ran for the stairwell. Rapp shouted after him but he ignored her. The radio was still going: *Gunshot wounds to the chest*. His feet hammered on the stairs.

"Who is it? Do we have an ID?" Zack's voice was sober.

"Young male."

Fairchild had reached the third floor. His chest constricted. He bent over. He couldn't get air into his body. He sank against the wall. It wasn't Rose. It wasn't her. He could forget the images his brain had made of her lying bloodstained in a dark cabin. He closed his eyes and made a forced effort to relax. With a long slow breath he filled his lungs. His heart rate began to slow. He sat, feeling weak. Rapp hadn't come after him; she wouldn't want to leave the bridge. Fairchild gave it a few more seconds and climbed to his feet. He felt sick but forced it back. He opened the door to the third floor and strode along the corridor. A soldier was standing by an open door.

"This the body?" asked Fairchild.

"Yep."

Fairchild leaned closer. It was one of the Japanese hackers, one of the students. He got on the radio.

"Zack, where are these hostages, for Christ's sake? Have we searched every floor?"

Zack came back. "Yes, we've searched every floor. You'd better get down here. Rapp as well."

The galley held the entire crew except for those who were on the bridge. There were about thirty of them, dour-looking Asian men watching everything. There were also four guys who were Japanese mafia, judging from their muscle and tattoos. They were being held separately with a much more significant guard. Fairchild arrived at the same time as Rapp.

"See any Hungarians here?" Zack asked them. "Or any of our hostages?"

Fairchild looked round. "They're not on board."

"We've looked everywhere?" asked Rapp.

"In all the rooms, and we've swept on and below deck."

"What about inside the containers?" asked Rapp.

"You're kidding. There are thousands of them."

"Is there any way they could have got off the ship without us noticing?" asked Fairchild.

"Maybe," said Zack. "There was some cloud cover earlier. We'd have to review the satellite coverage."

"Or we could ask," said Fairchild.

Zack glanced at the mobsters. "Good luck with that. I wouldn't want to be the one to rat out the boss."

"Not them. The crew. Starting with the captain."

"Good idea," said Rapp.

"I'd like to lead, if that's okay," said Fairchild to Zack.

"Knock yourself out."

"Hold on right there," said Rapp. "I should be leading. Why him?"

"Because I say so," said Zack. "But you should be there too. Get up there, both of you."

Rapp wasn't pleased, but then neither was Fairchild. He'd prefer to deal with this without the woman. But Zack didn't have all the options in the world. On the bridge, the two of them took the captain aside.

"We're not interested in the ship," said Fairchild. "It's the hostages we want. And the people who took them. If they're no longer aboard we'll leave you alone. But you have to tell us what you know. Your arrangement with your passengers and whoever runs this ship, that's not our concern right now. But we need our people."

The captain remained impassive. "I'm not keen on giving you information while you're pointing guns."

"We had guns pointed at us."

"Not by the crew."

"Immaterial. And we're here with the permission of the Japanese government. Some of the hostages are Japanese citizens. So unless you want us to take apart this ship container by container and fully disclose whatever we find to the authorities, tell us what you know."

"Okay. Some of them escaped in a rescue boat."

"How many?"

"Not sure. We don't have all details of all passengers."

"I see. And did others go after them?"

"We have another rescue boat, a spare. They took that."

"Who's 'they'?"

The captain didn't meet his eye.

"Was one of them the guy who boarded?" asked Fairchild. "The one you were waiting for?"

No response again.

"Did he call himself Milo?"

The captain looked up, recognition in his face. Fairchild and Rapp exchanged glances. "Which way did they go?" asked Fairchild.

"Back towards Tokyo."

"Are you in contact now with either of these boats?"

The captain shook his head.

"What are your instructions?"

"Wait here for another hour. If no word, back to port to reprovision."

"Reprovision? You've only just set off."

"We have no rescue boat. We can't sail like that."

"Well, it's good to know you have such regard for human life. I'm sure the guy lying in that cabin with three bullet holes in his chest would be gratified. Whoever he is."

Rapp cut in. "We got what we want. That's enough."

They passed the info to Zack. In the lift back to the galley, Fairchild said "Sorry. There's something about his pride in his correctness that gets me. He knows enough about what goes on here, but he chooses to ignore it."

"This is personal for you, isn't it?" Rapp was looking at him intently.

Fairchild hadn't anticipated how much he'd be affected emotionally. It had ended up with Rapp holding him back, not the other way round. "Yes, it's personal."

"Me too," she said. "My mother was in one of the hospitals that got the ransomware attack. She was there for an emergency procedure. They couldn't do it, so they transferred her to another hospital a couple of hundred miles away. She died on the way."

"I'm sorry," said Fairchild.

They rode down in silence.

When they got to the galley, Zack was already on it. "The copter is searching the bay. We're going over the surveillance video now. Christ, this place is big, though. They could have landed anywhere. Assuming they made land at all. If we don't get sight of the boats, they're invisible."

Fairchild's phone vibrated. It was Takao. Why was he calling at this hour? "What's up?"

"Fairchild. Problem. Big problem." He sounded on the verge of tears. "I'm at their hotel room. They're not here!"

"Start at the beginning, Takao. Whose hotel room?"

"Fiona and the children! I got missed call from Fiona half an hour ago. Couldn't get hold of her, so came over in a taxi. No answer at the door. So got the manager. Now we're inside. It's all messed up, Fairchild! Chair on the floor, clothes everywhere. Fiona's phone is here, all their stuff. But they're gone!"

Chapter 37

Mirai was on a mission. James was struggling to keep up with her, and he wasn't the only one. She led them round the promenade and it looked like she was going to head straight inland, but then she ducked sideways and disappeared. They almost went past the little cut-through that she took, but she called them back. How did she manage to know every little nook and cranny? Still, lucky she did. They ducked down and waited, and pretty soon several sets of running footprints echoed past them and faded.

"This way!" whispered Mirai, and led them in the opposite direction. At least with all this running about she was warming up a bit. James had been seriously worried for a few minutes in the boat. Or maybe he was just worried he'd be expected to undress the woman. Luckily it hadn't come to that.

Lost River Delta was the name on the building they were skirting now, an edifice that looked like one of those temples in Cambodia, as far as he could see, although he only caught the edge of it in Rose's torchlight as there was no other lighting. How did Rose still manage to have a torch on her after all this time? He must remember to ask her that. They were on a wide walkway with arches on one side and a stone wall on the other dotted with old-style street lamps, unlit. Beyond that, water. This place was huge, though normally it would be swarming with people, he supposed. They'd taken the kids to a couple of such places. He had to admit he rather enjoyed them. You had to enter into the spirit of it all.

They were still running, skirting water, then Mirai took them over a rather charming little hump-backed bridge. James was getting a little breathless by now, but they could never get too far away from those animals. Hopefully they could lose themselves in this labyrinthine world and stay put until help of some kind arrived. And here, coming up, was the arched entrance to a cave. A cave was exactly what they needed! Mirai took them in confidently though it was pitch black. Deeper and deeper they went, until it widened out into a kind of central gathering area with lifts that led, presumably, up – or down – to the main attraction, some rope barriers and so on, and a big screen. Finally Mirai stopped.

"What is this place?" asked Rose, who barely seemed out of breath at all. She explored every corner with the torch.

"Journey to Centre of Earth," said Mirai proudly. "My favourite."

"Okay, well, that's good, but if there's a particular reason for coming here—"

"Screen!" Mirai cut Rose off. "See?" She pointed. "It's controlled from a room. Door is here. I saw once. Screen wasn't working. Staff went through door here to fix it. Come, come!"

She led Rose and the torch along the wall.

"I say, you must have come here quite a few times to know it so well," said James.

"Fifty, hundred times, maybe," Mirai said.

Wow. That was a lot of trips to Disneyland.

They found the door. "You can open it?" Mirai asked Rose.

"Let's see. Hold the torch."

Rose got a set of tools from her pocket and began poking about with the lock. Odd, seeing your little sister calmly breaking and entering. Still, it was good she was around. They'd all be a goner otherwise. A silence fell, apart from an occasional clicking. Tomo and James were just standing about. The ladies were definitely running the show right now. Nothing wrong with that, of course. Perfectly normal chez Clarke, in fact. All power to their elbow.

A more satisfying click – more of a clunk, really – and Rose pushed the handle. The door opened. The others crowded in. Someone found a light switch. It was rather disappointing after the grandeur of the cave. Still, even Disneyland needed offices. Several fairly old desktop computers sat on the crammed-in little desks. They went round switching them all on.

"Okay, what we want now is to get a message out saying where we are," said Rose. "Can you do that, James?"

"I hope so." He sat at the nearest one and accessed the command prompt. "Do you have an email address?" He typed fast – but not too fast, James. No errors now. Not with everyone watching. Rose read out an email address.

"Who's that?" he asked as he typed.

"John Fairchild. One of the team." There was a teeny hesitation there. Interesting.

"So we want the back-up team now?"

"Now we do, yes. Now Milo is here. Now we've seen him shoot one of us. We're desperate, James. Just send the message!"

"Okay, okay! What shall I say?"

"Well, don't encrypt it, for goodness' sake."

"Of course not." He went for *Centre of Earth, Disneyland* and left it at that. He was just wondering if a bit more detail might have been helpful when the screen went blank and all the lights went out. The computers whirred to a halt.

"EeeehhhH?" intoned Mirai.

"What's going on?" said Rose.

Out in the main cavern area, things flickered into life and an orange-red glow appeared. There seemed to be some hissing and steam and recorded metallic banging sounds. They ran out of the office. The lights were flashing over the lift doors and a display cabinet holding old-style scientific paraphernalia was lit up brightly.

"Someone's got access to the power," said Rose.

A loud thumping noise emanated from somewhere and filled the cave. Then, a man's disembodied voice. A voice they all recognised.

"Hello! Hello, out there, theme park lovers!"

"Does he know where we are?" whispered James.

"Wherever you're hiding, I know you can hear this," said Milo, his voice sounding strangely loud and intimate at the same time. "You're in here somewhere."

"He must be using some kind of central tannoy," said Rose. "This is going out to the whole park." She sidled up to James. "How confident are you that the message went out?"

He'd been thinking exactly the same thing. "Fifty percent," was his honest answer. He wished he could be more reassuring.

"I don't think you realise yet who you're trying to run from," continued Milo. "My fault. Clearly I haven't communicated this well enough to you. Let's just say what you're doing is futile. You cannot run from us. We are everywhere. And we will have what we want."

The rhetoric was familiar from Fire Sappers ransomware attacks James had read about. But this Milo sounded like he actually believed in that omnipotence drivel. Clearly he was unhinged, which made him even scarier.

The tannoy cut out. They all looked at each other.

"He has no idea where we are," said Rose. "How can he hope to comb a whole theme park like this? He's bullshitting."

The lighting changed. The power in the office had come back on. That thumping again, and the voice returned. "You probably made some attempt to get help. So I'm guessing you can get onto the web from wherever you are. I think you'll want to see what I've got to show you. Or, I should say, who. Especially James." James suddenly felt breathless. "Try this." Milo reeled off an online address that James recognised as a dark web location. So did the Japanese two, he could tell. They ran back into the office.

The computers had powered up again. Between the three of them, they recalled the location. He typed it in. The screen turned into dark moving shapes.

"Ah, I see you! Thanks for coming," breathed the tannoy. "Let's have some light, shall we?"

The screen brightened, went out of focus, then sharpened again. James stood up. Something behind him fell over but he didn't care.

Fiona. Sophie. Henry. The three of them, sitting next to each other on a sofa, with their hands tied behind them. Looking terribly, terribly scared.

"No, no, no!" Everyone was looking at him. Rose had a hold of his arm.

"It's very sweet," said Milo softly. "They came to Tokyo to find you, James. They really made it easy for us. Now I think we need to talk again, don't we? We need to talk about how we can help each other. Do you agree?"

Chapter 38

The tannoy cut out again. Every muscle in James' arm was tensed. Rose had never seen him like this. That bastard Milo. There was nothing he wouldn't do. Rose had mis-judged Fiona as well – she'd never expected her to show up in Tokyo. Who was looking after them? Clearly they hadn't done a good job, but then who anticipated this? The guy was streets ahead of them.

Milo came back on with a click. "I suggest we continue this conversation face to face. It would make things easier, don't you think?" A message box popped up on James' screen. "Just tell us where you are, now."

His false gentleness made Rose feel sick. James stared at the message box, then at her.

"Not a good idea," she said. "We have an advantage at the moment. If we give away our position—"

Something changed on the monitor. In the room with Fiona and the children, something off-screen had got their attention. Then they turned and crowded closer to the camera, gazing in. They were talking – their mouths were moving.

"What are they saying?" asked James. "We need sound. Can we get sound? Please?"

Mirai and Tomo hunted around the computer. Mirai went back out into the cavern area.

"Ah! James-san!" she called. They all ran out. The big screen was also showing the hostages. Mirai felt around the edge of the screen and found a button. There was a crackle and the chamber filled with noise. Fiona was saying something:

"…if he's really there?" She was turning to someone in the room who was out of sight. "How we do know that? We can't see anything."

Henry and Sophie were gazing into the camera with frightened eyes.

"Oh, they're there," said a voice. "They can hear you, too."

Rose felt her body freeze. That voice!

Milo came on again. "Tell me where you are and you can speak to them. They can see you, even. We're not monsters, James. We don't want you all to suffer. Let me make it easier for you. No one will be hurt, I promise. I just want to talk. And you can speak to your family. How about that?"

James turned to Rose with pleading eyes.

"You believe him?" she asked. "He could storm the place and take us all."

"James?" That was Fiona's voice now. "James, are you there? Please, James, whatever they want, let them have it. I'm scared. We all are. I can't see you. Are you there?"

James was staring at his wife's face on the screen. He squeezed his eyes shut, then opened them again, turned and made for the office. Rose followed.

"Don't do it, James. Help is on its way."

"Is it?" He turned to her, furious. "We don't know that! We're on our own, Rose. What's he going to do to them?"

Before she could stop him, he'd typed into the message box: *Centre of Earth*.

"Don't send it! You're being a fool, James!"

She grabbed his hands off the keyboard and shoved him, hard. His chair rolled back, but he planted his feet and pushed her aside with a strength she didn't know he had. She fell to her knees, recovered, and came straight back at him.

But all he needed was a second. By the time she was at the keyboard, he'd sent the message.

"Ah, very good!" Milo intoned around them. "A wise choice. Expect me soon." He cut out.

"Idiot!" Rose snapped. "We put all that effort into getting away and you've led them right to us!"

Without waiting for a response she went back into the cavern.

"Mirai, is there only one way in and out of here?"

"Yes, I think so."

Rose looked around. "Stay together, all of you."

James had come back into the cavern. She could barely stand to look at him. She freed up a heavy metal barrier post, dragged it over to the display cabinet, planted her feet and swung the post shot-put style into the glass. It smashed, and the shards scattered everywhere. From inside the display she grabbed a heavy-looking metal tripod. It gave her comfort at least to have something heavy in her hand. She made towards the cavern entrance.

The shadows suddenly diminished. She looked round. The cave had brightened. Someone had adjusted the lighting. There was a shriek. It was Fiona.

"James! James, we can see you!"

James was spinning round, trying to see a camera.

"Here! Here!" They were waving at him. Mirai and Tomo were looking for the camera too. "Yes! Yes, that's it!" cried Fiona. The camera was up on the wall, though it was well disguised. Rose stayed back, one eye on the cavern entrance.

"You can see me? Can you see me now?" cried James, staring up.

"Yes! Oh, James! I'm so sorry!" said Fiona.

"No! No, it's my fault."

"We shouldn't have come. But no one was telling us anything and I thought if we all showed up—"

"Fiona, love, I think it's wonderful you came out here. Of course all of this isn't very wonderful, but you know what I mean. Are you all okay?"

"Yes, we're okay. They haven't hurt us." She glanced over to the side of the room.

"Sophie, darling!" said James. "I'm so sorry I missed your birthday! Are you all right?"

Sophie nodded shyly.

"Henry?"

"We're all okay, Dad."

It was such a timid grown-up voice, a scared boy determined to do the right thing. Rose felt tears in her eyes. A slight scuffling noise made her turn round.

"Shit!" Everyone else turned. Milo was standing at the cavern entrance flanked by two yakuza, each carrying a gun. Rose backed towards the others. This was it. James had led them straight here and they were defenceless.

"What's going on, James?" Fiona's voice echoed round.

"Keep them quiet, can't you?" said Milo, sounding irritated. He was pale; Haruma had done some damage to the man at least. Fiona and the children fell silent.

"Well, here we all are," said Rose. "Which one of us are you going to shoot now?"

"Rose, don't!" James' words were a plea.

"Yes, you're right, James," said Milo. "You can't always listen to your sister. Of course it's you we're interested in, none of the others. You already know what we want. But now you know us. Now you know our reach. We have friends everywhere. You can only continue if you work with us. And that's what you want, isn't it? For everything to carry on as it did before?"

His voice echoed away. Everyone was listening, the hostages too.

"Yes," said James simply. "That's what I want."

"Then give me what I ask. A back door to the wallet. Go home and carry on how you were. Create a way in for us. We will stay in touch. You do what we ask, everyone will be fine. That's the offer. Do you accept?"

"He's lying, James," said Rose. "He won't let us go, not now we've seen him. You know you can't trust him."

"I accept," said James quietly. "I'll do what you ask."

"James?" said Rose. "You can't! Think what that means! They're thieves! You'll be helping them steal money. And then what? They'll never go away. Whatever they ask for you'll have to give them."

James wasn't even looking at her. He was staring up at the screen, at his family, the three of them lined up, hearing every word.

"James, listen to me!" she said. "What about the people who get hacked? Some of them are not nice people. If they find out how it was done, you think they'll just accept it?"

"We look after our people," said Milo.

"Don't believe a word of it," said Rose. "You saw what he did earlier. He'll kill us all."

James lifted his chin and squared up to Milo. "Everyone in here walks free. Everyone. My family gets on a plane to the UK. Then I'll give you what you want. Those are my terms."

Milo nodded. "I accept."

"James!" shouted Rose.

Her brother turned and pointed a finger at her. "Now you listen, Rose. You said it yourself. Sometimes you do what you have to do to survive. I know you don't think much of us. With you it's all queen and country, and we're just living our boring, meaningless lives. But this is me, Rose. This is what's important to me. This is my world, my wife and my kids. They're everything to me. Everything! And I will sacrifice anything to keep them safe. I'm sorry you don't like it, but that's what I will do."

His voice echoed into silence. On the screen, Rose saw Fiona looking at her husband, and with such a look – pride, ferocity, intensity, love.

Milo nodded. "Good, good. Sorry, Rose. I guess you lost the argument this time. So! This is what happens next."

He took a breath, frowned and turned. Then everyone heard. From down the cave came heavy footsteps, running, shouting, a burst of weapon fire. Was this the rest of Milo's yakuza friends coming in? Rose moved forward, gripping the tripod in both hands. Hopeless though it was, she'd take a few of them out if she could.

But when the shouting got nearer, it wasn't the yakuza. She heard a woman's voice, one she recognised. "Get down on the ground! FBI! Everybody down!"

"No!" James ran forward. "No! Not now! They'll kill them!"

Armed officers were swarming into the cavern. The two yakuza had their hands in the air. James was running straight towards the soldiers. Rose stepped forward and tripped him with the tripod. He fell, and she pressed him into the ground under her knee. He struggled like a wild animal. "Don't let them!"

"They'll shoot you, James!" She held his face down. The soldiers passed round. With the echo it sounded like there were dozens of them. Voices shouted commands over the top of each other. Gunshots exploded: bullets then automatic fire. James screamed.

"Get them out of here!" That was Rapp.

"Get up! Get up now!" Two of them stooped either side of them, bulky with bulletproof gear. They grabbed her arms and pulled her up, wrestling the tripod out of her grip. They frogmarched her out of the cavern. They wouldn't even let her turn her head to see what was happening.

"No! You can't!" James was getting the same treatment as she was, but he didn't go quietly. He shouted and screamed the length of the cave as they were forced along.

They were almost out of the cave when from deep inside came the sound of more gunfire. What was going on back there?

Chapter 39

From the moment the helicopter touched down in the theme park, Fairchild clung to Rapp like a malevolent shadow. The way the situation had evolved, he had no choice but to pass on the location as soon as the email arrived. Theoretically Zack was in charge, but with Rapp at the forefront of an offensive, things might not necessarily go to plan.

They landed in a car park and ran past a battlement and over a bridge into DisneySea, the water-themed part of the park. A model sailing ship, a Mississippi steam-boat, some kind of volcanic structure: it was like a bizarre military training exercise. A few yakuza with guns were hanging around the outside of the *Centre of the Earth*. As they approached, one or two of them got a couple of shots off, but they were soon neutralised. Rapp wasted no time joining the advance team heading inside.

"Keep with her," said Zack. But Fairchild was already on it.

As they knew from the hastily-studied schemas, the cave curved round and led into a wide internal cavern. Rapp, already in there, was yelling at people to get down. The space filled with soldiers ready with their weapons. There were bodies flat on the ground. Two of them lay face down, one partially on top of the other. Fairchild slowed. It was Rose and James. For one horrific moment he couldn't see either of them move.

Some fool fired a shot. Idiot, shooting in a space like this! A short barrage of return fire downed the shooter, a yakuza. He wasn't going to be getting up again. Someone screamed. Another yakuza and a westerner had their hands up. The westerner was young, dark-haired, wiry. So this was Milo.

"Get them out of here!" Rapp seemed to be treating everyone in the cave as the enemy. The Japanese pair were led off, as were Rose and James. James wasn't going quietly. Fairchild hung back out of sight; they were both safe, and he needed to be here with Rapp. And Milo.

A huge screen on the wall was showing a live feed. Fiona, Sophie and Henry were in a room somewhere. All Fairchild could see of it was a sofa. They were staring with horrified expressions. They must be watching a feed of the cavern themselves. Milo had to be getting help with all of this; rigging something up like that was way beyond the skill set of those yakuza. Almost as soon as he saw it, the screen went dark. The connection had been cut.

It was only gradually sinking in how much his bargain with Tang had changed things. The Wong Kai boss's information had enabled this whole rescue. But Tang was angry. Tang wanted Fire Sappers, and thought that Fairchild was the person to deliver them. But Fire Sappers was elusive, and the only lead Fairchild had, anywhere in the world, was currently standing in front of Alice Rapp with his hands in the air.

Milo and Rapp were staring at each other. Rapp grabbed the man by the shoulder and threw him face down. He yelped with pain. The floor was covered in shattered glass. Everyone else stood staring. She knelt, grabbed the back of the man's head and pushed his face into the glass. He shrieked.

"Are you Milo?" she shouted. "Are you Milo? Answer me!"

Fairchild stepped forward.

"Rapp! It must be Milo. He was the only westerner here except for the hostages."

"You keep out of this."

"We need him to tell us where Clarke's family is."

"That's what I'm doing."

"By torturing the guy? Look at his face! There's blood all over it. His eye!"

"You're best buddies now, are you? You know what this guy did."

Milo spoke. "Let me go and I'll release them. You get them back unharmed."

"You're joking," said Rapp. "Let you go?"

"You won't find them otherwise."

"One of the mob will talk," said Rapp.

"No. Not them. They'll go to prison instead of that. It's what they're like round here, loyalty and honour, such a wonderful thing."

The guy was lying face down in shards of glass surrounded by armed soldiers, but he still managed to sneer. What a scumbag. Rapp was right about that at least. Fairchild squatted next to him.

"They won't let you go, Milo. Be realistic. If you cooperate, things will be a lot better for you. Tell us where they are."

Rapp pointed at Fairchild. "You back off. I'm leading this."

"Says who? Zack's in charge, remember?" But then it dawned on him.

"Quiet, isn't it?" said Rapp, watching his face. "The radios aren't working in here. Too much rock. Which means I'm the senior officer." She turned to the soldiers. "Detain this guy. He's trying to collude with the prisoner."

"I'm doing nothing of the kind and you know it."

But the soldiers moved forward.

"Take him outside," she said. "Get him out of here too." She pointed to the mobster. They hesitated. "Go!" she shouted. "All of you!"

"That makes no sense," said Fairchild. "Why stay in here alone with Milo? You've detained everyone now. We should all go out together."

"I'll be right behind you. Go, now!" Behind her on the floor, fear started showing on Milo's face. The soldiers encircled Fairchild.

"Why is she doing this?" he said to them. "Why aren't we staying together? You know this isn't right."

But they had no choice; Rapp was the senior officer and they had to obey orders. Two of them grabbed his arms. Another pair led the yakuza out in front, and one more followed Fairchild. They propelled him out of the cavern. Rapp and Milo were out of sight.

He let them take him twenty paces. The guys on either side relaxed. He could hear the one behind messing around with a pair of cuffs, slowing a little as he did so. The two in front with the thug were a few paces ahead. It was now or never.

He jerked backwards violently, pulling one of his arms free. He grabbed the other one's arm and twisted savagely. Anticipating, Fairchild's elbow and knee caught the other two as they came forward, winding them long enough to get out a kick and a punch and to grab a gun from a holster. Everyone froze. He pointed the gun at the nearest and backed off towards the cavern. The other two drew their weapons and aimed at him.

"Drop it! Drop it!" Their shouts echoed in the cave. It was a calculated risk. He didn't think they'd shoot.

"Come on, wake up! You know what she's doing in there!"

He turned and ran. He had to stop her. Milo was his only chance. But when he got to the cavern, he saw he was too late.

"Rapp! No!" Milo was standing, arms in the air. Rapp was aiming straight at his chest. Fairchild sprinted, but before he could reach them she fired twice in quick succession. Milo fell to the ground.

Rapp lowered her gun. She looked at Fairchild calmly. The other soldiers came up behind him.

"What are you doing?" Fairchild shouted. "We needed him, Rapp!"

"He was coming for me. I said I'd shoot, but he took no notice."

The soldiers bent over the body and straightened again. No point in hurrying: the man was dead.

"So where's his gun? Was he carrying?" asked Fairchild.

They already knew he wasn't. The soldiers turned to Rapp.

"He was coming for me," she repeated. "You think I should have asked him nicely what his intentions were? He could have grabbed my weapon. I have the right to defend myself."

"By shooting him in the chest?"

"There was very little time."

"You engineered the whole situation. There was no need for you to be alone in here with him."

"I had to take action, given you didn't seem sure what side you were on."

"Like hell. Milo wasn't a threat. He was unarmed."

"He could have got away. I couldn't take the chance, given the importance of the target."

"Got away how, exactly? The rest of the team is right outside!"

"We don't know that. We have no comms. The situation out there might have changed. I couldn't risk him escaping."

She was cool, he gave her that.

She stuck rigidly to her story when they all eventually emerged, Fairchild in handcuffs, Milo on a field stretcher, the two bullets efficiently fatal. Fairchild saw Zack's face when he cast his eye over the body. He knew exactly what he was looking at.

James was agitated; Rose was trying to calm him down. There was some friction between them, Fairchild could tell. "That's Milo?" said James, when he saw the body. "He's dead? Then how will we find them? Oh, God, they could have been killed by now!"

Fairchild recognised the expression on Rose's face: a restrained anger. Rapp was standing back, serene.

"One of those goons must know where they went," said Rose.

"They're not talking," said Zack. "Gentle persuasion didn't help either. What about the comms link? The screen? Can it be traced back?"

"No, it can't." James answered more calmly. "It was a dark web location. Untraceable."

"James-san," said the female Japanese hacker, her voice sounding tiny out here.

"What is it, Mirai?" James was close to tears.

"The yakuza have a place. A house. They took me there once. They kept me there long time." She bowed her head.

"Christ," said Rose. The other Japanese boy stepped up right next to Mirai.

"On the screen," Mirai said softly. "The sofa. The room. Not sure, but maybe same place."

"That's good enough," said Zack. "Where is it?"

"Sangenjaya."

"Yeah, that hasn't helped. Is it far?"

"Yes. Far."

"It's the other side of the city," said Fairchild.

"Well, let's get going," said Zack. "And why does everyone have cuffs on? Get them all off." He pointed at Rapp. "She's not coming. She's getting escorted back to base along with the body. The slow way. Everyone else – back to the copter."

Chapter 40

Rose sped up to approach Zack as they all raced back towards the waiting helicopter. Fairchild caught up with the American as well.

"I hate to rain on your parade," Fairchild said to Zack, "but do you have an idea of where we're going to land a helicopter in the middle of Tokyo? And won't they hear us coming? Assuming they're still there, which probably they're not because they already know Milo has been taken."

Zack had his phone in his hand and didn't slow his pace. Rose had to jog to keep up with the men.

"Yeah, there's a heliport at Minato base. Right in the centre."

"There's an American military base in central Tokyo?" said Rose.

"Sure. We used to occupy the place, remember? Never really left. Anyway, if you two will let me get on with things, by the time we get there we'll have a vehicle ready to drive us to San Gen whatever. We'll go in quiet and hopefully surprise them."

"They won't be surprised, Zack," said Fairchild. "They already know we have James and the others. They saw it on screen."

"Doesn't mean they've gone anywhere. They don't know Milo is dead. Maybe they'll stay put and wait for orders. Depends if there's anyone else there with a brain."

"There is," said Rose.

That got Fairchild's attention. "What do you mean? Did you see someone on the screen?"

"Not see. Hear. I recognised his voice."

She gave Fairchild a look which he'd seen before.

"Yeah, well, I'm open to other ideas about where to look for these folk, if you guys have any," said Zack. They didn't.

In the air decisions were made about who would go in the van. Mirai had to go with them. "We'll never find the place otherwise," said Zack. Rose noticed that she and Tomo were holding hands now.

"Fairchild, you're coming," said Zack.

"So am I," said Rose.

"Why? You're not part of the unit and you don't add anything."

"All that's true of Fairchild as well. If he goes, I go."

"I want to go," said James.

"No," said Zack. "Not a good idea. You should stay at base. We'll keep you up to speed, don't worry."

"No, I want to be there!"

"Come on, Zack," said Rose. "You'd want to go, wouldn't you, if it was you? He doesn't need to get out of the van."

Zack rolled his eyes. "Okay then. But it's your job to make sure he stays in the van."

A fresh team was ready and briefed by the time they got to base; all they had to do was climb into the vehicle. The journey was fast, Mirai up front giving directions as they got close. The place was above a shop and its entrance in an alleyway.

"Down there," said Mirai, her voice shaking, as they drove past. Whatever they'd done to her here, it had clearly traumatised her.

They parked out of sight. Rose and Fairchild followed the advance team and hovered at the end of the alleyway. But the door was hanging open. The soldiers filed in. Everyone else waited outside. The silence stretched on for an age.

Boots thudded down the stairs. "All clear," said a voice at the door.

"Really?" said Rose. "There's no one here?"

"Come and see for yourself."

Rose ran up the stairs and into the only room with a light on. Fiona, Henry and Sophie were inside. They'd been tied to chairs but were otherwise unhurt.

"Rose!" Fiona almost started crying when she saw her sister-in-law.

Rose helped the soldiers free them all. "What happened? Are you alone here?"

"They just left. When all the commotion started on the screen, they packed up the laptop and ran off. Just left us here."

"Fairchild!" That was Henry. Fairchild had just walked in after her. There were smiles all round. Typical he got more of a welcome from her family than she did.

"The house is clear," said Fairchild. "Nobody else here."

"Who was in here with you?" said Rose to Fiona. "It wasn't the yakuza, was it? The mafia?"

"No, they were outside. The two in here, one was a young guy, Russian I think. He was operating the laptop. The other one was older."

"Older?"

"Really old," said Henry.

"Everyone's old to you," said Rose.

"He was quite old, though," said Fiona. White hair. Well-dressed. Well spoken."

"British?"

"Yes, sounded like it."

Rose and Fairchild exchanged glances.

"Did they say anything about why they left you here?" Fairchild asked Fiona. "Did they not think about taking you with them?"

"He said, I'm not a monster."

"Which one said that? The older one?"

"Yes. That's all. Then they left."

"Daddy! Daddy!" The room exploded into uproar. James rushed in like a hurricane, and they were all over him with excited shrieks. Everyone seemed to be crying.

"You were supposed to stay in the van," said Rose, but no one heard. She backed off; she had no place here.

"Rose!" James called after her as she was about to head down the stairs. He came over. "What can I say? Thanks for being there. Thanks for not being ordinary."

"Glad I could help." They hugged, but it was strained. "You're pretty far from ordinary yourself."

She escaped into the street, taking big gasps of air, not fully understanding what was making her so shaky. They were meant to go back to the base to update Zack, but she was going to slip off. They could get everything she knew from other people. She needed time alone.

Fairchild had followed her down and was standing there.

"We need to talk about this," he said. He meant the man in the room, the older man, who claimed not to be a monster. They both knew who he was.

"We do. But not now." She walked off down the dark street, knowing he was watching her leave.

Chapter 41

Meetings and debriefs were still being had, repercussions considered and priorities revisited, a couple of days later, when on his way into the US Embassy, Fairchild bumped into Tim Gardner coming out. This was lucky as he'd been trying to get hold of the guy.

"Yes, of course, this favour!" said Tim as they greeted each other.

Fairchild wasn't intending to let him get away – he'd earned the favour, for sure. He quickly summarised what he wanted to know.

"Sutherland?" said Tim. "Well, you know, this famous Sutherland did serve in Japan for a short while. In the late sixties." Another thing Walter had never told him.

"He left under rather a cloud," Gardner continued. "Something to do with the loss of an agent. Anyway, I probably still have some details on file, if you're interested. I'll dig them out. You don't believe those rumours about the chap still being alive, do you? Sounds like nonsense to me."

Inside, Rapp was waiting for Fairchild in a meeting room. To say the woman was under pressure would be an understatement; she was facing scrutiny from the highest level. It showed on her face and in her manner: subdued, formal, dressed all in greys and blacks.

"So what's this about?" she said.

Fairchild sat down. "I've come to apologise."

That surprised her. She waited for more.

"Regarding what happened in the cavern. On reflection, and having revisited the incident in my mind, I feel I was mistaken about what happened."

A pause. The only sound was distant talking in another office. Outside the window the sky was a bright December blue.

"Go on," said Rapp.

"The team was under time pressure to locate the remaining hostages. The force you used to persuade the prisoner to disclose his identity was proportional, given the situation. There were very low levels of lighting in the cavern and it would have been easy not to notice the shattered glass on the ground. The facial injuries sustained by the prisoner were probably accidental."

"Accidental?"

"In my opinion. In the absence of radio contact with mission control, as high ranking officer you were in command. It was wrong of me as a civilian observer to question your orders, particularly in front of other officers. I regret that."

She raised her eyebrows but said nothing.

"Having pulled away from the officers ordered to detain me, I ran back into the cavern. I arrived there before the soldiers. I saw Milo try to overpower you, with the aim of grabbing your weapon. I saw you pull away from him, draw your gun and shoot him, having given him a warning."

Her eyes were on his face, trying to read him.

He continued. "Shooting the prisoner before he could get away was a reasonable action to take to avoid the risk of escape. Particularly given the seriousness of his crimes on American people. It was a fast-moving situation. I have no reason to think you were deliberately intending to kill him."

That bit stuck in his throat a little. Hopefully he wouldn't be called on to come out with all this too often. He'd struggle to carry it off every time. It might not work, of course. The whole situation looked bad for her, and she had an undeniable personal motive. But if others were inclined to give her the benefit of the doubt, Fairchild's testimony might tip the balance.

It wasn't for nothing, of course. She realised that. "Well, that's all very gratifying," she said. "So what happens now?"

"Regardless of his skills and expertise, James Clarke will not be a part of any future attempt to investigate or infiltrate Fire Sappers. He and his family go home. Any approach to any of them in relation to this will end badly for you. The same for the Japanese students. Agreed?"

She looked pained. "Agreed."

"All complaints that you have made about Rose Clarke will immediately be withdrawn."

A flash of amusement crossed her face.

"If it weren't for Rose Clarke," he said, "all of them would be out somewhere at sea by now. She brought you Milo. She brought you Fire Sappers. The fact that you then screwed up doesn't reflect on her. Any kickback on her will mean kickback on you. Agreed?"

"Agreed." Spoken like a sulky teenager.

"You have nothing but praise for the way Zack handled operations."

"Oh, please. Anything else, while you're here?"

He met her gaze with an uncompromising one of his own. "If I think of anything I'll let you know."

"You wouldn't have done the same? To a person who took someone you loved?"

"Not if there were other lives in the balance. Innocent lives. And besides, Milo could have taken you into their organisation. You think you're going to break them by shooting them one by one? You could have closed them down, with the information he'd have given you."

She stared out of the window. Her lips were pressed together.

"There are plenty of enemies you can't outgun," he said. "You have to outsmart them. It takes patience, and compromise. And working with people you don't want to work with."

"Thanks for the lecture, but I bet you've done plenty of outgunning in your time. How did you get away from those armed officers, anyway? You've seen your share."

"Maybe. Does it feel better, killing the guy who killed your mother?"

She turned to look straight at him. "It sure does."

That set something off inside him: regret, guilt, an awareness of unfinished business. Would he ever have the certainty he could see in Rapp's face? Instead, things seemed to be getting ever more murky and complicated. Particularly with Milo gone. Now another opportunity may have emerged to fulfil Tang's promise, but it was one he never thought he would have to take. The idea of it made him loathe himself.

He got up. "Remember me," he said, and left.

Chapter 42

Takao had suggested meeting outside McDonald's: prosaic but findable. The man had already apologised at length to Fairchild on the phone, but when they met face to face, Fairchild had to endure another round of breast-beating.

"Takao, really, it's not your fault. You're not a bodyguard. I didn't think his family would be in danger. This group was much more sophisticated than we thought. And they're all okay now, aren't they?"

"Yes, all okay," sighed Takao. "I offered them lift to airport. Least I could do. All turned out good in the end."

"All right, so let's get to the next thing then. The address?"

"Ah yes! I can find. Funny, it's just round the corner from Yonemura's place. You noticed?"

Fairchild had. That was why he'd picked it out from the confidential list of Sutherland's agents in his file, which for some reason had survived numerous paperwork culls over the decades. He was sure there was more to Yonemura's words than he'd managed to fathom so far. They found the place relatively painlessly, a dark wood-panelled house squeezed between two shiny new concrete apartment buildings. Overgrown plant pots crowded the veranda and a grimy air conditioning vent hung on the wall. The sliding door was sticky, and was persuaded open by a harassed-looking thirty-ish woman. As Takao explained to her who they were, the sound of children floated through from the back. Doing a project about people who've lived in the area a long time, said Takao. For a university. Maybe a book. Social history. Oral history. This house very historic. Anyone here who remembers this area in the 1960s?

She looked reluctant. More long-winded assurances weren't working. Takao was on the verge of offering to come back some other time, when a door inside opened and a hunched, grey-haired man came shuffling out. As was appropriate to their relative status, Takao focused his respect on the gentleman, who listened with his jaw hanging slightly open. Encouraged by Fairchild, Takao took the opportunity to mention that they believed there may once have been someone living here named Saburo?

The old man's face stiffened as though an electric bolt had run through him. The woman stepped forward, her hand up as a warning.

"Song-Ho!" said the man. "Song-Ho! Yes, Song-Ho lived here." He shuffled back and made some remark to someone inside.

Takao turned to Fairchild. "They're Korean. Maybe Zainichi. Been in Japan a long time."

"Their names aren't Korean."

"Some change their names. Makes things easier." A smoothing-over of the discrimination many Korean citizens of Japan experienced over the years.

"Come, come." The man beckoned them in with small, quick movements. The woman turned to him, concerned. He batted her away with a flick of his hand. She couldn't insist; in Japan, the elder of the home had authority. With one lingering look she returned to the children at the back of the house.

Takao and Fairchild entered. An old lady, with white hair in a bun, sat in an armchair, looking up from the floor when they came in but saying nothing. The man didn't sit; he was unsettled, walking around as if hunting for something. Takao started with the cover story, life here in the 1960's. It was harsh, said the man, as part of a description prompted by

Takao. That rang a bell; Yonemura had used a similar phrase. Fairchild had assumed he was referring to the era of the prints, the floating world, or fleeting world.

Fairchild prompted Takao in English. "Ask them about raising children, what it was like to raise a child."

That prompted more of the same, the food shortage after the war, the devastation, the factory jobs, things getting better. No specific mention of Saburo, or Song-Ho, though from the details in the file he must have been the younger generation.

"Ask them if they had children," said Fairchild.

Two, was the man's short response, followed by a silence. It felt like they wanted to talk but didn't know how, or didn't feel that they could.

Fairchild had the prints with him. He got them out and unrolled them on the tatami mat at the feet of the elderly couple. When he looked up they were pale, eyes wide. Angry, he thought. They were angry.

The man spoke, accusing now, pointing a weak finger. "They belong to you?"

Fairchild answered directly, in Japanese. "One of them belonged to my parents. But I don't know where they got it from or what it meant to them. The other one belonged to – someone else I've met."

They listened intently with none of the amazement he often got as a foreigner speaking the language. They were foreigners too, he supposed.

Fairchild carried on, gentle. "You mentioned Song-Ho. Is there some connection between Song-Ho and these prints?"

A slow turning of heads towards each other, though their eyes didn't seem to meet.

"Was he your son?" Fairchild asked.

The woman shuddered. He was being too direct, he knew. He looked at Takao, who came in with some softening phrases. They subsided into silence. Had he blown it, being too impatient? But there was something here. They knew these prints. As with Yonemura, the artwork seemed to conjure old feelings of great sadness – but here also fury.

The silence went on for so long he was about to ask Takao if it was time to leave. Then the man started up, his voice unnaturally loud.

"He loved pictures. Pretty things, colourful things. Mountains, trees, blossom. He didn't fit in at school, with the other children."

He gave a chesty cough, and carried on more quietly, with a warble in his voice. The woman watched him, expressionless.

"We worried about him. About what would become of him when he left school. But he got a job in the shop. It was perfect for him. He was in there all the time anyway, staring at the paintings, handling the objects. He knew all the facts. He could tell you everything about when they were made, who made them. He had a good memory. Facts and numbers, he was good at those. People, not so much."

He stopped. His wife reached out and touched his knee, briefly, then drew back.

His eye roamed the prints. Then he resumed. "There were three of these. He loved them. Knew all about them, everything. I'm sorry, my memory is poor. I can hardly recall any of that."

Takao leapt in with reassurances and gratitude. Fairchild asked a question via Takao. "The shop. Was it the shop of Yonemura-san?"

His eyes brightened, and the woman looked up. "Yes! Yes! Yonemura-san. His shop. These," – he pointed to the prints – "were in the shop a long time. Too high a price. People were poor! Not too many could pay. Then the Gaijin came."

He used the Japanese word for foreigner, with a certain emphasis – *the* Gaijin, not just any gaijin. This was a particular outsider, someone who particularly didn't belong.

"The Gaijin was friendly. They chatted a long time. He bought the prints, all three of them, paid a very good price. Song-Ho was proud of that. But it wasn't the end of it. Song-Ho talked a lot about the Gaijin. He came back. Very often. They became friends, Song-Ho said. He'd never had a friend before. He was delighted. We weren't sure. But what could we say? He was so enthusiastic. They would talk about the paintings and the objects, other parts of the world. The Gaijin had been everywhere. Then came the little tests. The Gaijin would give him puzzles."

"Puzzles?" That word again – it kept cropping up.

"Codes, games with numbers and letters. He knew the Latin alphabet. He was good at them. But he became secretive."

He cut off and nodded at his wife who stared at him. It was a shared look, no words necessary. "He hid papers in his room. He thought we didn't know. But we did, of course we did. He thought he could hide things but he'd never tried it before. Then we heard noises in the room, crackling, voices. He had a radio up there. What for? It was bigger than just an ordinary radio. We looked, when he wasn't there." He seemed ashamed of this act of dishonesty. "Then he got very excited. Something was happening. But he went very quiet, too. He was out every evening, up during the night in his room. I said to him, Song-Ho, you don't leave this house again until you tell me what's going on. He cried. He cried!

He said he couldn't tell me, it was a secret. But I insisted. So, he said, he's going on a mission."

"A mission where?" said Fairchild.

"To Korea! To Korea!" The old man's voice cracked.

"You mean North Korea?"

His eyes filled. "My son, in North Korea! It was madness! But he wouldn't listen. The Gaijin had got into his head. It's important work, he said. To reunite our country. Japan is our country now, I said. No, he said. Korea is our country. One Korea. I can help. They need someone good with codes and numbers on the radio. I can be useful. Oh, he was so eager!" His face was wet with tears. "We tried again and again to dissuade him. But he stopped talking to us, came and went without saying a word. Then one evening he left and never came back."

A long silence. The end of the story, except for the decades of hope and dread and wondering and suffering and guilt. Fairchild had known decades like that. But he couldn't put it into words, not in awkward Japanese. He muttered some sympathetic sentiments. Takao managed something more eloquent.

"Did no one come to explain?" asked Fairchild. "What about the Gaijin?"

"No, not him," said the man with sudden bitterness. "Not him. But someone came. His wife."

"His *wife*?"

He couldn't keep the shock out of his voice. Never in the years of talking about Sutherland and his legacy had anyone, ever, mentioned a wife.

"What was she like?" he asked. "You'd never met her before?"

The man's face lightened a little. "Nice lady. Not Japanese. A westerner, like you. Beautiful. Afraid."

"Afraid?"

"Afraid to come here, I think, but she did."

"What did she say?" asked Fairchild.

Now the old woman lifted her head and looked him full in the face. She spoke for the first and only time. "She said sorry."

When they came out, the younger woman was hovering by the door, a dark cloud of disapproval.

"Why you dig up the past? It changes nothing. Just makes them unhappy. Better to forget."

She hurried them out and pulled the door shut. Her shadow hovered on the inside of the screen until they walked away.

Chapter 43

Rose had asked Gardner for a restaurant recommendation. It was a good choice, an upscale place with a Mediterranean menu: quiet, linen tablecloths, heavy cutlery, an unrushed atmosphere. She got a table with a view over the central square of a shopping mall. Not very special-sounding, but at this time of year the tall spiral statue at the centre glowed with ever-changing rainbow colours, and every branch of every tree around the edge was outlined in delicate white fairy lights. It may only be a retail outlet but there was something magical about it. Or maybe Rose had been in Japan too long and it was all going to her head.

She was early, and so was Fairchild, although she got there first. Right from the start, she regretted the dinner invitation. They should have just met for coffee instead. Making small talk, looking at the menu, choosing wine, it was false, false, false. This was how things were now – they'd spent so much of their time in extraordinary situations that the ordinary felt unreal. Fairchild seemed nervous as well. This was all a mistake. The sooner they moved on from chit-chat, the better. Fairchild clearly felt the same, and once they'd ordered he got straight in.

"The man in the room with James' family. Are you sure it was Grom?"

"I'm sure. He spoke on the live feed. It was his voice."

"You didn't see his face, though."

"It was him. And the description they gave was spot-on."

"But even Grom seems a little on the old side to be at the forefront of a global hacking enterprise."

"He doesn't have to be at the forefront, just connected in some way. Someone else was with him, remember, this

Russian doing the technical stuff. He still has allies among his former FSB colleagues. The way they got Fiona and the children out of that hotel room required some skill. People in hotel uniform with ID badges went to the door. We don't see their faces on the CCTV. Fiona said they had guns. They knew how to get them out quietly, no fuss. He's using his secret intelligence expertise to help Fire Sappers. That's what he can offer them."

"Maybe Milo getting killed will bring this partnership to an end."

"Let's hope so. But it could be an opportunity, a power vacuum at the top. He could take advantage of it and step in as a leader. On the ship, Milo said that someone had persuaded him to come to Japan in person. Now I'm wondering who that might have been. Coming here certainly made him more vulnerable. Maybe Grom had an ulterior motive and wanted Milo to take a risk."

"If Grom is being fed information from someone within MI6, and that information starts being used by Fire Sappers…"

"Exactly. It makes them a much greater threat, to security as well as economically. And do you think it's a coincidence that Grom ends up in Japan at exactly the same time we are?"

"No, I don't. He knew you were coming here, or that I was. It may be that he latched onto Fire Sappers because they were already looking at James. But you can't get that kind of inside information trawling the dark web. Someone tipped him off."

"The same person who told Grom I was in Nice."

Fairchild hesitated. "Have you spoken to Walter about this?"

"I have. I really don't think Walter is working with Grom, Fairchild. It was Walter who wanted to go after Grom in the first place. And he specifically gave me a team to do that. He had to persuade Marcus Salisbury to authorise it."

"He could just be covering himself by doing that. The more I find out, the more I realise how much Walter has been holding back all this time."

"You've found something out?"

"I tracked down an old colleague, someone who knew my parents, and Walter, and Sutherland, as he was then. Name of Penny Galloway."

"Means nothing to me."

"She's been retired a while. Like all of them, she didn't give much away, but I know something happened. Something they want to keep buried. Then there's the prints."

"Was Gardner any help there?"

"He happened to mention that Sutherland served in Japan in the late sixties, a fact that Walter has failed ever to mention despite me specifically asking him about the Japanese prints."

That was one hell of an omission on Walter's part. "Okay, I admit that's unhelpful. I've asked him about those prints himself and he was cagey."

"And there's more. A lot more."

Fairchild told her about the visit to the old house and Sutherland's naïve young recruit from Yonemura's store. "It makes sense," he said. "The CIA was parachuting covert teams into North Korea right through the sixties. MI6 was probably helping find recruits. Most of them were Koreans living in Japan. Their job was to foment unrest and overturn the regime."

"But a boy like that!" said Rose.

"Exactly. He was totally unsuitable. Grom was sending him to his death, and probably condemning the rest of the cell to the same fate. Yonemura was trying to tell me about Song-Ho. I thought when he said things were lost, he meant the places in the prints. But that had nothing to do with it. It was the person he associated with the prints he meant. His young employee who disappeared."

"And those poor people got nothing by way of explanation? Sounds about right."

"They did get a visit, though. Not from Sutherland. From his wife."

"What? His wife? Sutherland was married? Did you know that?"

"Nope. Another small fact that Walter failed to mention."

"My God. Did they say anything about her?"

"She was a western woman. It sounds like she went there to apologise on behalf of her husband. And they thought she was afraid of him. But that's it. That's all."

There was anger in his voice. Rose had thought his edginess was down to the awkward dinner date, but it was probably more about this.

"So what now?" she asked.

"Keep digging. Go back to the beginning and ask everyone about his wife."

He sunk into himself, as if defeated by the scale of the job. But there was no way he was going to step away from it. She didn't blame him. And she didn't want him to, either, for her own reasons.

There was something else she wanted to discuss with Fairchild, she'd realised. Why she'd invited him to dinner in particular. This was more than a coffee conversation.

"Walter's pulled me out of the field," she said. "He's given me an analyst role in London. Says it's temporary."

"Why?"

"He says I'm losing my humanity." Rose outlined what happened in Paris and the counselling report they argued about.

"Nonsense," said Fairchild. "Sounds like misdirection to me. He has another reason for wanting you out of the field."

"That doesn't make sense, Fairchild. It was Walter who sent me after Grom in the first place. I'm starting to wonder if he's right."

"What makes you say that?"

"In the cave, James was ready to give Milo what he wanted. When they had Fiona and the kids, he agreed to help Fire Sappers in exchange for everyone's release."

"You think he was right to do that?"

"No."

"You wouldn't have done it?"

"No. But now I'm starting to wonder if that's just because nothing's mattered to me as much as the family matters to James."

Fairchild swilled his wineglass. "Love trumps everything? A very Romantic idea. By that I mean it came in with the Victorians. But what is unconditional love? If you fell in love with someone, committed to them for life, then found out they were a paedophile, would you still love them?"

"That's different. I'd have found something out about them I didn't know before. But what if this love of mine was put in danger and to save him I had to condemn other people?"

"Would you do it?"

"It would depend. Not necessarily. I wouldn't think that he particularly deserves to live because I happen to like him. But a lot of people would, wouldn't they?"

"A lot of people would. But you're not a lot of people. These considerations are part of your job."

"Would you?"

A pause. "It would depend."

Rose filled up their glasses. "James and Fiona were both angry with me. They think I don't care and that I look down on them. That I see them as boring because they're ordinary. But I'm supposed to be doing this job for ordinary people. What's better about having secrets or knowing how to use a gun? Or using a gun? They've made me wonder if I've passed into some kind of closed-off world where people don't behave like people any more."

"You could make it up to them. See them more often. While you're in London, certainly."

"I suppose." Though maybe she didn't want to because she felt awkward around them, a sole entity witnessing a family unit, reminding her of her solitude. But she didn't say this.

"If you'd lost your humanity we wouldn't be having this conversation," said Fairchild. "You care and you still want to do the job. It would be easier to walk away and leave it to other people to screw up, but you don't want that. You do a job that might crush the care in you if you let it, but you're not letting it. You're afraid the decisions you make will rob you of the ability to care, and that fear is a good thing. That fear is keeping you human."

He was more sympathetic to her situation than she was expecting. Afterwards, she couldn't remember what she said back to him, but she did remember feeling lighter, and another bottle of wine was involved. They drifted somehow into conversation about other things. Fairchild suggested going on somewhere else. Rose was tired; she'd barely slept after the kidnapping. But she didn't want to be on her own just yet. Talking felt good.

They ended up in a piano bar on a top floor somewhere in Ginza, all padded black leather sofas and dramatic views. They settled back with gin and tonic and a bowl of nuts and listened to the music, and talked about people they both knew: Zack, Zoe, Pippin, Jinpa, Roman Morozov, Alice Rapp. In the lulls Rose got sleepy but she didn't want to leave. Not yet. Not back to hotel rooms and packing and an analyst desk in London.

It was late, it was late. She shifted in the sofa to get more comfortable, a little closer to Fairchild. He didn't pull back, didn't move forward. It felt okay. They were cut from the same cloth, after all. She was only just starting to realise that. She'd be okay with him.

They listened to the piano. Her eyelids became heavier and heavier.

"Madam! Sumimasen, Madam! So sorry!"

She opened her eyes. A waiter was leaning over her.

"Madam! Your taxi is here, Madam."

"Taxi?"

She looked around. Fairchild was gone.

Chapter 44

Fairchild walked fast. It was only the forward momentum that stopped him turning round and going back. Sitting on that sofa with the music, the gin, the view, and Rose, Rose relaxed, beautiful, comfortable in his presence, able to be with him – wanting to be with him – shifted the nucleus of every cell in his body. He belonged there with her, watching her sleep, enjoying the luxury of looking at her face, tracing every shape and light there. Being the company she needed, at a distance if that was what she wanted. Whatever she wanted. But he couldn't. Watching her sleep was when it all fell into place, what he had to do, and it was partly because of what she herself had told him. She would hate him for it, but he had to go. He had to go because of a promise he'd made to another woman. And when that woman was Darcy Tang, it was a promise you had to keep.

It wasn't far. Ginza was the traditional heart of Tokyo night life, the streets stuffed with glitzy new arrivals, but many of these bars had been here since the post war years, quietly providing female company, often innocent – just places to socialise and network for serious hardworking corporate leaders and politicians. After walking three or four streets he entered a building and went up in the lift to the fourth floor. There were six other bars on other floors in the same building, and this was one door of many, on one street of many.

As he stepped into the bar the *Irrashaimase!* was in no means diminished by his being a westerner, or a stranger, or on his own, although all of those things would have made him unusual to the slim ever-busy Shin-Mama running the place. It wasn't large inside; sofa seats lined both sides and a karaoke machine took pride of place in front of the window at the end. The hostesses were sitting chatting to the clients, a bottle of whisky on each table.

"I'm here to meet with Mr Hamilton," said Fairchild to the Shin-Mama. "I understand he comes here regularly."

Shin-Mama's movements ground to a halt. She stared at him. "One moment." A tiny bow and she glided off. She was gone for several minutes, then returned. "Your name?"

"John Fairchild."

"Please, have a seat."

Another long wait, during which Fairchild was honoured by a visit from the Mama-San, who emerged in full kimono expressing the highest intricacies of respect, and expecting something similar back. She was shorter, rounder and friendlier than Shin-Mama. She asked very little of Fairchild but her curiosity shone through. She withdrew to bestow similar favours at all the other tables before vanishing again.

Fairchild continued to wait. He asked for whisky, an extravagance, as he'd have to buy the whole bottle, but they'd keep it for him if he ever came back. It was at least half an hour before Shin-Mama returned.

"Please, a car is outside."

Downstairs, the car was waiting for him at the kerb. The rear door opened automatically. Fairchild glimpsed a beige leather seat. He hesitated, then got in. The door closed and the car moved off.

"Mr Hamilton, is it?" he said. "How many different names do you have?"

"Good evening to you, too," said Grom. "Or morning, I should say. It's half past bloody two."

"I was busy earlier."

"Oh, the woman! Of course. You want it all. Why not? You deserve it. How did you know I was in Tokyo?"

Fairchild was hoping he wouldn't ask. Grom watched him hesitate. "Ah! The woman again. I like your style. And how did you find out about the hostess bar?"

"Tim Gardner gave me your file."

"The whole thing? Timothy!"

"There wasn't much to it."

"I was always bad at paperwork."

"You weren't here long."

"Yes, well, that too. You're not one to stick around in one place either, it seems."

It was the first time they'd met in person since Lake Baikal. Grom was thinner, hungrier, older of course like they all were, but his energy was still there, his life force. He was looking distinguished today though tired, an ageing corporate man enjoying the benefits of retirement, you'd have thought.

"Don't think I'm like you," said Fairchild. "I'm not. I have my reasons for this."

"Well, exactly. You can be as contemptuous as you like, but it was you who reached out to me, remember."

"To talk."

"Of course. Always to talk. Talking makes the world go round, does it not. And what is it you'd like to talk about?"

"You had a wife."

"I've never been married. Check my records."

"Your records are meaningless. A woman claimed to be your wife."

"She may have said it."

"So there was a 'she'."

"Yes, there was a 'she'. A long time ago. Plenty more before and since. Don't get hung up on any of them, Fairchild. They're not worth the trouble."

Fairchild looked out of the window. The streets of Ginza slid past in the light of dozens – hundreds – of neon signs. Even at this hour, men in suits and women in kimonos passed by. Taxis dropped off and picked up. There was more he needed to ask. Always more.

"You sent a vulnerable boy to his death."

"Is that what they said? Don't believe everything they tell you, Fairchild. Haven't you learned that yet? I'm not a monster."

"So you like to say. But I didn't hear it from some spook."

"Really? Oh, the parents. They're still alive, are they? Well, lucky for you the Japanese populace enjoys such great longevity. In most other places that story would have died a long time ago. And I say story, Fairchild. They're all stories, these tales of the past."

"It's what 'she' thought. She apologised for you."

"She betrayed me."

"Is that why you kept the prints?"

"I keep lots of things. Kept. They're all gone now. Fire, the Kremlin, light-fingered public servants. Don't hold on to stuff, Fairchild. Hoarding isn't healthy. The world of physical things is over anyway. All value is in the virtual world now. A life in bytes, ones and zeros. Money, identity, power, that's where it is. It's accessible anywhere and you can be whoever you want to be. It's the future. The present, actually."

Fairchild wouldn't be distracted. "You only had two of the prints. One at your Monaco apartment and one at the villa. My parents ended up with the third. How come?"

Grom pulled a regretful face. "Well, I suppose, if she had been a wife she could have considered it part of the divorce settlement. Actually, she stole it. Sloped off in the middle of the night. Took that and a few other things besides. As I said, she betrayed me."

It was so much the essence of the man. These prints were significant to him because they reminded him of a supposed betrayal. They stoked up a need for revenge that justified a pattern of behaviour that had caused the death of Fairchild's parents and plenty of others, attempts on his own life and so much more. It was the way Grom was wired; resentment at how the world treated him was what fired him up.

"My parents helped her get away from you, didn't they?"

"You're making me sound like a monster again, John. We were good together. But other people got into her head, whispered things about me. The half-truths of lie-masters. You know them. You know how they befuddle you."

Fairchild steeled himself to say the next thing. "I do. I've had enough of it. I want the truth, all of it now. That's why I'm here. You were right, what you said at Lake Baikal. This latest thing has made me realise I could spend my whole life guessing, turning up one fact after another, year after year. I just want to know."

Grom was watching him, evaluating him. He looked back at the man, mirroring his expression. The car continued through the streets of Tokyo.

"This woman, Rose," said Grom. "She's important to you, isn't she?"

"Not as important as this."

He hated how those words sounded. They weren't true, at least he didn't think so. In any case, his decades-long quest for answers wasn't why he was here right now; his motives were much more current. But Rose couldn't know that he was doing this. She'd already suffered from Grom's callous, playful ruthlessness through her association with Fairchild. The path Fairchild was taking was for him alone.

He carried on. "I have no affinity with who she works for. Her values aren't mine. Walter's her boss and he's been lying to me for decades. He'll never tell me everything. You said you would. You said I could get the truth from you."

"Well, you can," Grom said quietly.

"And what do I have to do in return?"

"Let's talk about that."

The car kept moving.

Chapter 45

James sat at the bar in one of those pretend pubs they like to have at airports. He was tempted by a beer, but decided against it in the end. It would only be a disappointment. Better to wait for the real thing. He looked at his watch. Not too long now. It was all looking very Christmassy here at Narita: Santa on his sleigh, tinsel and gift-wrapped boxes, ginger and toffee specials at the coffee shops, jaunty red and green hats and scarves. It really was true that a life-or-death experience made you look at everything in a different light. Even just being able to sit here, warm enough, plenty of food inside, a Wi-Fi connection when he needed it, seemed like luxury aplenty. All he needed now was Fiona and the kids, and he'd be seeing them soon enough.

A man came up to the bar and asked for a beer. A Brit, by the sound of it. Trim figure, blue eyes. He glanced across.

"Not like the real thing, of course," he said. Odd how people sometimes seemed to know what you were thinking. "Got a long wait?"

"Not too bad, considering."

His beer arrived. "Mind if I join you?" He pulled up a stool. "Latest Test a bit of a disappointment. You're a cricket man?"

"I certainly am, though for how much longer on their current form, who knows?"

They talked cricket for a few minutes, then the chap stuck out his hand.

"Timothy."

He did the same. "James."

"James Clarke? I was wondering if you was you. Wasn't sure, though. I'm Tim Gardner."

"Ah, right! Good! My sister mentioned the name."

"Did she now? Well, interesting time you've had of it over here. I expect you're glad to be heading home."

"Actually, I'm not going home. I'm waiting here to meet Fiona and the kids in Arrivals. We decided to stay on here for a while. Things were getting a bit stale, to be honest. Too much in the groove. Nothing shakes things up like a change of scene. Turns out the kids were very taken with the place, despite the circumstances. My company has an office here so we're going to give it a go. Not forever, I'm sure, but it'll be an experience."

"Well, good for you! If you want any tips from a longstanding expat, you know where to come."

"Thanks, yes, I'm sure we will. Takao's being pretty useful. Turning into something of a family friend. Maybe Mirai and Tomo could as well, although I'll have to work on Fiona a bit."

"Good stuff. Well, let's stay in touch."

"Oh, right. That's how these things work, is it?"

Gardner seemed befuddled by his question.

"Sorry, I mean I really don't know anything about these situations."

He still looked blank.

"Well, I mean, you working with my sister and all?"

"Rose and I are in the same line of business, if that's what you mean. I don't work with her directly. In fact I believe she's already on her way back to London. Anyway, happy to exchange details if you're hanging around in Tokyo for a while." He put his business card down on the bar.

"Yes, well, here's the thing." James felt slightly awkward. "I realised something, thinking about it all afterwards. I mean, in that cave – you heard about the cave, I take it?"

"Oh yes, I heard." He sipped his beer patiently.

275

"Well, back then I'd have done anything for Fiona and the kids. Sold my soul to the devil, whatever."

"Perfectly understandable, James. I wouldn't worry about it. I mean these people are all about coercion in the nastiest of ways."

"But I was wrong!"

He looked startled.

"Well, I was, wasn't I? Rose was right. I'd have given them everything with no guarantee from their end that they would have kept their side of the bargain. I'd have been in their pockets for the foreseeable."

"Yes, but in the circumstances—"

"Well, exactly. What else could I have done? They wouldn't have brooked a refusal. Which just makes me realise what dreadful people they are. I mean, the way they treated those poor students. It was a real eye-opener, you know. I never thought I'd witness someone shooting someone else in cold blood like that. You can't tolerate them or explain it away. There's nothing someone like that wouldn't do, is there? You know, I really didn't think that people like that existed in the world. I've lived a very sheltered life, I expect you'll say."

"Well, there certainly are some despicable people around. And plenty who won't be shedding a tear now that our friend Milo is no more."

"But there'll be others. That kind of game won't just stop. I know enough about hackers myself, but I hadn't seen the evil side of it. What you can do with those skills if you don't have any humanity. It's – well, it's made me reconsider a few things."

"Yes, well, the depths of the human psyche certainly give one pause for thought." Gardner looked philosophical as he reached for his beer. Goodness, was he doing this deliberately? These spies were supposed to be intelligent, weren't they? Or maybe this was some kind of technique to get James to spill exactly why he'd reached out to Gardner in the first place. It was a big deal, actually, going behind Rose's back and putting a call in to the British Embassy to try and speak to the fellow. Hopefully it wouldn't be for nothing. It looked like James was going to have to be a bit more forthright.

"I've worked out how to do it," he said.

"Do what, old chap?"

"The back door. The cold wallet."

"Sorry?"

"The thing that Milo wanted. I know how to encode the wallet's encryption so that it can be accessed with a secret key. A key only I know."

"And that means…"

"Well, if the need arose, I'd be able to sneak a quick look into the account of anyone with one of those wallets. And keep a record of when and where they've gone online. It's going to launch quite widely, this. The cutting edge of crypto security, you might say. People who value their privacy will be interested in this product, for sure."

Now the fellow looked interested. "Really? Well, I can see that might be useful." His head started nodding. "Yes! But how would this work, exactly?"

"Well, to clarify a few things. I would have the key. Only me. No one else. If you want something, you come to me. This is for looking only. Discreet observation. A quick peek. And only when there's a damn good need. No arbitrary nosing about just to see what people have been up to. And I decide who and when."

"Right, right." Gardner was deep in thought. "Well, of course, we'd be relying on you for the intel, so it's your rules.

I mean, from our side, we're interested in the nefarious types who abuse these confidential networks to oil the wheels of terrorist groups, for example. Life and death, that's what's on the table as far as we're concerned. So there'll always be a damn good reason. That's a useful offer, James. Though I have to say I'm surprised. I'd have thought after everything you've been through, something like this would be the last thing you'd want."

"But as I said, it's taken this run-in with Fire Sappers to make me realise what's at stake and who you folks are dealing with. So I'm yours, Timothy, if needed. That's what I'm saying to you, if that all makes sense."

The man did at least look chuffed. That much was gratifying. "Absolutely. That's very welcome news. Delighted to have you on the books, so to speak."

"Yes, well, one more thing, then. This is strictly confidential."

"Oh, of course! Goes without saying. You don't have to worry on that front. We know what we're doing there."

"No, I mean, strictly confidential. Not a word of this to my sister. Ever. She doesn't need to know, so we don't trouble her with it. I wouldn't want her getting all protective on me. It's my decision after all. You understand?"

"Oh yes," said Gardner. "Perfectly."

Chapter 46

On the flight to London, Rose tried to think of some ways of making her time back in Britain bearable. Seeing more of James and the family would have been one idea, but now they'd made a snap decision to go and live in Tokyo for a while. It seemed like the last place they'd want to spend time, but clearly she didn't know them as well as she thought. At least they were safe and out of the woods now, free to pursue normality again when it suited them.

At Heathrow she switched on her phone and found a text from Walter: *I'm at the airport.* Her boss was coming to the airport to meet her? This was unheard of.

He was waiting for her at the arrivals gate, a grim, pale figure among the Christmas decorations and hugs and kisses of holiday season reunions all around.

"What's up?" she asked, coming over.

"I need you on something urgent. There's a car waiting." They started walking towards the exit. "Fire Sappers is becoming a problem. The risks to British security have been massively upscaled. Dark web monitoring shows them forging links with various fringe political groups that have issues with the west, and the UK in particular. They're supporting groups that see Britain and British interests as terrorist targets."

"This is Grom," said Rose. "You said he'd behave like this if he got the chance. He mobilises people to serve his own ends. He's recruiting other causes to stir things up against us."

"Indeed, but it's worse than we thought. He's been joined by someone else, which compounds the problem."

"Who?"

"Can't you guess?"

"No." She really didn't know what Walter was getting at.

The man sighed. "When did you last see John Fairchild?"

Fairchild? She'd been trying not to think about that. He hadn't bothered getting in touch since walking out on her in the piano bar. She cringed inwardly at the thought of that evening, that she'd felt able to trust him with her feelings. If she ended up with a slap in the face it was what she deserved. But this?

"A couple of nights ago. But you can't think Fairchild has joined them, Walter. No way."

"An anonymous source from Fire Sappers sent a message to a disguised MI6 inbox. It was pretty clear. Someone who knows us wanted to tell us that Fairchild is working with Fire Sappers."

"And is it verified, this message? Confirmed via another source?"

"Not so far. But it won't be easy to verify. We need to assume for now that it's true. What did you talk about when you met with Fairchild? What state was he in?"

Rose's heart sank. "He was angry. He'd found out that Grom used to serve in Japan. And that he had a wife."

"Ah. Oh dear."

"Why didn't you tell him these things, Walter? This is why he's so bitter. He goes to enormous lengths to uncover this information and then he finds out you already knew."

"I had my reasons, but I fear this may be what's caused Fairchild to turn around. Regrettable."

"Regrettable? You trusted him. I trusted him. It was me who told him Grom was in Japan. And he was badgering Tim Gardner for information as well. Grom working with Fairchild against the British would be a disaster. I'm not sure I believe it, Walter."

"You need to factor in Grom's ability to manipulate. Fairchild could have killed him in Russia, remember? He was pointing a gun at the man. But somehow Grom talked himself out of it. Did Fairchild ever tell you what he said?"

"No." Fairchild had deliberately avoided telling Rose what Grom had said to him that day. "I told him everything, Walter. We'd been working as a team."

"Well, I blame myself as well. Clearly I mishandled things. But this isn't a time for beating ourselves up. The analyst role will have to wait. The FBI task force is enlarging and going international. It'll pursue Fire Sappers wherever they are in the world. With your experience you need to be a part of this, Rose."

A slap in the face? This was so much more. But it was her own fault. She'd let her guard down. She thought she could reach out, somehow not be alone. Feeling sorry for herself, seeing James and Fiona and the kids and what they had, she thought she could have it all. But she'd made her choices years ago.

Learn, Rose, learn. Make up for it. And don't let it happen again.

"When do we start?" she asked.

"Right now."

The Clarke and Fairchild series

Thank you for reading *The Secret Meaning of Blossom*! If you want to stay in touch and hear about new releases in the series before anyone else, please join my mailing list. Members of the Clarke and Fairchild Readers' Club receive exclusive offers and updates. Claim a free copy of *Trade Winds*, a short story featuring John Fairchild and set in Manila. It takes place before the series starts, and before Fairchild and Clarke meet. Another short story, *Crusaders*, is set in Croatia and features Rose Clarke's fall from grace from the British intelligence service. These stories are not available on Amazon but are free for members to download. You can unsubscribe from the list at any time.

Visit www.tmparris.com to sign up!

Reviews are very important to independent authors, and I'd really appreciate it if you could leave a review of this book on Amazon. It doesn't have to be very long – just a sentence or two would be fine – but if you could, it would provide valuable feedback to me to and to potential readers.

Previous books in the series are *Reborn* (Book 1, set in China and Tibet), *Moscow Honey* (Book 2, set in Russia and Georgia), and *The Colours* (Book 3, set in Monaco and the south of France). In Book 5, Clarke and Fairchild will meet in Hungary, where Rose has to come to terms with Fairchild's betrayal and her true feelings for him, and Fairchild will unearth some startling revelations about his family. All of this takes place against a backdrop of some of the most explosive issues of identity and nationalism that are current today.

I hope you stay with us for the journey.

The Real Takao

Takao is a name borrowed from a real person. I met Takao in Tokyo through some mutual friends, a couple of Australians. He was an investment banker, but clearly an unusual one. He'd lived in the UK and the USA and found the Japanese business environment constraining and frustrating. Several weeks after we first met, he got in touch and, astonishingly, offered me a job working for him. Confident that the sluggish Japanese stock market was on the verge of recovery, he wanted to set up an office in Tokyo so that he could provide advice and stock recommendations to European clients. He needed an administrator to keep everything together while he went and did his day job, so he offered me a post, along with an apartment. At that time, an offer of a free place to live in Tokyo was pretty incredible. A number of people did suggest he was trying to set me up as his mistress – not all that unusual, apparently – but I trusted my instincts and there was never any suggestion of that. It was the business that interested him.

The job, or at least the job as Takao wanted to do it, also involved travelling around Japan in style visiting companies to assess their investment potential. This took us to numerous places, the most memorable of which to me were Hiroshima, with its sobering museum and epicentre memorial, and Hokkaido, the snow-clad island in the north hosting the fabulous ice festival. Of course these trips were fun and social – it wasn't just about work – but it was never more than that, and gave me a great chance to go places I probably wouldn't have been able to afford on a humble English teacher's salary. My 'training' also involved sending me off to Amsterdam for a week, and a few days in Hong

Kong where, amongst other things, he'd just bought a yacht and roped me in to help launch it.

In the end, Takao was wrong in his optimism about the Japanese stock market bounce. I don't know what happened eventually, because after a few months I bowed out and went home. We ended up parting on bad terms. Though I remember Japan incredibly fondly, I didn't find it an easy place to live and eventually felt alienated and became quite unhappy. I took it out on him and treated him very badly in the final couple of weeks. In the Japanese tradition, I'd like to apologise to him for how we parted ways, but his name is a very common one and I've never been able to find him on social media and have no other details for him.

So, I've put him in this book, or a character at least partially reflecting some of his attributes, and I dedicate this book to him, with apologies and thanks. Perhaps some day he will read this.

Takao and the author at the Sapporo Ice Festival, c.1994

Sources

Twice Booker Prize winning author Peter Carey wrote a short memoir called <u>Wrong in Japan</u>, recounting a trip to Japan with his twelve-year-old son who at the time was obsessed with manga and anime. This is a lovely introduction to these worlds, and an insight into and refresher of the delights and eccentricities (to the visitor) of modern day Tokyo.

On the same bookshop trip I picked up <u>Japan Journeys</u> by Andreas Marks, a beautiful book that connects some of the loveliest classic woodcut prints to specific places in Japan. Within this book you can find the renditions of places such as Ochanomizu and Yoshiwara as I've imagined on Fairchild's prints. Descriptions of what these places are like now owe much to Google Street View.

In the black and white world of current affairs media, everything tends to be deemed either success or failure; if a country isn't growing in leaps and bounds it's "stagnating". <u>Bending Adversity</u> by David Pilling puts Japan's recent economic performance into context. It includes the observation, articulated by Takao in the novel, that GDP per capita is still growing while the economy itself may have shrunk – or just not grown very much – in response to population decline. It's Pilling who quotes a visiting MP from the North of England, who, on seeing Tokyo's bustling streets and busy shops, said "If this is a recession, I want one."

<u>The Code Book</u> by Simon Singh was influential, particularly in its explanation of the development of current encryption standards and the underlying principle of

multiplying prime numbers. It's basically a history of codes and code-breaking going back in time – a fascinating read.

Researching crypto currency and related security, I read numerous blogs and articles and am grateful to PixelPlex for educating me on the role of hot and cold wallets and the features of blockchain technology. Bitcoin and Blockchain Without the Bull by Andrew J. Smales provided some valuable context to the current crypto hype from the perspective of a knowledgeable enthusiast. My online reading also took in the connections between crypto and criminality, the state of play with hackers, ransomware and the FBI, Bitcoin mining and a real example of the theft of electricity to this end, and numerous examples of international hacking groups and the tactics and language they employ.

More online research informed my depiction of the Japanese mafia, in particular their involvement in the pachinko industry; manga and cosplay generally, though the specifics were generally fabricated (including the themed restaurant in Akihabara); DisneySea (it wasn't there when I lived in Tokyo, though I did go to Disneyland twice); travelling on a cargo ship (this is now on my list of things to do before I die); working on a cargo ship including the mechanics of launching a lifeboat and/or a rescue boat; how to escape from a building using bedsheets; whether satellites can see through cloud; how to email someone your location without using a computer's operating system; and the location of the Minato US military base right in the heart of Tokyo. Other descriptions are generally from memory, and as ever, accuracy at all times was subservient to the demands of the story.

Thanks

A huge thanks to the contributions from my beta readers, those at Hidden Gems and also Chris Lewando, Julia Blewett and Snyman Rijkloff. Ryan O'Hara as ever has created a magical book cover. Thanks also to those people who have reviewed The Secret Meaning of Blossom – it's hard to articulate just how much of a difference this makes. If you haven't left an Amazon review yet, please do so, and consider yourself thanked!

About the author

After graduating from Oxford with a history degree, T.M. Parris taught English as a foreign language, first in Budapest then in Tokyo. Her first career was in market research, during which she travelled extensively to numerous countries and had a longer stay in Hong Kong which involved visiting many of the surrounding countries. She has also taken sabbaticals for a long road trip in the USA and to travel by train from the UK through Russia and Mongolia to Beijing and around China to Tibet and Nepal.

More recently she has played a role in politics, serving as a city councillor in Brighton and Hove on the south coast of the UK.

She currently lives in Belper, a lively market town near the Peak District National Park in the centre of England.

She started writing seriously in 2011. She published her first novel, Reborn, in 2020, the first in a series of international spy thrillers. She is drawn to international settings and the world's most critical political issues, as well as the intrigue, deception, betrayal and secrecy of clandestine intelligence services.

Crime and action thrillers are her favourite book, film and TV choices. She occasionally plays the trumpet or the Irish flute. She enjoys walking, running, cycling and generally being outdoors in beautiful countryside, as well as cooking and baking and, of course, travelling.

Email: hello@tmparris.com
Facebook: @tmparrisauthor
Twitter: @parris_tm

Printed in Great Britain
by Amazon